Cover Design: Jay Aheer

Editing done by Jenny Sims Editing4Indies

Proofing Julie Deaton by Deaton Author Services

Interior Design by CP Smith

Parker and Cooper

If you were real I would want to hug you and thank you for making my dreams come true.

It's a Stone thing..

THIS IS FOREVER

THE THIS IS SERIES

☐NE

JUSTIN

"*J*USTIN, GETTING KNOCKED out of the playoffs in the first round is obviously not what you were hoping for." Standing in front of my locker, I am already irritated by the reporter's question. I mean, it wasn't like we were going to win the Stanley Cup, but when the underdogs beat us in round one, I don't want to discuss it. "Are you planning on taking the summer off, or will you be training?" Looking at his suit, I think he's overdressed, but what do I know? I'm wearing basketball shorts and a team T-shirt with the matching baseball hat.

I put my hands on my hips and look down at the floor, something that my big brother Matthew taught me a long time ago. Having been in the NHL for over twenty years, he knows what he's talking about. Always think about the question before saying what you really want to answer. My first instinct is to tell him to fuck off and get out of my face. I want to tell him to strap on a pair of skates and tell me how easy it is for him to get to my stats, but I don't.

Instead, I look up and say, "Yeah, for sure. Going out in the first round isn't what anyone wants, but I have to give it to Vegas. They came out to win, and the better team won." I look at him, and he nods his head, waiting for the answer to the second part of his question. "I'm taking a month off, and then I'm coming back to start the first ever Justin Stone Summer Hockey Camp." I smile, proud of what I've put together. "I'm excited to start this first ever summer camp. I think there are a lot of talented kids who don't have the means to get extra time on the ice. We have five kids coming in from every level, from mite to midget. It's going to be mostly one-on-one hockey, and I am super excited about it."

"That sounds great," he says, ignoring it, and then asks another annoying question. "With many of your team members becoming free agents, how sure are you about the success of the team next year?" I look at him.

"I have no idea, and to be honest, that isn't my job. My job is to go out on the ice and give it my all. Who I do it with is just a bonus," I say, and then I turn to grab my Gatorade, hoping he takes the hint and fucks off.

"Thank you for answering the questions, Justin," he says with a smile, and I nod. "See you next season."

I look around, seeing a couple more reporters in the room. Apart from the last game of the year, this has to be the most depressing. Everyone came in today to "clean out their lockers." Glancing at my watch, I realize my meeting with the GM is in ten minutes, so I grab my phone and head toward his office. My phone beeps in my pocket, and when I take it out, I see that Matthew just texted me. Matthew is my older brother, retired NHL god, and now the GM for the New York Stingers. And if that didn't make it hard enough to follow in his footsteps, my father is Cooper Stone. *The* Cooper Stone who holds all the records across the board. The same records I try to beat every single year but always come short of.

Matthew: What time do you land, and are you staying with Mom and Dad?

I don't text him back. In fact, I hate fucking texting. I always, always call, so it's no surprise when he answers the phone laughing. "I think you are the only twenty-four-year-old kid who hates to text." I hear honking in the background, and I know he must be in the city.

"I just don't see the purpose of it when I can pick up the phone and call you," I say, walking down the blue carpeted hallway. "I get there tomorrow morning. I changed my flight to give me extra time to pack up my condo and shit."

"You mean you changed the flight so you can bang one more time before coming home." He laughs, and I shake my head.

"No," I say, trying to sound convincing but failing. Am I exclusive? No, I've never been. I have yet to find the person I want to be exclusive with. When I look around and see that all four of my siblings are happily married with kids, I wonder if I'm ever going to find my person. "Besides, if I got the flight out, I wouldn't land in New York until midnight."

"Where are you staying?" he asks. "I spoke with Dad ten minutes ago, and he said Mom is fixing your room."

I groan out loud. "Why does she keep doing that?"

"Because you're her baby," he says.

"I have chest hair and a beard. I think I'm past the baby stage," I say, and he laughs. "I'll call her now. I was hoping to spend some time in the city. Viktor said I can crash at his condo and so did Max." I mention my two brothers-in-law. "I have a couple of people I want to hit up while in the city."

"I bet you do," he says, chuckling. "Just remember to come home without a mark on you."

"I can't be held accountable about that," I say. I think back to the time I went home and had scratch marks all down my back when I took off my shirt. "Fuck, I think she even drew blood," I say out loud.

"Okay, well, call Mom and tell her what your plans are, or she's going to start planning a welcome home barbecue like she always does."

"I'm staying for two weeks," I say, and he gets quiet. "I set up a two-week training session with Ivan at his ranch." Ivan is a Russian hockey coach who kicks my ass every single summer. He makes me come back bigger and better.

"I heard that he makes the guys barf the first day of training." I nod my head.

"He's the most intense off-season coach out there. I have that hockey camp for the month, and then I want to see if I can go back to him for another couple of weeks before preseason starts."

"Come out guns blazing, I see," he says. "I have to run but give Mom a call."

"I will," I say and disconnect just in time because the GM, Hartley, comes out of his office.

"Justin, right on time," he says and stretches his hand to mine, and I shake it. I walk into the pre-camp meeting and sit on one of the empty chairs as we go over what I thought of the season and things I want to change. When I get up and walk out of the room, I grab my bag at the same time as the metal door shuts behind me.

I'm closing my trunk when I hear my name being called, and I look over to see Ryder, the defenseman. "Have a great summer. Hit me up when you get back."

"Will do," I say. When I get into the car and put on my glasses, I have no idea how this summer will change the rest of my life.

TWO

CAROLINE

One Month Later

"**D**YLAN!" I YELL from the bathroom while I attempt to apply mascara, but it's so old that it's dried out. "Ten-minute warning," I say, turning the knob on the rusty sink to slowly add some water to the mascara. I swirl the brush in the tube, and it helps a little bit but not much. After one coat, I give up, closing it and opening the cracked mirror medicine cabinet. The bathroom is from the seventies, for sure, with moss green tiles everywhere. What used to be white grout is discolored to a dark yellow now. The tub is the same moss green color with lines of rust down it.

Walking out of the tiny bathroom, I turn off the lights, then step right into the living room that holds the small kitchen table with two chairs. Dylan sits on his knees while he eats his cereal, holding my phone in his hand as he watches YouTube videos about hockey. All he does every single time he has my phone or is on the computer is watch hockey plays or highlights. I think it's why he got so good. That and the fact he loves the ice.

"I'm going to go get dressed," I say, but he barely looks up from my iPhone. Walking into the bedroom I share with him, I open the closet door and see the six items that I own hanging. I grab the pair of jeans I wore yesterday and pair it with my gray and white striped short-sleeve shirt, tucking it in the front of my jeans. Then I pick up my black running shoes and slip them on.

The sound of my phone beeping lets me know that it's time to go. "Mom!" Dylan shouts. "Time to go," he says, and I walk out of the room and look at him. He takes his bowl to the sink and gets on his tippy toes to turn on the water and rinse it out. His shorts from last year are way too short for him this year and a bit too tight around his waist, but until I get my paycheck, they will have to do.

"Are you ready?" I ask him, smiling when he turns around wearing his own smile. His happiness lights up the room and my heart. He's missing his two front teeth, his eyes are a baby blue just like his father, and his hair is a mixture of blond like me.

"Ready," he says. Wiping his hands on his shorts, he nods his head and grabs his hockey bag at the door. I look at it, and I know that by the time the new season starts, he's going to need a bigger bag since his equipment also needs an upgrade. He opens the door, and I close it behind me, locking the door. We walk down the hot hallway, then the five flights of stairs toward the parking garage.

Opening the trunk, I put his bag in there and hold his hand as we walk around the back of the car. I open the door, the squeaking noise echoing in the empty parking lot. "Get in, baby," I say, and he climbs into the car and sits in his booster seat. I buckle him in, kissing his neck at the same time.

"Mom," he squeals. I close the door, walking around to the driver's side.

Another squeaking door when I open my own door, getting in and putting the key in and turning. It turns over three times. "No, no, no," I say under my breath. "Please, please, please, please," I send out another silent prayer. This time, the car starts, and I have to wonder how much longer the car is going to last. According to the guy in the garage, I should have scrapped this car last year, but with thousands in credit card debt and a minuscule salary, there is nothing else I can do.

The drive to the arena is smooth without much traffic. When Dylan's coach called me two weeks ago to tell me that he enrolled him in a hockey camp, my heart immediately sank because I knew no matter how many days I ate ramen noodles, I wouldn't be able to afford it. Then he told me the best news; it was all paid for through the Justin Stone Foundation. When I told Dylan about it, the smile and excitement on his face was everything. I knew I would eat all the ramen noodles in the world just to see him that happy.

Getting pregnant in my last year of high school was not something that we thought would happen. I was on the pill, we used condoms, and when I found out, it was the same day Andrew got the letter accepting him into the University of Edmonton for football. It was what he had worked for his whole life. Breaking the news to our parents was not an easy decision and deciding to keep the baby was even worse. My parents said it was me or the baby, and when I chose the baby, they kicked me out of the house. Thankfully, Judi, Andrew's mom, took me in, and two days before Dylan was born, I married Andrew.

He wanted us to have his last name, and with his scholarship, we'd have housing since we were married. I had this idea of what it would be like to be married and have his child, but once Dylan arrived, my idea of perfect and Andrew's were very different. He was riding the wave of his football until he tore his ACL and had to have surgery, and well, then he went down the rabbit hole of drugs. Though he did it so sly and sneakily, I had no idea how far down he'd gone until two guys showed up at our house and beat him right in front of me and one-year-old Dylan. The scholarship was toast, we were kicked out of the housing, and to add the cherry to the sundae, he had used all his scholarship money on drugs. By the end, he was addicted to fucking meth.

"Mom, will anyone I know be there today?" Dylan asks from the back seat, and I look in the mirror, watching him watch outside.

"I don't know, but the good news is you make friends fast," I say over my shoulder. The rest of the ride is quiet with him singing some of the songs from the radio.

"Okay," I say, putting the car in park and looking in the back. "This is it. How ready are you?"

He unclips his seat belt. "How long am I on the ice for?" he asks when I open the car door and get out, going to the back and opening his door. "Is it all day, you think?" He jumps out of the car at the same time a truck pulls up and parks next to us. Walking to the back, I pull his bag out, and I'm getting ready to carry it when he grabs it from my hand. "I got it, Mom." Picking up his bag, he struggles to carry it to the door. It's so heavy, he ends up dragging it halfway there.

We get to the front arena entrance at the same time as someone else, and when I reach out to grab the door, a big hand covers mine.

"Let me," he says. I look over my shoulder to thank the person, and all I can do is stare at the man behind me.

"Are you Justin Stone?" Dylan asks from beside me, and the man smiles, which makes his brown eyes turn just a touch lighter and golden. His hand drops from mine, and he squats down in front of Dylan.

"I am Justin Stone, and who are you?" he asks, his plump lips making me stare. He has to be the most handsome man I have ever seen in my life.

"I'm Dylan," he says, and Justin holds out his hand to shake Dylan's. Dylan looks up at me, and I just smile at him as he reaches out and shakes his hand.

"So you must be Dylan Woods," he says, smiling at him and then getting up and looking at me. "And you must be Dylan's mom." His hand comes out, waiting for me to shake it

"I'm Caroline." I smile, shaking his hand.

"There you are," a woman's voice says behind us. "You are ten minutes late," she says as she walks toward us. Her swinging hips make her hair swoosh perfectly. I look her up and down, and she is wearing the best of the best. Her skirt is perfect and tight and looks like it cost the same as six months of my rent. I don't even want to know what she paid for those shoes.

"I was just talking to Dylan," he says, looking down at Dylan. "I couldn't start the day without him." He smiles at Dylan, his whole face lighting up. "Are you ready?" he asks, and just for one second, I wonder how many people are lucky enough to get that smile from him.

"Dylan," I say, trying to ignore the two people standing around us. "Let's go get you settled. I have to get to work." I open the door now and wait for him to walk in with me. I try not to look over my shoulder, but I fail. His eyes are on us while the blonde talks his ear off, and then he turns to her, and she smiles at him, and he just nods.

"Welcome." A woman is standing at the bottom of two staircases. I look around. This venue is huge, much bigger than the arenas we play at. "To the Justin Stone Summer Hockey Camp," she says, and she has a blue shirt that says the exact thing. "My name is Malika, and I am going to be checking you in today and giving you all the information."

"Thank you," I say, looking down at Dylan, who is watching everything in awe.

"Can I have a name please?" she asks, going to her boards on the table beside her.

I'm about to answer but Dylan beats me to it in his excitement. "Dylan Woods," he says with a megawatt smile on his face. She flips through the manila envelopes to find his name.

"Here you are, Dylan," she says, handing me the envelope and then walking to the side where it looks like the gym bags are sitting. She grabs one and comes over, and I see that it's blue with "Justin Stone Summer Hockey Camp" embroidered on one side. She turns it to the other side, and Dylan's name is also embroidered on the side. She hands me the bag, and it's heavy. "In that bag will be everything he needs for the month-long camp. There are two pairs of running shoes, five pairs of shorts and T-shirts, along with socks, a jacket, and hats. His jersey and hockey socks will be given to him in the dressing room." I look over at Dylan, who stands there with his mouth open. "If you can have him change into shorts and a shirt, we are going to be talking to the kids group by group before their first activity. All the information is in the package along with the meals that will be provided." She looks at her watch. "For today, breakfast is done, but if he gets here by eight, there is always hot breakfast being served." My head is spinning at all this. "If you have any questions or concerns, everyone's contact information is in the envelope."

"Thank you so much." It's the only thing I could say, and I'm trying to blink away the sting of tears hitting my nose. "What room is he in?"

"He'll be in room number three," she says. "You can go to the right side, and it's on the right corridor." I nod at her and then walk around the staircase to the right. We pass two vending machines and come to another staircase, but there are hallways on both sides with a sign in front of it, telling us that room three is on the right. We walk down the corridor and see the rooms are open, and some kids are already inside getting changed.

When we get to room number three, we are the only ones in the room for now. Brown benches line the white cinder block walls. Off to the side is the bathroom and then there is a half cinder block wall on the left side that leads to the shower. "Where do you want to sit?' I ask Dylan, and he walks over to the bench, sitting in the middle. I put his equipment bag down in front of him and open the blue gym bag, taking out a royal blue pair of shorts with match-ing shirt. The shorts have Justin Stone on one leg and then Woods on the other. "Let's get changed," I say, and he un-dresses faster than he's ever done before, slipping on the shorts and then the matching shirt that has his name on the back. He sits down, and I grab the blue running shoes out of the bag and tie his laces for him even though he wants to do it himself. By the time we finish, two other kids have walked into the room with their dads along with Justin.

"Is everything okay in here?" he asks, looking around. I look at Dylan, who just nods.

"Great. How about we get things started by going up-stairs and getting our spots for the meeting?" he says, clapping his hands. Two more kids who are a bit older walk in the room and freak out when they see Justin, who just smiles. He gives the kids high-fives, and then he looks up at me. When our eyes meet, he just smiles, and I have to look away because my heart just started to beat faster.

"Let's go get you set up," I say to Dylan and rush out of the room and away from the man with the brown eyes.

THREE

JUSTIN

*M*Y EYES FOLLOW her as she walks away from me as if I'm in a trance. The minute I pulled up and got out of my car, my eyes went to her as she walked with his hand in hers. I almost jogged to make sure I would get to the door so I could hold it open for her. I was only planning to help her, but then she looked up and her green eyes knocked me back and made my chest tight.

"Justin," Amy says from behind me, and just the sound of her voice makes me shiver like nails scraping down a chalkboard. "It's time for you to go upstairs." I turn to look at her and try to stay out of her grabby hands. She's been working with the foundation for six months and has tried to get me in her grasp since then, but it will never happen. One thing I've learned is you don't fuck with anyone who works for you.

When we walk out of the room, and she starts to tell me

everything I need to do and say, I zone her out. Climbing the back stairs, I come to the tables where the kids are sitting and the parents hang out in the back. I nod at everyone and try to find her without making it too obvious, but I don't see her when I look around. Dylan sits at the table with another child, and when I step up to the front, the kids get quiet. Looking around, I think back to how I got here. I mean, if you think about it, there really was no other choice for me. I was born a Stone, and anyone who knows hockey, knows the Stone name.

I started skating as soon as I could walk, and I even have a picture in my condo of me on the ice with my father holding me up. I loved it, and it was a good thing because we were always at the rink, whether it was for my father or for Matthew, my brother who was drafted first overall. We have that in common, but that is where it stops. Where he got drafted to Los Angeles, I got drafted to Edmonton, and we both handled it differently. He went out and partied while I sat in my room missing home and everything about it. Mind you, Edmonton is no LA.

It was so fucking hard, and I suffered from homesickness so bad that my parents would come out every other week. Slowly, I got into the groove, and now six years later, I've settled, knowing that I will probably never leave Edmonton. They have me signed for another two years, and I'm not one to toot my own horn, but the stats don't lie. I'm at the head of the leaderboard every year, and just last year, I finally beat Evan, my brother-in-law who plays with New York and is married to Zara, one of my twin sisters. My other brother-in-law, Viktor, who is married to the other twin, Zoe, finished third, and from what he told me last week, the next season will be his last. Better to go out on top than be asked to leave, he said to me. That and Zoe wants to have another child, and he wants to be home for it all this time.

The sound of clapping makes me turn my head to see what is going on, and I see everyone getting up and the parents coming over to me. I look at Amy and see her smiling. "Thank you so much for doing this," one of the dads says with tears in his eyes. "It's not easy to get him on the ice, and then I try to bring him to the outdoor rinks, but it's hard." I shake his hand and thank all the parents for trusting me with their kids. When they finally leave, it's time to get on the ice. I walk to my locker room where the other hockey coaches are. I'll be on the ice with the kids the whole day, and I've hired people to direct the activities off the ice as well as three extra pairs of hands on the ice to run the drills I set up.

Once I get on the ice, the doors open and five kids join me. One loses his balance, but he gets up again, and when I look down, I see that Dylan is the first one who skates to me. "Okay, today we are going to do five drills over and over again." I explain to the kids what they are going to do during the drills. Standing on the side, I watch as they do the first drill, and I have say Dylan is good. He can skate faster than all the other kids, and he uses both hands to help skate and speed up, which not all kids know to do. He can skate backward and do crossovers better than all of them.

"Dylan, how old are you?" I ask him when he finishes the fifth drill before everyone.

He looks up at me through the cage of his helmet. "Eight."

"How long have you been playing hockey?" I ask him, and he shrugs.

"Not a lot," he says, and I shake my head. Having nieces and nephews, I get that it can either be all the time or once or twice.

"What team do you play for?"

"I only played a little bit last time because I didn't have any equipment." I look at his skates, and you can tell they are well worn in. "Mom tried to get some skates, but there were none." I shake my head, not thinking about how that might hold someone back.

"Well, looks like you have skates now," I say with a smile while the other kids finish. Then I blow the whistle. "Okay, let's do it again," I say. Dylan skates to the first cone, and I drop a puck for him. "Try to do it with a puck," I suggest.

He takes the puck and then stick handles it better than any kid on the ice. When his hour is over, I call him over and ask him to stay on the ice again with the older kids, and he stands out even with kids who are ten. After three hours, we skate off the ice, and I expect him to complain that he's tired, but instead, he grabs a water and then looks at me as he takes off his helmet. His blond hair is stuck on his head from sweat. "Are we going to do that every day?" he asks as he drinks the water.

"I can make it happen if you want." I smile at him, and he just nods and walks back to his locker room. I follow him since he was left back on the ice, and I didn't know where his group was. I sit down with him while he takes off his equipment, and his elbow pads are too small for him. His shin pads don't fit properly, and don't even get me started on the chest protector. He puts everything in the bag and then grabs the shorts and the T-shirt. "You hungry?"

"Yeah," he says, and I get up from the bench. "Follow me. I have to change my skates, and then we can get some grub." I turn to walk out of the locker room and run smack into Amy.

"I was looking for you," she says, and I just turn to walk toward the locker room where my shoes are. "I was thinking we can sit together at lunch and go over a couple of things."

"Yeah," I say. "I'm having lunch with Dylan, but you can bring what you want to talk about," I say and walk into the locker room. Dylan sits on the bench next to me, swinging his legs. "You can meet us up there."

"Okay, yeah sure, or if anything, we can do it over dinner."

I know what she's doing. "Lunch will be good, Amy," I say, and she just nods and walks out. I put on my sneakers, and we head up the stairs to the food. There are a couple of kids at the table, and some are watching the other kids play hockey from the viewing windows overlooking the rink. I grab a tray for myself and one for Dylan. "What do you want to eat?" He shrugs his shoulders. "Do you like veggies?"

"No," he says and then looks at me, "but my mom said I have to eat them to grow." I try to hide my smile.

"Your mother is right. My mom used to make broccoli every single night," I say, and he looks at me in shock. "I used to give it to the dog. Don't tell anyone."

"We don't have a dog," he says, and I grab a plate of chicken and pasta and put it on his tray. "I love pasta."

"Me, too." I grab my own plate and walk over to an empty table. He sits down, and I don't know if I should cut the chicken for him or not. "You need help?" I ask him, and he just shakes his head. The chair beside me pulls out, and Amy sits down.

"If you want, I can find his team coach and take him to them," she says. I look over at Dylan, who isn't even listening while he tries to cut his chicken after giving up eating his pasta.

"It's fine," I say, leaning over and cutting his chicken, and he just nods as he puts a piece in his mouth. Amy goes over the things happening this week and lets me know that a couple of my teammates will be coming by on Wednesday to get on the ice with me for a couple of hours.

I look over at Dylan who finished his whole plate and is now drinking the apple juice that I put down for him. "Can I go watch?" he asks of the game taking place in one of the rinks. About five other kids are standing over there to watch, so I just nod.

"I can call and see if my brother and my brothers-in-law want to come and lend a hand," I suggest, and Amy nods. The bell rings somewhere, and the kids look around. One of the coaches claps his hands and tells all the kids to go into their locker room for the second part of the day.

I finish my lunch and then walk back to the locker room, taking my phone out and sending a group text to Matthew, Max, Viktor, and Evan.

Me: Do you old men want to get on the ice in a couple of weeks? I can get some canes to help you out.

Before I have a chance to put the phone back into my pocket, Evan answers me.

Evan: M&M are dinosaurs. Can they even skate?

I laugh. When Evan started dating Zara, he gave Matthew and Max that nickname, and it's stuck ever since. Forget the fact that they hated each other when they first met, but then Max eloped with our sister, Allison, something that Matthew refuses to let him forget. But now they are both working for the Stingers organization.

Not bothering to answer, I tie my skates and get on the ice with the older kids. This is why I do this; the kids are so good. There is one kid, in particular, who flies on the ice. His hands are the best I've ever seen, and he has hockey sense.

I blow the whistle, and they come over to me. "How long have you been playing hockey?" I ask the five kids who are huffing, trying to get their breathing under control.

Everyone says since they were six except the kids with the hands. "Two years," he says. I look at him and make a mental note to ask him more questions after.

The time flies, and by the time I look around, it's five o'clock, and I get off the ice. Taking off all my stuff, I change into shorts and a shirt. I grab my phone and see that I have forty missed texts and shake my head, laughing as I read through them.

Matthew: Who you calling old? Max is older than I am.

Max: I'm like fine wine; I get better with age.

Matthew: I just threw up in my mouth.

Viktor: I'm in.

Evan: We should just have the family vacation there instead of up north.

Max: That sounds good to me. I'll mention it to Allison.

Matthew: The sister you stole.

I laugh at the back and forth, and I'm about to answer

29

when I see Dylan sitting on the step facing the front door.

"Hey there," I say, putting my phone away. "Whatcha doing?"

"I'm waiting for my mom," he says, trying to blink away tears. I sit next to him.

"Mind if I wait with you?" I ask, and he just shrugs. "Do you want to call your mom?" I take out my phone when he nods.

I give him my phone, and he takes it and dials her number. She must answer right away.

"Mom," he says softly, and she must be telling him something. "Okay," he says. "I will." He hands me back the phone. "She'll be here in ten minutes."

"That's okay. It'll fly by," I say. "Are you hungry?" He just shakes his head. "How did you like the first day?"

"I really like it," he says and then looks at me. "I like the ice the best," he says, and I just nod at him.

"But in order to be faster on the ice, you need to do lots of stuff in the gym," I say. "When I was your age, all I wanted to do was be on the ice, but my father forced me to go to the gym and made me use a jump rope." I lean in to him. "I hated it," I whisper, and he smiles and laughs.

"Did you do it?" he asks, and I nod.

"I had no choice. He wouldn't let me on the ice unless I did it." I see a car pulling up, and a woman climbs out of the back seat. She runs into the arena and looks around, the fear all on her face. You can see that she has been crying; her eyes and the tip of her nose are red.

"Mommy." Dylan calls her name, and she runs over, her eyes looking at him and then at me. She looks a little shocked I'm still here.

"I'm so sorry," she says, taking Dylan into her arms. "I'm so, so sorry."

"It's okay," he says softly. She kisses his head and then leans back and takes his face in her hands. "Did you have fun?" She tries to hide the tears in her eyes.

"I was on the ice a lot," he says, and then she looks over at me.

"I'm so sorry. My car died, and I had to get an Uber, and there was traffic," she says and then gets up. "Thank you so much for sitting with him."

"Not a problem, Caroline," I say, and my heart starts to beat a bit faster. I want to pull her in for a hug, but instead, I put my hand in my pocket.

"Let's go, buddy," she says. Bending down and grabbing his camp bag, she puts it over one shoulder and then picks up the bag with the equipment.

"Do you want me to carry that?" I ask, and when she smiles at me, I see that the smile never reaches her eyes.

"No, thank you. You've done enough for the day," she says politely. "Let's go." She holds out her hand, and Dylan grasps it and then looks at me.

"Bye, Justin," he says, walking out with his mother. When I grab my stuff and walk out, I see that they are walking down the street. I get into my SUV and watch them walk to the corner and stand at the bus stop, and my stomach burns. I pull out and then stop the vehicle at the corner where they wait.

"What are you doing?" I ask, getting out of the car and walking to them.

"We have to take the bus because Mom's car didn't

work," Dylan says, and I look at Caroline, who looks like she wants the ground to open up and swallow her.

"Why don't I give you guys a lift?" I offer, and she just shakes her head.

"No," she says, standing tall. "It's more than okay. It's not that much of a ride."

"Right," I say, "but my mother would kick me in my a—" I stop myself from saying the word and then look down at Dylan. "Butt if she knew I didn't drive you home. Not to mention, what my father would do to me." I smile at her. "So technically, you would be saving me."

"Do you still get time-outs?" Dylan asks, and we both laugh at him.

"Actually, you would be surprised," I say, then I look at her. "Let me drive you home, please."

"I don't want you to go out of your way," she says. "The bus should be here any minute."

"I have nothing else planned, and I am just going to end up following the bus to make sure you get home safely, so it's just easier if you let me take you."

"You really don't—" she starts to say, and I stop her.

"I know I don't have to," I say, and she looks at me, her eyes still a bit red, "but I want to." I look down. "Let me take you and Dylan home, Caroline."

"Okay," she says softly. "If I'm honest, that would be really great." She turns to walk to the SUV, but I stop her and take the bag from her shoulder. She just smiles at me shyly and tucks her falling hair behind her ear. She is a mother to one of your kids, I tell myself, so she could be someone's wife. And just with that thought, I feel a sudden sense of loss, and I have no idea what is going on.

FOUR

CAROLINE

"*HE* NEEDS A booster seat, right?" Justin asks me when he opens the back door to his SUV. He goes to the trunk, taking one out, and my stomach sinks even more than it did before. I watch his arm muscles while he puts the bag in the trunk. His baseball cap hides the dark hair that I know he has because I may have googled him for one hot second when I left the arena. I don't know hockey; I know nothing about hockey except that my kid loves to play it, and according to everyone around us, he's really good at it. I also try to make sure he is at every practice and every game, but I didn't know how expensive the equipment was, even when bought secondhand. He had to sit out a couple of games once because his skates were just too small for him. I kept going back to the secondhand shop, hoping they would get a pair in his size. Luckily, the coach came through with a secondhand pair that I could buy.

"Let's get you in," Justin tells Dylan, who grabs his hand and gets into the SUV. He buckles him up like an expert. I stand here, not sure what to do or where to go when he shuts the door and looks at me. His brown eyes are a bit darker than they were this morning, and I avoid them when he starts to really look at me. The phone beeps in his pocket, and he takes it out and types something back and then looks at me. "Do you want to give me your address so I can plug it in?"

"Um, yeah," I say, giving him the address, and he types it in.

"That's almost an hour from here," he says, and his tone is tight. I suddenly just want to grab Dylan from the back seat and go about my way. I've had the worst day so far. My car finally died, and no amount of praying and cursing would bring it back to life. One of the workers at the office looked at it, and he just shook his head. I had to borrow Amy's Uber account to get here. She's the closest thing I have to a best friend, but she has her own issues. I know that money is tight for her, too, but she wouldn't take no for an answer.

"I understand if you can't take us," I say, trying to keep my hands from shaking by crossing them together.

"How long would it have taken you to get home on the bus?" he asks, and I don't know where he is going with these questions.

"I'm not sure. Probably longer than an hour," I answer him. I don't even dare tell him that I would have to take two buses. Something that we will have to do tomorrow also. We are going to have to be out of the house by six to make it here by eight, and I've already arranged a lift with another co-worker who will pick me up at the arena on her way to work.

"He's had a long day," he says. "He was on the ice for over three hours." I look at him, expecting him to say more except he doesn't. He gets into the driver's seat, and I stand here, wondering what he was actually getting at. I walk around the passenger side and get into the front seat. The car has a new car smell, a smell I recognize from when my parents got a new car right before I left home.

Reaching behind me for the seat belt, I fasten it while he looks in the back to make sure that Dylan is okay and then starts driving. I have to force myself to look out the window, or I'm going to gawk at him the entire ride.

"Thank you," I finally have the courage to say. I look at him, and it's the wrong thing to do or maybe it's the right thing to do, who knows. One of his hands holds the steering wheel while the other arm rests on the door. "You really didn't have to go out of your way like this."

"I have sisters," he says and then looks at the road. "I would hope that if any of them were stuck, someone would help them." I nod. "Why do you think I have a booster seat?"

"I have no idea. I assumed you had a child," I say, ignoring the pit in my stomach.

"No, my sister Allison came to visit a couple of months ago, and I needed two, so then I keep one in my other car and one in here just in case," he says.

"Do you just have one sister?" I ask him. I don't know why it even matters.

"No." He laughs. "I have four siblings." My mouth flies

open. "Yeah, and I'm the baby."

"Oh my gosh." I laugh. "So you must be the spoiled one."

He shrugs and smirks, and it just makes him so much better looking than before. "I say no, but everyone else says yes."

"Are you the only boy?" I am suddenly so curious about his family.

"No." He shakes his head. "Matthew, who is twenty years older than me, is the firstborn."

"Wow, he could be your dad," I point out. When he throws his head back and laughs, my thoughts immediately wonder what it would be like to lean over and kiss his neck, right below his ear. I shake my head, making the image go away. *Don't go there.*

"He sometimes forgets he is my brother and not my dad," he says. The car stops, and I look forward at the three lanes of traffic. Justin looks down at his phone. "It looks like there is an accident."

"I'm sorry if this puts a damper on your night," I say.

"I told you I had nothing planned, so it's all good." He looks ahead and then looks at me again. "Do you want to stop somewhere to eat? By the time you get home, it'll be really late to start dinner." I swallow, and it feels like my tongue just swelled in my mouth.

"No, we really can't," I say. "I already have dinner for us," I lie. The last thing I want to tell him is that I have seven dollars left in my bank account, and that I'm going to use most of it on the bus rides now. He just nods, and I don't say anything for the rest of the way home.

When he turns on our street, my heart starts to beat

faster. It's going to be no surprise that we live in a not-so-great area. And that the five apartment buildings placed in a baseball diamond shape are for the low income.

"You can just drop us off here," I say when he pulls between building one and two. He pulls over, and then when the car shuts off, I undo my seat belt and get out. Justin is already out of the SUV and opening the back door to help Dylan out. I stand in the back, not sure how to even open his trunk. He comes over and opens the door, handing me the hockey bag and Dylan the gym bag. "You go to bed early tonight," he tells Dylan, holding out his arm to fist bump him. "Don't stay up late watching television."

"We don't have a TV," Dylan says. My eyes fly to Dylan's as my heart speeds up. "But I'll go to bed early," he says and comes to stand next to me.

I look at Justin, who just stands there, and the bottom of my neck starts to get hot. "Dylan, say thank you to Coach Stone."

"Thank you, Justin," he says and fist bumps him again, and then turns to walk to our apartment building.

"Thank you so much," I say and turn to walk away. I don't look behind me. One, I'm afraid he'll catch me looking at him, and two, I don't want to see that look of pity on his face at the fact we don't have a television. Dylan's hand slides into mine, and blinking away tears, I look down at him, knowing how much he has suffered through all this.

"What do you want to eat for dinner?" I ask him, and he shrugs. "How about some mac and cheese?" I suggest his favorite meal, and he just smiles. As we walk up the stairs, it gets hotter and hotter. I'm not even going to think about how hot it is in our apartment.

Unlocking the door, I walk in, not looking at anything, and then I hear Dylan shriek, "Dad!" My head snaps up as I see Andrew sitting on the couch. The hockey bag drops on the floor at the same time Dylan runs to him and Andrew hugs him. It's been two months since we've seen him. Two months of peace for me. I close the door and toss the keys on the small kitchen table.

"Go take a shower, Dylan. I'm going to start dinner," I say, and he looks at me and walks to the bathroom. I wait for the door to close and the water to turn on before I turn back and look at Andrew. The man I used to love, the man who promised me everything would be okay, the man who's lied to me over and over again.

"What are you doing here, Andrew?" I ask him, folding my arms over my chest.

"I missed you guys," he says, and I roll my eyes.

"I have no money for you," I say. "And there is nothing left for you to sell either."

"I'm not here for that," he says, and I look at him and see the shell of the man he used to be. His dirty jeans, his yellowed shoes, his gray shirt with stains all over it, but more importantly, the needle marks up and down his arm.

"You really have to go," I say.

"Why are you being like that?" he says, getting up and coming closer to me. He smells like he hasn't showered in weeks. "I just need a place to crash for the night."

I'm about to tell him to get out of the house when the door opens and Dylan sticks his head out. "Mom, can I wear one of the new shirts to bed?"

"Yeah, honey," I say, grabbing the new bag and looking over to see Andrew's eyes go from me to the bag. "Keep that in there with you and then put it in the bedroom when you are done with it."

"Okay, Mom," he says, closing the door, and I turn back to Andrew.

"You can't stay here," I say.

"Why not?" he whines, and I just shake my head.

"Because the last time you came here, so did your dealer," I hiss. "Then he came back every freaking day until I paid him the five hundred dollars you owed him!" I shout.

"I'm going to pay you back," he says, and I turn around, walking to the cabinet and taking out a pot. "You know I just have—"

I fill the pot with water then put it down on the burner and turn around. "I don't want to hear your excuses, Andrew. I really couldn't care less."

"God." He shakes his head. "You can be such a bitch."

"Yup," I say, turning around to ignore him, while he goes to the couch and grabs his jacket.

"All I wanted was to spend some time with Dylan, and you give me shit about it." I look at how his beautiful blond hair is now dark and stringy, and his blue eyes are so sunken in you can barely look at him.

"Last time you did that, we left, and you stole the fucking television," I say.

"Whatever. I don't have to stay for this bullshit," he says, storming to the door and slamming it closed behind him. I walk over and lock it. Although it obviously doesn't matter if he broke in here before. I close my eyes, and the tears

41

come no matter how much I try to fight them. I work my ass off to make sure Dylan has everything he needs, and just when I think I'm getting ahead, Andrew comes in and knocks all my cards down.

The phone rings in my back pocket, and I don't even look at who is calling. "Hello," I answer, my low voice almost a whisper.

"Um, Caroline." His voice comes through, and I open my eyes. "It's Justin."

"Um, yeah." I wipe away my tears as if he can see me. "Did I forget something in your vehicle?"

"No," he says, and his voice goes soft. "Are you okay?" he asks, and I don't know why I want to tell him that I'm not okay. That I haven't been okay in a long, long time.

"I'm fine," I say. It's the answer I give everyone because this is my life. As my parents said, I made my bed, and now I have to lie in it. "What's the matter?"

"So I was thinking that I really don't use my vehicle during the day," he starts, "and I know that you're stuck."

"I can't do that," I say. "I'm not your problem."

"I never said you were. I'm saying that my vehicle will be parked in a parking lot doing nothing," he says, and his voice goes softer. "Just take the favor, Caroline."

"I can't," I say, closing my eyes. The door to the bathroom opens, and Dylan comes running out. "I have to go," I say, disconnecting and looking at him.

"Where's Dad?" he asks, and I look at my son, who I will protect with everything I have.

"He had to go to work," I say. "He said he'll see you soon." I watch his lower lip tremble, and he blinks and rushes to wipe away the tears. I take a step toward him, but he shakes his head.

"I'm tired," he says and then runs to the bedroom and gets into the bed. I walk to the bed and sit next to him.

"I'm so sorry, honey," I say, my fingers playing with his hair, and I lean down and kiss his cheeks.

"Whatever," he says, and I hear the hissing of the stove and run to see that the water I turned on is no more. I turn off the burner and put the pot in the sink. I catch my breath for just a second before I have to go back into the room, and I find that Dylan's already asleep. I turn off the light and head to the shower, and only when I'm under the water do I let the tears escape.

Five

Justin

I DON'T HAVE a TV. His voice plays over and over in my head. I couldn't help but call her. I actually wanted to go to her apartment and take her to Walmart and buy her a TV or even ten. I didn't care. Instead, she answered me in tears. I know she did because I heard it, and more importantly, I felt it. It's fucking insane that I have this pull to her. It's because of Dylan, I keep telling myself. You are drawn to the kid.

I slam my car door, then walk into my condo, and the cold air hits me right away. Closing the door, I walk over to my couch and grab my laptop to bring with me to the island in my kitchen. I have a huge open floor plan, and my sister came down one weekend to make sure I had all my stuff.

Pulling up the documents I got with every kid coming to the program, I type in his name, and it comes up right away with a picture from his school. I read all his information, or I start to, and then I stop. My foot starts to bounce up and down, thinking about whether I should read it or not. I want to read it, but I also don't want her to feel like I'm snooping. I look at one thing before I decide to shut it down. Single mom.

After shutting the laptop, I walk over to the fridge and open it, grabbing a bottle of water. I close my eyes and think about what they are doing. I take out my phone, and I almost call her again, but then I can hear my sisters' voices in the back of my head calling me a stalker. I walk toward the balcony and sit outside, watching the lights from the buildings start to shine brighter as the sun goes down. So many things are going through my mind that I don't know where to start. "This is either the best thing ever, or it's going to blow up in my face," I tell the universe while I make my plan for the next day.

I hit the road at four thirty, not even sure what time she has to leave home to take the bus, but either way, I'm going to make sure I don't miss her. I pull up and see some people hanging around. A couple of women who have seen better days look my way when I pull up to the curb and turn off the car. I watch as the building slowly comes to life as the minutes tick by. People taking the bus come out every five minutes, and right at six a.m., I see her walking down the sidewalk with a sleepy Dylan beside her and get out of my vehicle. She is holding his hand and looking tired herself. Her blond hair is pulled back in a high bun on her head.

I wait for her to look up, and when she finally sees me, she stops in the middle of the sidewalk. I walk to her, her green eyes locking on mine as she stands there with her mouth hanging open. Dylan stops moving and looks at her, and then his eyes fly to me, and he just smiles. The big hockey bag is hefted over her left shoulder. "What are you doing here?" she asks me, almost in a whisper.

"Well, I figured if I asked you if you needed a ride, you would tell me no, so I decided it would be better to just show up." She looks down in order to hide her smile. "So now that I'm here, will you accept that ride?"

"What time did you get here?" she asks, and I reach over and slowly take the bag from her shoulder. She lets me but only because I think she's still in shock that I'm standing here.

"Hey, buddy," I say to Dylan, who rubs his eyes.

"Hi, Justin." His voice is sleepy.

"Did you just pull him out of bed?" I ask, and she just nods her head.

"Yeah, if we wanted to make it to the rink by eight, we had to take the six o'clock bus," she says, and we walk over to the truck.

"Why don't you get him into the SUV, and I'll put his bag in the trunk?" I say, and she opens the back door.

I close the trunk at the same time she closes the back door. "Are you okay?" I ask as she just stands there.

"Seriously, what are you doing here?" she asks, standing in front of me, and the wind picks up and some of the loose hair flies into her face.

"I," I start, but I don't even know why I am here. "Listen, you need a lift, and there was no way you would have taken it had I asked."

47

"So you just show up here?" She looks around at the traffic of people coming our way.

"Answer me this." I look at her, and I suddenly want to step closer to her. "Had I called you and offered you one, would you have taken me up on my offer?"

She doesn't hesitate for even a second. "No," she says. "You had to go out of your way yesterday to drive me home, so I wasn't going to let you do it again today."

I'm about to argue with her when the back door opens. "Mom, I'm hungry."

"What are you in the mood for, buddy?" I ask him.

Without missing a beat, he just blurts out, "Pancakes, waffles, eggs, and some bread." I look at Caroline, and I want to put my hand on her neck and bring her close to me and kiss her, but instead, I just shake my head.

"I think we should get him fed before he adds lobster to that list." I see the worry set into her eyes, and I know she's probably thinking about paying the bill.

"I owe you breakfast," I say. "It's on me."

"How do you figure you owe me breakfast?" she asks.

"You're letting me take you, and you aren't giving me a hard time about it," I say. "So thank you." I nod at her. "Now get in. I'm hungry, too." I turn and walk to the driver's side, and I don't even realize that I'm holding my breath, waiting for her to get in the SUV. She gets in and then shakes her head. "Are we all ready?" I ask. Looking behind me, I see as Dylan nods his head to me.

Pulling away from the curb, I make my way to the arena, stopping at a diner halfway there. I get out, and when I walk around, Caroline is already getting Dylan out of the vehicle.

It looks like she is telling him something, and he just nods his head at her. "Everything okay?"

"Yes," she says, and I look at Dylan who just nods.

We walk up to the entrance, and the bells on the door ring as soon as I pull it open. "Sit where you want," the older white-haired lady says, rushing from behind the counter to the back.

"Pick a seat," I tell them, and Caroline walks in front of me to a booth along the window. She waits for Dylan to climb into the booth and then follows him in, and I sit in front of them. I grab the menus tucked behind the salt and pepper shakers, handing one to Dylan and then one to Caroline. Then I look down at my own.

The lady who told us to sit comes over with three glasses of water. "Hey there, what can I get for you?" I look at Caroline to go first.

"Um," she starts to talk and then looks down at the menu, and I see her eyes roaming over the menu.

"I can order first," I tell the lady who holds the pad in one hand and the pen in the other. "I'll take pancakes, waffles, two eggs over easy, two eggs scrambled, some hash browns, six orders of toast, and three orange juices." The lady just rolls her lips, trying not to laugh, and I look up at her. "Just put the plates in the middle, and we can all share."

"Got it," she says, and then looks at Caroline. "Did you want to add some fruit with that?" Caroline just shakes her head. "Coming right up."

"Do you know how much food you just ordered?" Caroline leans over the table and directs her question at me, but her voice is louder than she intended.

"Well, you took too long, so I ordered for us," I say, grabbing the water and taking a sip, my mouth suddenly dry.

"Can we talk?" Caroline says. "Outside." She gets up. "Honey, I'll be right outside."

"Okay, Mom," he says.

I smile at him. "Don't eat all that food before I come back." He smiles back and shrugs. I follow Caroline outside, ignoring the fact that the yoga pants mold her ass like a second skin and should be worn with a long shirt to cover it. I wonder to myself if I have a jacket in the car, and then I almost stop in my tracks. What is happening to me? I don't have time to think about it because we are outside in front of the window, and she looks in to see if Dylan is okay.

"I can't afford to pay for this meal," she says, her head held high and her shoulders back. "There is no way I can even imagine what that bill will be, but …"

I hold up my hand to stop her from talking. "When did I ask you to pay for anything?"

"I can't afford to pay this. Not now"—she talks faster now—"not next week, not even next month. I am not a charity case."

"Are you done?" I ask and wait for her to indicate she is listening. I step into her space, and she takes one step back, which pisses me off to no avail. Suddenly, I want to sit her down, and I want her to tell me everything. I want to know everything about her, but something says to tread lightly. "I'm not doing it for charity, and I don't expect you to pay me back. Not this week, not next week, not even next year. I don't know your story, Caroline, and I'm not even sure you would tell me, but I want you to listen and to pay attention

50

to the words I'm about to say. I'm doing this because I want to and because I can. I'm doing this because sometimes people come into your life for certain reasons. I don't always know what that reason is, but I know that I want to be your friend, Caroline. And as your friend, this is what people do."

"I don't have many friends," she says, and I smile. "I mean, if you think about it, I probably have maybe one friend. But she's more of an acquaintance."

"Well, I'm happy I'm your first." I try to make a joke but see that her eyes are filling with tears, and it kills me to see her cry. "Don't," I say softly, and my hand flies out to touch her face and catch the tear that falls out of her eye. "Don't cry." Her skin is soft like silk, and I want nothing more than to pull her to me.

"I'm not crying," she says and steps out of my grasp. "It's just I usually do things on my own."

"Yeah, I can see that," I say, then look in and see that the waitress is there with the food. "It doesn't make you less of a person to accept help. Now, I don't know about you, but I'm pretty sure that kid can eat everything I ordered, so I think we should go in and make sure he doesn't." I walk away, and when my hand touches the door handle, she speaks.

"Thank you," she says softly, and I turn back to see her standing there with her hands in front of her. "I don't know what your reason is, but I want to just say thank you."

"You're welcome, Caroline," I say to her softly, and my heart speeds up. This tiny woman who comes at me with guns blazing and ready to go to war doesn't even know how much she is worth.

51

Caroline

"*T*HANK YOU." IT'S the only thing I can say to him. My heart is beating so fast I can't even focus on anything else. From the minute I saw him standing there waiting for us, my knees have been shaky. I didn't know what he was doing, and I have no idea what's going on. It's just too much.

"Let's go eat," he says, and I have to stop looking at him because all it does is make me want something I can't have. He holds the door open for me, and I walk in with him following, and he is not wrong. Dylan is already eating one waffle and is grabbing a pancake to add to his plate. The syrup is already in front of him, and there is syrup on his plate.

"I was going to wait," he says to me with his cheek full of food as he takes another bite. It looks like he hasn't eaten in a month.

"Oh, I forgot to order bacon and sausage," Justin says,

sitting down on his side of the table. He holds up his hand, and the sleeve rises and shows his arm muscle, and I suddenly wonder how many people got lost in those arms. Is he with someone right now? Did he have to sneak out to come and pick us up, or did he tell her all about the poor lady with the kid whose car broke down? "Can we get some bacon and sausage?"

"Coming right up," the waitress says, and I look at the full plates of food on the table. I don't even know what to eat first when I hear him.

"Eat." Justin's voice makes me look at him, and I roll my eyes, taking my empty plate and filling it with some scrambled eggs and then a slice of toast. The waitress comes over and adds two more plates to the table. "Meat," he says, grabbing the plate of bacon and putting some on my plate and then on Dylan's. "Have some sausage," he says, putting two on my plate and then two on Dylan's, who just nods his head and eats another pancake.

I pick my fork up and scoop up some eggs, and they melt in my mouth. We rarely, and by that, I mean never, go out and eat. So this little diner is everything. "Are we going to be on the ice again today?" Dylan asks Justin, who is eating from his own huge plate. Between the two of them, there is barely any food left, and I eat the little I have slowly so Dylan can get the rest if he wants it.

"Yeah," Justin says, drinking his orange juice. "We are making new groups today. After the evaluations yesterday, we are going to make new groups every week," he says. "And there is a special surprise today."

I look over at Dylan and see that his eyes are as big as

saucers. "More surprises?" He looks at me and then at Justin. "What is it?"

"I can't tell you that." Justin smiles at him and takes the last drink of his juice and then looks at me. "Did you eat enough?"

"Yeah," I say, looking down at my empty plate. I don't grab the last piece of toast, and it's a good thing because Dylan snatches it up and then turns to me.

"Can you put peanut butter on this?" he asks, and I lean over to grab a small square plastic container, then peel the top off and spread it on the toast. "Thanks, Mom," he says as he bites into it.

The waitress comes over. "Well, I take it the food was good?" She stacks the empty plates to clear the table, and I smile at her. When she walks away, Justin gets up and follows her, and I know he's going to pay the bill. I'm trying not to think about how much it is, but I can't help it. When I pulled out the menu, my heart sank at the prices. The lowest was six dollars for the two eggs plate. I grab the menu now and try to do a quick calculation in my head, but my mind starts to spin when I get past the fifty-dollar mark.

"Did you eat good?" I ask Dylan, grabbing my own orange juice and drinking it while he nods and finishes his toast. Justin comes back over and sits down in front of us.

"You are going to be a bullet on the ice today," Justin tells Dylan. "My father used to make me eat the biggest breakfast in the morning," he says. "I used to hate it." He shakes his head. "All I wanted was to get on the ice."

"I like the ice best," Dylan says.

"One day, I didn't eat breakfast, and I went on the ice. I

couldn't even skate," Justin says, and Dylan just listens to his story.

"What happened?" Dylan asks, all worried.

"Well, I went to skate, and then I was going on a break-away, but I just didn't have the energy to skate it all the way to the goal line, and they stole the puck from me."

"Was your dad mad?" he asks, worried for him. "Did he yell at you?"

"Nah, my dad never yells at me. My mom sometimes." He smiles and looks at me. "Most times. Are you guys almost ready?" he asks, and Dylan nods.

"You need to go wash your hands and mouth before we leave," I say, seeing the peanut butter across his cheek. Looking down at the syrup drops on the table, I bet he has some of that on him as well. I get out of the booth, and I'm about to go with him when Justin gets up.

"I don't think you have the parts that belong in the men's bathroom. I have it," he says. I stand here with my mouth open as they walk away, and I sit back down, not sure what else to do. He's been around me for a day, and my whole world feels like it's shifted.

Sitting here, I wait for them to come back out, and when they do, Dylan is laughing at something Justin just said. "Ready?" I say, getting out of the booth. Justin looks over my head at the waitress, who nods at him, and he walks past me, grabbing a brown to-go bag.

"Is that your lunch?" Dylan asks him, and Justin just smiles at him. Opening the door, Justin gestures for me walk out before him. He opens the door for Dylan and makes sure he's seated and buckled, and I get in, looking in the back.

Justin gets in and starts the vehicle, pulling off and making his way to the arena. "All the papers are in the glove compartment," he starts saying to me, and I shake my head. "I have AAA in case something happens," he says, pulling into the parking spot, "but I want you to call me and then call them."

"I can't believe I'm doing this," I say, and I have to be honest. I have no choice. My boss at the call center is amazing, but he can only do so much, and me missing work and leaving early is something he is already covering for me. Because of hockey camp, I'm arriving late this whole summer.

I get out of the car the same time as Justin and then Dylan, and Justin hands me the keys like it's nothing. "Let's go get the surprise," Justin says, and Dylan skips beside him.

I walk beside them while Dylan asks questions, and Justin opens the door and waits for me to walk in. Dylan walks up to the lady who greeted us yesterday.

"Good morning, Dylan," she says with a smile and then looks at me. "Good morning." Then she must see Justin behind me. "Morning, Justin."

"Hi, Malika," I say, smiling and putting my hands on Dylan's shoulders.

"We have a special surprise today," Malika says, and Dylan jumps up and claps his hands.

"I'll take them there," Justin says, and she just smiles.

"Have a great day, guys," she says while Dylan follows Justin around the staircase. When we get to the hallway, he turns and walks into the first room. Stopping at the door, I see tables against all four walls with equipment on it.

57

"Grab one of the bags," Justin says to Dylan, gesturing to the stack of empty blue hockey bags in the corner. "Now let's fill up the bag."

"What?" Dylan asks, looking at him.

"You need a chest protector," he says, going over to the table and grabbing one, and another man comes in the room.

"Hey, there he is," a man says, coming up to Justin.

"Dan," he says, holding out his hand. "So glad you could make this happen."

"When Justin Stone calls, I come running," he says, and I just watch him in action. "Who is this one?'

"Dylan Woods," Justin says. "His mother, Caroline."

"Dylan, let's get you geared up," the man says, grabbing Dylan and bringing him over to get him elbow pads. I have to wipe away a tear, and when Justin looks at me, I look down and try not to let him see. He's never had new equipment before. He's never had anything that was brand new and his own. Everything from his clothes to his shoes have always been secondhand.

"I have to go," I say to the floor and walk around him to Dylan. "I'll see you tonight."

Turning, I start to walk out of the room and then remember Justin needs to get his lunch, but when I turn around, I run smack into his hard chest. I know it's him because it smells exactly like him. His hands catch my arms to steady me, and I breathe in and out, which makes it worse since now his smell is all around me.

"Um," I start to say, and then I look up, and his brown eyes are dark with just a little gold on the inside. "You forgot your lunch," I say softly, and he smiles a big megawatt smile. It's a smile that lights up his whole face like you would when you win a race or, in his case, win some cup.

"It's not my lunch," he says, his voice soft. "I figured you didn't pack yourself a lunch." I'm about to ask him what he's talking about, but then I hear a female voice calling his name.

"Justin, there you are." I step out of his hold and take two steps back, looking over and seeing the woman from yesterday. This time, she's dressed in black pants and the nicest top I've ever seen, and her hair is perfectly set. She walks like she owns the world, and it takes one second for me to realize that these two fit. This is who he'll end up with, so it's only logical that she would fit.

"I'll be back tonight," I say and make a beeline for the exit. I walk a little bit faster than normal out into the hot sun. Getting into the car, I smell him all around me. I adjust my seat and make my way to work. The SUV drives so smooth. I have no idea what to do with the radio or what button to press, so I just leave it off and get lost in my own thoughts, which go right back to Justin where they shouldn't be.

SEVEN

JUSTIN

"GREAT IDEA TO get the kids new equipment," Amy says. "Some of them have equipment that needs to be retired." I look at her, and I'm almost tempted to fire her, but then who the hell would help run this shit.

"Have some respect, Amy," I say under my breath as kids run out of the room like it's Christmas morning. I walk in, looking for Dylan, but don't see him anywhere.

"He went to his locker room," Dan says while he helps a kid try on skates.

"Thank you so much." One of the fathers comes to me and shakes my hand with his eyes filled with tears. "It's more than you know."

"It's my pleasure," I say, and then I point over at Dan. "He's the one who made this happen."

"Your parents should be very, very proud," he says, and I smile.

I lean in and whisper, "I'll remind my mother of that the next time I miss her curfew when I'm home."

"Always her baby," he says, and I nod. "Have a great day."

"You as well," I say and turn to walk down the hallway while I hear some of the kids freaking out.

"These are the newest skates on the market," one of the kids says. "He has to mold my foot tomorrow."

"This hockey stick has the best flex," another says, and I finally find Dylan in one of the locker rooms all by himself.

"Hey there, did you get your stuff?" I ask, sitting on the bench and looking around.

"Justin, look at the new skates I got," he says, taking them out of his bag and holding them up to me. "The laces are so white." He looks down, and his smile fills his face.

"I saw. Did you try them on?" I ask. He comes to sit next to me and takes his running shoes off and puts his foot in one.

"Will you help me tie them?" he asks, and I get up and stoop down in front of him. "Usually, Mom helps me."

"Does she tie them really tight?" I ask as I tighten the lace at the bottom.

"Yeah," he says and then looks at me. "But the other dads do it tighter. Don't tell her."

I try not to laugh, and then my heart hurts for him to never have a father tie his skates. "I won't tell her. My mom used to try also."

"Not your dad?" he asks, and I look at him, grabbing the other skate and putting it on him.

"Yeah. Most of the time it was my dad, but sometimes when he had a meeting, it had to be my mom," I say. "Sometimes, if I was really lucky, it would be my big brother." I smile at him. "He used to come home and come to some of my games, and I would always try to score a goal for him."

"Did you score?" he asks, not even realizing that I finished tying his skates.

"Most times," I say. "What about you, do you score?"

"Yeah," he says, getting up. "I even got a trophy for most goals in the season," he says. "I got five goals in one game," he says, and I get up.

"Wow, that's better than me," I say. "Walk and see how they feel," I say. The bell rings, letting everyone know it's time to get to your place.

"They hurt my feet," he says, and I nod at him.

"That's new skates for you. It'll take a bit to get them worn in," I say. "Let me go get my skates, and I'll help you get ready for the ice." I get up, and three kids come into the room who are older than Dylan.

"Is this group four?" one of them asks.

"Yes," Dylan says, taking off his skates. I walk outside and find one of the trainers. Actually, he's the one I picked myself. Ralph plays with me for Edmonton, and his contract is up next year. He is the best on the ice, and you can't even try to deny it. Stats don't lie and neither do the results once he hits the ice. He's also known as the pretty boy on the ice, and one of the few defensemen who still has all his teeth.

"Hey, Ralph," I call him over. "Dylan Woods, he's in there with kids who are twelve."

"Yeah. Did you see him on the ice?" he asks. There were five people in the stands evaluating the kids to make sure they were placed in the right level to help them get better.

"That kid plays like a thirteen-year-old. He just doesn't

have the height," Ralph says.

"He's eight," I say. I knew he had it, but I had to have someone else say it so I knew I wasn't playing favorites.

"Yeah, well, the kid has it," Ralph says. I walk away to the room to get my bag and wonder if I should go back to him or not. I grab my bag without thinking twice about it.

Walking back into the room, I see he's almost already dressed. He slips his jersey over his head and then steps into his skates again, and he looks up and sees the kids tying their own skates so he doesn't say anything as he tries to tie his own skates. "You good?" I ask, and he looks at me while he tries to tighten it.

"Here," I say, putting my own skate on and showing him how I tie it. "You grab the one on the top and pull up." I show him, and he ties it all the way to the top.

"I did it," he says happily and then gets up, doing the other one. He grabs his new helmet and puts his mouth guard in.

"How did you get so good at skating?" I ask.

"I use the outdoor rink," he says. "When Mom is cleaning the rooms, she lets me skate outside."

"She cleans hotel rooms?" I ask, and he nods his head.

"Not all the time, just on Saturday and Sunday," he says. "I have to go with her because she doesn't have anyone to watch me."

"She's a good mom," I say, my head swirling with the information he just told me. She works two jobs and doesn't even have money to buy breakfast. I want to ask her all the questions, but who the fuck am I that she is going to answer me. I'm just some guy who took her to breakfast once.

Dylan walks over to the wall and grabs his new stick. "I'm going to tape my new stick tonight," he says, and I smile, grabbing my own helmet and following him on the ice.

He gets on before me, and I'm expecting him to wobble a bit, but instead, he just glides on like he was born to be there. I get on after him and blow the whistle. "Two laps," I say, twirling my fingers and then blow the whistle again and watch the kids take off. I stand in the middle with Ralph.

"Doesn't it make you laugh?" He starts to talk. "Some rich kids out there are paying two hundred dollars an hour for someone to train them, and they will never be as good as half of these kids." I watch the kids go around in the circle, and I spot Dylan right away by the way he moves. "Look at that kid," Ralph says, pointing at Dylan. "Look at the way he skates. He uses his whole body, which makes him even better."

"What about if you put a puck on his stick?" I ask, and he smiles at me.

"My favorite part," he says, going over and getting the pucks and throwing them on the ice. I watch as Dylan slides over and takes a puck with the back of his blade and then kicks it to the stick like it's no big deal. He skates around and moves the puck right and left. The whole time, his head is up, and not once does he lose control of it. "His hands are better than the fifteen year olds. If this kid has the opportunity, he might beat your dad's records."

I throw my head back and laugh. "If you're right, I'll pay you a thousand dollars."

For the rest of the practice, I watch Dylan closely, and every single time he's given something to do or works on a drill, he just excels and pushes himself. When the hour is over, the kids skate to the bench and take a drink of water. "Okay, three-on-three game," Ralph says. I watch as Dylan skates to center ice, and I stand back as he gets into position exactly like I do. He skates in a circle and then leans forward with his stick in his hands. He gets ready for the face-off, and he doesn't look at the kid; he looks at Ralph who holds the puck in his hand. He leans in just a touch and drops the puck. Dylan ducks down, and his stick goes out winning the face-off.

He skates past the kid, going straight to the puck, and there is only one kid on defense, so it's almost like a one-on-one. He skates to the right and then to the left, and when he thinks the other kid is going back to the right, Dylan pulls his stick back and aims for the net, his puck hitting the back of the net. "I should have doubled the wager," Ralph says, skating to go get the puck.

"Hey, Justin, did you see that I scored?" Dylan says, skating to the bench and letting someone else take his place.

"I did see it," I say. "Smooth."

He just nods his head, smiling, while he takes a squirt of water. By the end of the game, he's scored ten goals. He skates off the ice, and the only time I see him again is at the end of the day when he comes out of the locker room with his hair wet.

"Hey, is my mom here?" he asks, looking around. I look toward the door and see her walking in. I smile, just thinking about her, but when she looks up, I see that she's been crying. Her eyes look like they are bloodshot, and I look at Dylan, who sees her and runs to her. She sees him and smiles at him, showing a brave face, and my heart can't stop the hammering. It can't stop even if I told it not to, even if I know she has the ability to shatter it.

I don't go to her. Instead, I watch how she buries whatever she is going through to smile at Dylan. "Did you have a good day?" she asks, opening her arms and kissing his head when he reaches around to hug her waist.

"Yeah, we got all new stuff," he says, and she looks up and finally sees me.

"Hey," she says, her voice coming out monotone. "Thank you so much for helping today," she says, holding out the keys for the SUV. "And for the lunch." She does a fake smile and then looks down at Dylan. "Let's get going."

"How are you getting home?" I ask, and my stomach somehow burns with anger.

She is about to answer me when Amy comes out, calling my name. "Justin." She swaggers over, and I turn my head to look at her. "We are still on for tonight, right?"

"Yeah," I say and then my name is called again, this time by a parent who walks by, and when I turn back around, Dylan and Caroline are gone. I jog out to see if I see them, and I can't spot them anywhere. I turn to walk back into the arena, and I'm almost run down by Malika, who isn't looking up.

"I'm so sorry," she says, and I can see that she is really upset.

"Is everything okay?" I ask, and she just looks around.

"You are doing a good thing here," she says. "The kids who come here, this is huge for them. And the parents, I can't even begin to tell you how blown away the parents are. They aren't freeloaders, and they deserve to not be judged." I almost have to take a step back.

"I would never judge anyone," I say.

"I know you don't," she says and then looks down and then up again. "But not everyone working for you does. I'll see you tonight at seven," she says and then walks away. I watch her walk away with more questions that I have to do, and I make a mental note to talk to her tonight after the meeting. I also take my phone out and call Caroline, and it goes directly to a generic message.

The customer you are trying to reach is unavailable. Please call back.

I hang up and text her right away.

Me: Where did you go?

I look down at my phone, expecting her to answer, but she doesn't.

"Hey," Ralph says when he sees me looking down at my phone as I wait for Caroline to answer me. "Do you have a minute?" he asks me, looking around.

"Yeah," I say, looking at him and seeing he is unsure of whatever he has to say. "Let's go into the office." I lead the way into the offices and go inside one of the empty ones and close the door. "What's up?"

"Listen, I think what you are doing here is amazing," he says, then he runs his hands through his hair. "You are giving these kids a chance to be something." I just look at him. "All of us are here for one reason or another, but Amy"—he shakes his head—"I just can't."

"What happened?" I ask him, my blood starting to boil.

"A father just went up to her to hand her his new contact information, and she refused to take the paper from him because his hands were dirty." He shakes his head. "She told him to put it down on her desk and she would take care of it. The way she jumped when he tried to hand it to her. Dude, it was …"

"That is unacceptable," I tell him. "This is my name. It's the Justin Stone Foundation. If you work for me, you represent me, and she definitely does not represent me when she acts like that. What is wrong with her?"

"That is a loaded question, and my mother told me to be kind to women," Ralph says, laughing. "I just thought you would want to know."

"Thank you," I tell him, and he walks out of the room. Taking a seat, I look down at my phone, and I decide to go to her after the meeting.

I walk into the meeting already tense and on pins and needles to get this show over. I sit at the head of the table, and my team sits around the table. Ralph is also there as well as Malika, who is taking notes.

"One thing I was thinking of," Malika starts to say, "is a weekend program." Looking over at her, she continues, "Many of these parents work on the weekends, so we could have a free skate day on Saturday or a Sunday Family day."

I start to say something when I hear Amy pffts out, and all eyes go to her. "You don't think maybe these parents are taking advantage of this program already? I mean, seriously some of them are taking advantage of the whole system. Get a job. That should help you get off food stamps," she says, and I want to slam my hand down on the table. But instead, I rein it in and push away from the table.

"Amy, I'd like to talk to you outside," I tell her, and I'm already out in the hallway when she comes out with a huge smile on her face. I don't think she realizes how angry I am. Is she that clueless? I don't even beat around the bush. "Amy, we are going to have to let you go."

Her smile fades and in its place is the leer. "What the fuck does that mean?"

"It means that you're fired," I tell her. "It means that you take your stuff and don't come back."

"But why?" she asks, trying to act as if she's hurt by all this.

"Well, just off the top of my head. You are rude and condescending and aren't a nice person." I take a deep breath. "What I'm doing here is helping the kids, and it's helping the community. It's called giving them a chance and not judging them. It's called being a decent human being."

"This is bullshit." She starts to throw a hissy fit, and as my sisters would say, a tantrum. "I have given this everything I have." I swear she stomps her foot. "You can't fire me."

"Oh, but I can," I inform her, "and I just did. I started this foundation when I was nineteen years old. I saw my family do things like this when I was just a kid. My brother-in-law has the biggest foundation I've ever had the privilege of being a part of, and I want to have one just like him. I want people to have nothing but amazing things to say abut my foundation, and having you represent me and my foundation the way you have is not okay."

"This is not the end of me," she says, pushing past me. Going into the office, she grabs her purse and then comes out. "You are firing me without cause. I'll be contacting a lawyer."

"You do that," I tell her, and she storms out. Putting my head down, I look at the phone in my hand with still no word from her. I walk back into the meeting, and I don't even know what we discussed after that because the only thing on my mind was Caroline.

EIGHT

CAROLINE

"*I*'M TIRED, MOM." I hear from beside me as we sit on the bus, making our way home. To say that today has been a giant disappointment is the understatement of the year. "Are we almost there yet?" he asks, putting his head on my shoulder, and I just nod, looking outside.

The two-hour commute has turned into almost three hours and counting since the first bus broke down, and then it took over thirty minutes to fix. "We should be home soon," I say, trying to keep the defeat from my voice.

When we are finally walking up the stairs, I'm ready to collapse on the couch. Opening the door, the heat hits you right away. The thickness of the humidity makes it hard for you to even breathe. "Why don't you get in the shower, and I'll start making dinner."

"Okay, Mom," he says, dumping his new hockey bag by the door and walking into the bathroom. I walk over to the window in the corner and open it up, not sure if it is going to help. When I finally pull the thick wooden window up, a slight breeze comes in. Tying my hair up, I walk to the bedroom and strip out of my jeans, the thick envelope I got at the end of the day heavy in my back pocket. Taking it out, I open it and sit on the bed. Being summoned to the boss's office fifteen minutes before the end of your shift never has a good outcome. Walking in and looking at him not making eye contact with you was a second alert. Starting the sentence with I'm so sorry was what cemented what I knew was coming. Hours have to be cut and the last one in usually takes the brunt of it. Even though I'd been there for over six months, I was the last one in.

A tear escapes my eye, making it hard to stop the other tear that comes after. Putting my hands over my face, I let the disappointment run through me. I don't know why I'm surprised. Usually when something is running smoothly is when it turns to shit shortly after. I was finally able to see a little bit of light at the end of the tunnel but then with me getting fired and getting a two-week severance, the light is now covered in black. I have no idea what I'm going to do. I called Karla right away and asked her if she had more cleaning shifts at the motel, and even though I was almost begging, all she had was my regular weekend shifts. Tonight after Dylan goes to bed, I'll take out all my papers and see how I will stretch this last check.

The water turns off, and I tuck the letter and the jeans in the drawer and go over to the stove and start frying eggs. We have three eggs left, so I make two for Dylan and slip the last two slices of bread in the toaster. I would also have to go down to the church and see if I can get anything from their emergency fund. I open the fridge and go to grab a slice of cheese and realize I don't have any left. Instead, I grab the small container of ham that I bought last week and take out a couple of pieces and fry it in the pan with the eggs. The bread pops up, and I grab the little bit of margarine I have left just as the bathroom door opens. "I'm done," he says, coming out, and this time, all he's wearing is his boxer briefs, knowing it's too hot for anything else.

"Just in time," I say over my shoulder, grabbing a plate and putting his eggs on them and the ham, cutting the bread in half. "Here you go."

"Thanks, Mom," he says, and I wait for him to eat before cracking open of the last eggs for myself. He looks up at me. "Why aren't you eating?"

"I had a big lunch," I say, thinking of the lunch bag Justin left in the car. It was actually a chicken club sandwich with a bag of chips and even a drink. "Do you want more?" I ask him, and he just shakes his head. I turn back around and think about breakfast in the morning. Knowing I don't have much left, I put the last egg in the fridge for him tomorrow.

"Can I watch some videos on your phone?" he asks, and I nod my head, thankful we can get free Wi-Fi.

"But not for too long. You have a big day tomorrow," I say, and he nods his head and goes into the bedroom. I clean the little kitchen, my mind going around and around, thinking of everything. I'm not even working on plan B; I'm working on plan C, and then I'm working on worst-case scenarios. The thought of the two of us having to move again is making me sick. There is no way I can find another apartment as cheap as this for what we get. I know it isn't much, but at least it's clean. The other places we found were roach-infested or in an even seedier part of town.

I finish cleaning with tears streaming down my face. I wipe the tears when I finish and then splash some cold water on my face. Walking to the bedroom, I see he's already sleeping, so I grab the phone from the bed and see that I have a text message.

Justin: Where are you?

I don't answer him. Instead, I close the window just a bit and get into the shower. After peeling off my tank top, I step under the cold water, but the pressure is nonexistent. My eyes burn from all the tears, and when they finally stop, I get out. After putting on the same clothes, I open the bathroom door and check on Dylan, who is sleeping like a starfish. I walk over to the drawer and take out the white looseleaf paper I've been working on for five years now. I walk to the table with it in my hand, my arm feeling like it's carrying a thousand pounds. I walk over and turn on the faucet to fill a glass of water, and for once, I wish it was something stronger. Walking to the bedroom, I grab my phone and see that five more texts have come through, but I don't even want to read them.

I sit at the little brown table that isn't steady since one leg is a touch shorter than the other. Unfolding the white paper that is starting to be yellow, I make sure not to tear it where the creases are.

On the top of the page in the middle is Debt list, and under it is the amount I still owe: $17,405. That is what I still have to pay to the five credit cards that Andrew took out in my name that have been closed and sent into collections, and no matter how sorry they feel for me, they can't do anything about it. The interest will go up now that I will have to stop the payments. Rubbing my head, I ignore the ringing phone, looking up just in time to catch Justin's name. I shake my head and decline the call. I had actually put it on airplane mode before, but Dylan must have turned it off while he was watching videos.

It rings again, and I just take a deep sigh and decline it. When it happens four more times, I'm about to decline it again when I hear a soft knock on the door. I get up, not even sure who it could be, and when I open it slowly, Justin's standing there. "Do you know how long I've been trying to get in touch with you?" he asks me and storms right into my apartment. I stand here with the door in my hand. He turns to face me, and I have to take him in. His hat is finally off, and you see his long black hair on the top but then short on the sides. "I have been calling and calling. I swear I was about to contact the hospitals."

"What are you doing here?" Is the only thing that I can say. "How did you know which apartment I lived in?"

"You filled it out on the application," he says, and he looks around, and I have to wonder if he is judging me because of the apartment. I know it's not much, and his closet is probably the size of my whole apartment, but it's clean, and it's ours. "Why didn't you answer my calls?" His eyes are now on mine, and I see that his jaw is tight.

"I didn't get them," I say, closing the door and closing my eyes before turning around and getting ready to lie out of my ass.

"Really?" he says, never once blinking. "So the four times I just called and you didn't answer, you didn't hear?"

"How …?" I ask, and he holds up his hand.

"I've been standing outside your door for the past thirty minutes," he says. "I didn't hear anything, so I called." He puts his hands on his hips. "I thought something happened to you."

"Well, as you can see, we are fine," I say, ignoring the fact that my heart just skipped when he said he was worried about me. I don't think anyone has ever worried about me. "So if that was all you came here for …" I'm about to tell him he can go when there is another knock on the door, and this time, it's not soft like his was. Suddenly, my neck starts to burn, and my heart beats faster for a whole different reason. "Were you expecting someone?" he asks, and I just shake my head. He must see that my hands are shaking when he walks past me and opens the door, coming face-to-face with a man who I knew it would be only a matter of time until he paid me another visit.

"Who are you?" he asks, and he makes my skin crawl. I spot him dressed up in his usual camo pants and white T-shirt and a jean jacket. He is wearing a jean jacket to probably hide the fact he has a gun tucked into the back of his pants. He looks over Justin, spotting me, and calls my name. "Caroline."

"Can I help you with something?" Justin says, and Vince laughs and looks down and then up.

"He isn't here," I say, walking to the door and trying to stand in front of Justin, but he puts his arm out and stops me from standing in front of him.

"Where is he?" Vince looks at me.

"I don't know," I say softly.

"He owes me five large," he says, and I close my eyes. "Took off with some of my shit."

"Well, he isn't here," I say again.

"That doesn't help you," Vince says.

"Well, I guess she tried," Justin now says.

"This puts me in a difficult situation," Vince says. "I'll drop by tomorrow." He turns and walks away, and I sigh that he didn't say anything else. But now that he's walked away, Justin closes the door.

"I'm sorry," I say, walking to the table and picking up the glass of water that is shaking in my hand, "that you had to be here for that." I turn and face him.

"What would have happened if I wasn't here?" he asks, and I just look at him. "Say it," he hisses out.

"I would have to come up with the money, which"—I throw my hands up—"is what I'm going to have to do anyway," I say, and at that moment, I've never regretted anything more in my life.

NINE

JUSTIN

𝒯HIS IS NOT a good idea. I need to calm down before we continue this conversation. The meeting was a clusterfuck to end all clusterfucks. I was so angry because I was worried about Caroline and Dylan, and I had no idea why I was so uptight. It was like my body was one nerve, and everything that was said wrong just set me off. I kept checking my phone and sending Caroline texts but never got any answers.

When I got in the truck, I didn't even realize that I was driving toward her apartment until I got on the highway and approached her building, and then I pulled up her application and got her address. Walking into the apartment building, I hated every single second I was in there. There was yelling going on in one apartment, and I could swear I heard the sound of someone getting smacked, but I had one goal and that was to make sure she was okay. When I got to her door, I looked down at the rinky-dink knob, and my blood started to boil. She shouldn't live here; they shouldn't live here. I listened and called her phone and heard it ringing and then stop. After the fifth time, I just knocked on the door, and when I saw her standing there looking like she'd been crying again, my heart stopped. All I wanted to do was take her in my arms and tell her that no matter what, it would be okay.

But instead, what I did do was barge in and demand to know why she didn't answer my calls. Then that knock on the door had my heart sinking because I thought she had a man. She had a man to protect her, and here I was standing in the middle of the room secretly hoping she'd want me to protect her.

Opening that door made my blood run cold. There was so much I didn't know about her, so many questions I had to ask her, but one of them was answered right away.

"He isn't here." Her words lingered in my head even after the guy walked away from her door, and I knew he would be back. Those men don't just give up. No, they keep coming back for more.

"What would have happened if I wasn't here?" I asked her, and she stood in front of me, her eyes bloodshot and her shoulders slumped in defeat. "Say it," I hiss, knowing the answer but wanting her to confirm it.

"I would have to come up with the money, which"—she throws her hands in the air, aggravated at me for asking these questions—"is what I'm going to have to do anyway."

"Is it your debt?' I ask her. She shakes her head. "Then why would you have to pay it?"

"Justin, what are you doing here?" she asks. Instead of keeping it to myself, I come out and tell her.

"I have no idea," I answer honestly. "I texted you, and you never answered, and then I texted you again." I drag out the again. "And when I got into my vehicle, before I knew it, I was parked outside. Then I sat there wondering how the fuck I would find you. I thought for sure I would have to go door to door, but then I remembered that I had your application."

"So you just show up?" She puts her hands over her face, rubbing her eyes. "This is crazy, and you need to go."

"I'm not going anywhere until you talk to me," I say, holding my ground.

"This has nothing to do with you." Her voice gets louder, and I look behind her toward the bedroom where the soft light shows that Dylan is sleeping in the middle of the bed.

"Well, whether or not it has anything to do with me"—I shrug my shoulders—"I'm in it now."

"That isn't how this works, Justin," she says. A tear sneaks out of her eye, and she angrily wipes it away. "This has nothing to do with you. This is my problem."

"What about the guy he's looking for?" I ask, and I watch to see if maybe she has feelings for him, but all I get is anger from her.

"That's also my problem," she says. "And no matter how I try to not make it my problem, it always seems to become my problem. Because that is the choice I made when I married him." Her voice trails off at the end.

"You didn't make the choice to steal from that man," I say. "You didn't make the choice for him to come knocking on your door. Sooner or later, you are going to see that you deserve better than this."

She looks at me and smiles sadly. "The only one who deserves better than this is Dylan, which is why I bust my ass to make sure none of this touches him."

"That is where you are wrong," I say. "You." I want to step into her space, but instead, I point at her. "You deserve it also. Do you still love him?" I ask that, and even if I don't want to hear her answer, I'll do whatever I can to help her.

"No," she answers softly, and the breath I was holding comes out. "The minute he lied to me and did what he did, I knew it wasn't love."

I nod at her, knowing that she opened up to me more than she wanted to. "Will that guy come back?"

"Even if he comes back, I'm not answering," she says. "He usually doesn't come back into the night, but I don't really know his schedule, so I can't say."

"I'll be back tomorrow morning at seven to get you guys," I say, and I turn to walk out before she starts making excuses. "I'll text you when I'm on my way." Opening the door, I look back. "I expect you to answer." She rolls her eyes, and I close the door and wait to hear the lock click behind me.

I walk away from her door with my heart heavy and my feet almost like they're in cement blocks. I push open the front door and start walking to my vehicle, and I see him leaning against it. "There he is," Vince says to me, standing up now, and I see that his own Cadillac is parked next to mine.

"What do you want?" I say, and he looks at me and smirks.

"I was hoping I can speak to you, man to man," he says, and I roll my eyes.

"A man doesn't go after a woman and child for shit that has nothing to do with them," I say, and he nods his head.

"I'm not the bad guy in all this," he says, and I just walk around him to get into my SUV. "I'm the least of her problems right now." The way he says it has me stopping in my tracks. "He's making deals with the wrong people. People who won't knock on her door, but instead will bust it down."

"It has nothing to do with her," I almost shout.

"Yeah, except he gives her address as his," Vince says, and I don't know who this man is, but I already want to put my fist through his face. "He brings the danger to her door, and he doesn't care."

"How much does he owe you?" I ask him, and he looks down and then up.

"This time, he owes me five hundred," he says, and my heart sinks for Caroline, knowing that it will take her years to pay that back.

"Why the fuck would you let him get away with that?" I ask.

"Because he said he had a buyer and gave me a deposit," Vince says, and I have to wonder if we are actually talking about the same thing. Why the fuck would a drug dealer take a deposit? "Needless to say, after he got my shit, he went underground. People saw him here yesterday."

"I'm dropping her off tomorrow night. I'll have your money. You don't tell her, and also, after this, you don't go to her for his shit. She is not in this," I say, and he just looks at me.

"I have no interest in working with Andrew again," he says and then walks to me. "She doesn't deserve the shit he's putting her through, and she doesn't deserve the shit that is going to come."

I get into the driver's seat and slam my door, and I want to pound my fist on the steering wheel. I have never in my life felt more powerless than I do at this moment.

I don't sleep that night; I toss and turn, and when the sun starts to come up, I'm out the door. I pick up coffee and sandwiches for us, and when I walk into the apartment building, it's quiet. I make my way to her apartment and softly knock on the door. I wait a couple of minutes, and when I'm about to knock again, the door opens just a touch, but it's Dylan who greets me.

One of his eyes open while he smiles. "Hey, buddy," I say, and he walks back, and I see that the apartment is still dark with just a little light coming from the bathroom. "I brought you food, sausage and egg sandwiches," I say. He grabs the bag of food, walking over to the table and sitting down. I walk over and sit with him, grabbing my own breakfast. The bathroom door opens, and she comes out and she's wrapped in a towel with her hair piled on her head. She stops when she sees me and walks back into the bathroom, closing the door. When she comes out again, she's dressed in what she was wearing last night.

"I brought coffee," I say softly. "And breakfast." She looks at me and then looks at Dylan, who doesn't care what's going on. All he knows is that he's eating.

"Can I talk to you?" she asks, and then I get up, grabbing a cup of coffee and bringing it to her. "Thank you," she says softly and turns to walk into the room. "I'm going to talk to Justin for a second."

"Okay, Mom," he says.

"I bought you two," I say, and he pulls his arm back and whispers yes.

I stand in the bedroom that I know she shares with Dylan, and I wonder how much longer it will be until he takes over the whole double bed. "This has to stop," she says when she turns to me. "You can't just come here and give me lifts and buy us stuff."

"Why?" I ask, and I have to think she is the proudest person I have ever met.

"Because you just can't."

"What if I want to?" I say softly. "What if I want to take you to dinner?" I ask.

"I don't think that's a good idea," she says.

"I don't care," I finally say, and she looks at me in shock. "I don't care what is a good idea and what isn't. What I care about is that I want to get to know you, and I want you to give me a chance."

"You just feel sorry for me," she says, trying not to let her voice get louder.

I look at her, and it takes me two seconds to step really close to her. "I feel a lot of things for you, Caroline, but sorry isn't one of them." I'm so close to her, she stops, and I hear her take a deep breath. "Now get dressed because I brought you breakfast."

I don't let her answer. Instead, I turn around and walk out of the room. Closing the door behind me, I try to get my hard-on to go down before Dylan sees it.

TEN

CAROLINE

$\mathcal{J}$USTIN CLOSES THE door softly behind him, and I have to sit on the bed, or I will fall to the floor. He's come into my life, and I feel like this roller coaster I'm on is finally slowing down. When he walked out of the apartment last night, I watched him walk to his SUV and have a conversation with Vince. I can only imagine what was said. I thought for sure Vince would tell him all my dirty secrets—well, not mine but Andrew's—and once again, I hated him.

I didn't go to the bed. Instead, I went to the couch and lay down, but my mind never shut down. No matter how many times I closed my eyes. So many things are up in the air that I don't know what will happen. I got up and woke Dylan once, stepping into the shower. Walking out, I never expected Justin to be standing there with his hair all over the place and his white shirt pulled across his chest with his shorts low on his hips. All I could do was go back in the bathroom to steady my heartbeat. I knew we had to have a talk. This needed to stop, literally now!

"Mom," Dylan says. I get up, opening the door, and I see them sitting at the table eating and laughing while they discuss hockey. "How many goals did I score in one game?"

"Which one?" I ask him, and he looks at Justin.

"Name one," he says. "I scored in all of them."

"Cocky," Justin says and then looks at me, but his look is different this time. It's soft. "Come eat."

"I'm really not hungry. Dylan can have mine," I tell them, knowing that there is nothing in the fridge today.

"He already had two," Justin says, getting up. "Come and sit and eat something."

I walk over, my pulse picking up as he holds out the chair for me. "Go get dressed," I tell Dylan, who gets up and walks into the bedroom. Justin walks around the table and sits where Dylan just left. "Do you work today?" he asks, and I look down and then look up at him.

"No, not today," I say, not ready to admit that I got fired.

"What are you doing today?" he asks. I think of all the errands I have to run, but I just shrug.

"Not much. Just laundry," I say and take a bite of the sandwich that he brought. The buttery croissant melts in my mouth, and I take a sip of the hot coffee.

"Do you want to drive us to the rink and take the SUV again?" he asks. He leans back in the chair and stretches, his shirt coming up just a touch, giving me a glimpse of his lower abs.

"No," I say, trying not to look but failing miserably. "I don't need it."

"Okay," he says. "What are your plans this weekend?"

"I have to work," I say. "Saturday afternoon and Sunday all day."

"What about after work?"

"I have no idea," I answer him. "I usually never make plans."

"Good," he says, smiling, and I just look at him. "We'll have a barbecue at my place, and then we can go swimming."

"Um ..." I try to come up with an excuse that sounds good or at least something better than the fact I don't own a suit. "I don't know. Why don't we see how we feel after the day is over?"

"Sounds good," he says, and then Dylan comes out of the bedroom dressed in his uniform for camp. "Ready, buddy?" Justin gets up, and I follow suit, not sure I'm okay with him taking Dylan without me.

"Give me a hug," I tell Dylan, who comes over and hugs me around the waist, and I kiss his head. "Have an amazing day."

"You, too, Mom," he says, and I lean down to kiss his lips. He walks away from me, and Justin is suddenly at my side.

"Have a good day," he says, his voice soft. He comes closer, and I don't breathe. I don't do anything really; all I know is that my neck starts to get hot, and my heart starts to echo in my ears. His face comes close to mine, and then he leans in and kisses me softly on my cheek. "I'll call you later," he whispers, and then he's gone.

Walking out of the door with Dylan by his side as he asks him questions, Justin closes the door softly behind them.

All I can do is stand, my hand flying to my cheek where the soft kiss still lingers. I don't move until my phone rings, and I walk to it and see it's Justin.

"Hello."

"You didn't lock the door," he says, and then I hear him slam the door and start the ignition. "Did you lock it now?" I roll my eyes, and before I can say anything, he continues, "Let me hear you lock it now."

"You're kidding me, right?" I ask, annoyed, then pissed. "I've been taking care of me and Dylan ..." I don't finish that sentence either.

"Yeah, and you've done a great job of it, but"—his voice goes low—"can you just do this for me, please?" I want to tell him no, that I don't need to lock the door because I can look after myself, but having someone worry about me is a strange feeling—one I don't know what to do about—so I walk to the door and turn the knob, locking it.

"There, are you happy?" I ask, not sure if he heard the click or not.

"Very," he says, and I don't know why, but I can see him smiling like he is standing right in front of me. The dimple on the left side of his cheek calling for me to reach out and touch it. But before I get ahead of myself, I close my eyes and remind myself there is no time, and Justin definitely doesn't need me in his life. "I'll call you later."

Putting the phone down, I get my stuff together. An hour later, I'm walking out of the apartment and making my way toward the church. I pull open the big brown door, and the incense hits me right away along with the silence and the instant peace that I always feel here. I walk down the aisles with wooden pews on each side. The church has seen better days—some of the ceiling paint is peeling and the stained glass colors are fading. I walk past the altar to the side where an open door leads you to two bathrooms and the stairs going to the basement.

I walk down the stairs and see that a light is on. Peeking my head in, I see Father Rolly placing papers on the chairs that are set up in a circle. "Knock, knock," I say, and he looks up, his white hair falling onto his forehead and his face lighting up with a smile.

"Caroline," he says and gestures for me to enter the room.

"I'm sorry for interrupting, Father." I smile at him and look around. "I was looking for Murielle." Gesturing to her office, I see the door is open, but she isn't behind her desk.

"She isn't here," he says and then sits down in one of the steel chairs. "She had to move to Vancouver to take care of her ailing sister," he says, and my stomach sinks even more. "Did you need something?"

I try to think of something, and I even look down while my heart beats fast and my chest starts to hurt, tears starting to sting at my eyes. "No," I say, ignoring his question and smiling. "I was …" I can't even come up with a good excuse.

"You know that you can talk to me, right?" he says, and I drop down on one of the chairs. "You've been coming to us for the past four years, and I know she's helped you when times are tough."

I put my hand to my mouth to try to stop the tears from coming, but no matter how much I fight it, they just pour out. "I lost my job." The worry comes over his face. "I'm looking for another one," I say, "but I was hoping she could help me out with some bread, butter, and some milk." I hold my head high and take a deep inhale. "But it's okay," I say, getting up. "We'll see you Sunday." I smile. There isn't much I believe in since my life went downhill, but every single Sunday, we come to service, and every single Sunday, I say the same prayer, hoping that someone, anyone is listening to me.

"Do you have some time to help me?" he says, and I look at him. "We have the AA and NA meetings back here every day. Murielle usually helps me, but I've been doing it by myself."

"Of course," I say even though I need to get out of here and start looking for a job. "What can I do to help?"

"You can start the coffeepot and then fix the table in the back with white Styrofoam cups. There is a basket of sugar in the kitchen." He points at the door at the end of the room.

"On it," I say and walk to the back of the room and into the kitchen. The kitchen looks like it was from the 1970s, and the beat-up round tin coffee machine sits on the corner of the counter. I walk to the counter, taking it off, and then open the top. Luckily, I helped Murielle set up for a barbecue once, and she explained to me how it works. It takes me four minutes to get everything ready, and then I carry it over to the table, plugging it into the wall and waiting for it to do its thing. I walk back into the kitchen and open the cupboards, looking for the cups and some sugar. I get everything that I need out along with some stir sticks. I walk over and start setting up the table as people slowly start arriving. Looking over, I see that Father Rolly is standing by the door talking to someone, and then he looks over at me, pointing.

I stand here and look around the room, noticing some people sitting and waiting for it to start. "Excuse me," Father Rolly says and then comes to me. "It is just about to start," he says, smiling. "Luckily, Patricia is going to run the meeting." I smile at him, and I'm about to ask him if he needs anything else when he holds out his hand. "Would you come this way please?" He walks toward Murielle's office and steps in, waiting for me to follow him in, and then closes the door behind me. "Sit, sit," he says, and I sit in the chair I always sit in when I have to come and ask Murielle to help us out.

He sits in the chair next to me, and I am suddenly nervous. Can one be kicked out of church? Can one be refused entry? "Relax, dear." He chuckles.

All I can do is wring my hands together. "Easier said than done."

"You know I always say everything happens for a reason," he starts, and I just look at him. "Just like you coming in this morning while I was setting up. I was thinking to myself that I really needed to get going and hire someone to take over Murielle's position."

"She really did a lot here," I say, knowing full well she ran the whole church.

"She did, and I know that it's going to be hard to fill her shoes." He smiles. "But I think you can do it."

I look at him shocked, my mouth opening and closing and then doing it again, but nothing comes out. Finally, I whisper, "What?"

"It seems we have been pushed together for a reason," he says. "I will be here with you every single step of the way, and I'm sure once you get used to it, you'll be able to do everything with your eyes closed."

"I don't know what to say," I say, along with the tear that slips over my bottom lid.

"You could say yes," he says, smiling. I just nod my head, afraid if I say anything, a sob will rip through me. "Now to get to the nitty-gritty stuff. It pays sixteen dollars an hour." My eyes open wider as I think about the extra three dollars I will make per hour. "The hours are very flexible. I know Dylan finishes school during the year, at three, so you can either have him in the after-school program, or you can take off at that time."

"I don't know what to say." I shake my head. "I think the only thing that I have been saying is that I don't know what to say." Laughing now, I wipe away a tear with the back of my hand.

"Why don't we start tomorrow after you drop Dylan off at camp?" he says. I'm so overwhelmed that all I can do is nod.

"I don't know how I can ever repay you," I say honestly, and he reaches forward and grabs a tissue that is on the desk and hands it to me. "Thank you."

"You can repay me by doing the job I know that you'll be amazing at." He smiles. "And in the meantime," he says, getting up and going over to the desk drawer to take out a checkbook, "this is going to be an advance. We can take out twenty dollars a week until it is paid back." He continues writing and then hands it to me. I look down and see that he wrote a check for two hundred dollars.

"I don't need this much," I say, shaking my head. "It's too much."

"Well, then put some of it away for a rainy day," he says,

and I want to scoff at him. It seems like every day is a rainy day.

"Now if you will excuse me, I have to get things ready for later," he says. "I will see you tomorrow."

"Yes," I say. "I will be here tomorrow."

He turns to walk out of the room and closes the door after him. I put my hands on my face, and the tears that I kept at bay start to fall. This time, though, they're not tears of sadness or despair but tears of happiness. I wipe my eyes, and when I'm finally calmer, I walk out quietly just as the meeting finishes. I smile at some of the people walking out.

I push open the church door, and the sun hits my face, and for the first time in a long time, I look up and smile.

ELEVEN

JUSTIN

"YOU NEED TO skate up the wide more." I look down at Dylan. "You skate to the middle too much." He looks at me, his chest heaving after his play. It was a good play with him skating to the middle and then shooting the puck. "It worked this time, but when you go too much down the middle, you can get blocked in by the defense before the puck even hits the goalie. If you skate in the side, the goalie is usually stuck to one side of the post, giving you a big opening on the other side." He just nods his head, and I know he'll understand it if he sees it. "Watch Ralph." I call over to the other side of the ice where Ralph is teaching another play and raise my hand to tell him to come here. He skates over and stops in front of me. "I want to show Dylan how to skate down the side with the puck and not to the middle. Do you think you can play defense?" I joke with him, and he just smirks.

"It's summer, right?" he asks, skating backward in front of me. "Which means I don't really have to go easy on you." He tilts his head to the side, and I look at the bench and see that all the kids are watching this one-on-one.

"You think you can stop me?" I goad him, skating to the middle of the ice and dropping a puck.

"No one is here to tell me to go easy on you." He winks at me, and I just shake my head. "Golden boy, my ass," he continues, and I skate around in a circle before skating over to the puck and making the play. I've been practicing against Ralph for the past five years. He got drafted to Edmonton the year before me, and when you are number one on the team, they make you train with the number one defenseman, and that is Ralph. His eyes aren't on the puck; instead, his eyes are on me. Another thing he does better than anyone is read the play. I skate to the right, and the puck hits the blade of my stick. I skate to the left, and my eyes go to Ralph, who skates backward never leaving or moving with me. My hands slide the puck right and left as I make my way down the ice, and I move more to the right. Once I pass the blue line, I pick up speed, and he stops skating and makes me move right to left to see which way he is going to go. His body is now close to mine, and he knows that if he gives me just a touch more space, I'm going to slap in the puck. But he doesn't; instead, he sticks out his stick and tries to poke check me, giving me just enough room to shoot the puck under his raised hand and into the net. The kids on the bench cheer loudly, making Ralph laugh and then push me away. "You got lucky."

"No such thing as luck." I wink at him this time and skate

back to the bench as the horn sounds, letting us know it's time to rotate the groups. "Okay, that's it for you guys."

I watch them walk off to the changing area and then feel Ralph looking at me while he drinks some water. "What?"

"Nothing. I'm just wondering if Justin Stone has finally met his match?" I've been asking myself that same question.

I shrug at him. "No fucking clue. The only thing I know is that I can't walk away."

"Don't tell me that the biggest bachelor in hockey is finally going to be taken?" He goads me with the title that I've gotten through the years, making me roll my eyes and look away. I skate off the ice and see that it's lunchtime. Unlacing my skates, I walk outside, pulling my phone out of my pocket to call Caroline. My hands suddenly get clammy. I wait for her to answer, and when she does on the third ring, it sounds like she's out of breath.

"Hey," I say softly and then hear traffic in the background.

"Hey," she says, and it almost sounds like she's running.

"Where are you?" I ask, going over and sitting on the bench outside the rink.

"I just left the grocery store," she says, and her breathing doesn't let down. "I'm on my way home."

"Are you running home?" I ask and smile, thinking about her. Her green eyes that light up only when she looks at Dylan.

"No." She laughs, something she doesn't do often, but something I want her to do more. "I'm walking home. I somehow didn't think about the walk when I was filling the cart," she says.

"You're walking home?" I ask as I sit up, my voice coming out harsher than I mean to.

"Yes," she says, ignoring my tone. "I thought about taking the bus, but it just made more sense to walk."

"How far?" I ask, and she lets out a big breath as if my questions are annoying her.

"Did you need something?" she cuts me off and ignores my question.

"There are a lot of things I need," I say. "The first thing is for you to let me in." I close my eyes when the words tumble out of my mouth.

"Justin." The way she says my name, it is almost like a breakup. I'm waiting for her to start with the "It's not you, it's me" speech.

"God," I say, wishing I could hang up and start this over again. "I was just calling to check on you and see what you were up to."

"I went grocery shopping, and now I'm on my way home," she says. "How is Dylan? Is he okay?"

"Yeah," I say. "He's fine."

"Okay, I have to let you go. The bags are slipping out of my hands, and I'm trying not to drop the phone. Gotta go," she says and hangs up. I look at the phone, and I dial the one person who I know I shouldn't, but I do anyway.

"Grasshopper," he says, answering the phone, and I laugh.

"Will you ever not call me that?" I ask Matthew, who now laughs.

"Nope." He doesn't miss a beat. "What's up?"

"Does something have to be up to call my big brother?" I

say, but even I don't buy it.

"The last time you called me, you wanted me to break it to Mom that you didn't want to come home Christmas because the girl you wanted to bag bought a bunny suit."

"That is not what I said," I say with a groan. "A bunch of people were going to Colorado to ski."

"And were you not bringing a girl with you?" he asks, and I don't answer. "And did she not put bunny ears on?"

"It's a Snapchat filter," I say.

"I honestly have no idea what that means," he says. "And I don't really want to know. Sounds like some dirty shit."

I laugh. "I'll explain it to you again when I see you."

"I can't wait," he says sarcastically. "Now to what pleasure do I owe this phone call?"

"I need to ask you something, and before I do, I need you not to bust my balls about anything," I say, suddenly regretting my decision to call him.

"Why do you do this to me?" he asks.

"I also need for you not to tell anyone." I add that in even though I know he'll tell Karrie.

"Jesus, did you get a girl pregnant?" I know he's talking between clenched teeth. "How many times did I tell you to wrap it up? Jesus," he says and doesn't stop. "Are you going to marry her?"

"Okay. One, I didn't get anyone pregnant," I say. "That's your job."

"Hey," he snaps. "I was always going to marry her, but I just had to convince her."

"You mean trick her," I joke with him. He and Karrie met when she was his chaperone, and then she got pregnant.

There was no denying he loved her with everything that he had, but he was also a caveman. "Anyway. I met someone," I say it out loud, admitting it to the universe.

"Okay," he says, waiting for the rest.

"She's a mom, and her son attends the hockey camp."

"Justin," he says my name almost like a warning.

"I know what you're going to say." I lean forward on the bench, putting my elbows on my knees.

"There is a lot I want to say, but the first thing I'm going to say is that if you don't think you can give her what she needs, then you need to walk away."

"I know that, Matthew."

"No, I don't think you do. This isn't just one person," he says as if I don't fucking know. "You can't think with your dick this time."

"Matthew," I hiss. "It's not like that."

"What are you saying?" he asks, and I take a deep breath.

"I mean that I like her a lot." My heart beats fast, but then my chest constricts when I tell him the next part. "She's had a rough time. I don't know the details, and I'm afraid to ask, but she isn't giving me the time of day. I want to just help her," I say softly. "I want to just be there for her."

"You have to knock her walls down," he says.

"I don't know how," I say. "I've never been here. I've never wanted anything more in my life than for her to sit down with me and tell me everything. I want her to know that I don't want to solve her problems but to help be by her side."

"Have you told her this?" he asks.

"No," I say quietly, almost whispering. "I'm afraid to." I look up at the sun. "She has a lot to her past. I don't know much, but I met one of them, and he isn't the friendly neighborhood type."

"Fuck," he hisses. "How in are you?"

I think about my answer just as I've been thinking about this whole thing for the past couple of days, and that is what it has been … a couple of days. But just the thought of not seeing her hurts my heart. The thought of going a day without her makes it almost hard to breathe. "I'm all in."

"Then you need to sit with her and put all your cards on the table. You need to tell her."

"What if she …" I start. "What if she's overwhelmed by it?"

"Then you show her," he says. "She has probably had people promise her things before." His tone is soft. "But they were probably empty promises, so you have to show her that you are a man who stands behind his promises."

"Yeah," I say, and then I hear my name being called and look back to see Ralph is trying to get my attention. "I have to go."

"Okay. Call me for anything," he says. "You hear?"

"Yeah," I say into the phone and then hold up my hand to Ralph. "I'll call you later," I say, disconnecting, then getting up and walking to meet Ralph. "What's up?"

"Nothing, but Dylan was looking for you," he says, and we turn to walk inside.

"Is everything okay?" I ask. My heart had started to beat faster, thinking he was hurt, but then I see him playing basketball with the other kids, and he looks up and sees me.

"Justin," he yells, "I got a three-pointer!" His eyes beam with pride, and his smile is so big that his eyes crinkle at the sides. "It even went swish."

"That's amazing, buddy," I say. Standing, I watch the game with my hands on my hips, already setting a plan for tonight into motion.

I get into the truck after buckling Dylan in and call Caroline's number. "The customer you are calling is unavailable at the moment. Please try again later." I look at the phone and then hang up, and during the forty-five-minute drive, I spend most of the time speeding and trying to tell myself that she just turned off her phone. I try not to think about the trouble she could be in or the trouble that is always lurking around her.

We get there, and now I'm about to crawl out of my skin when I grab the hockey bag from the truck and walk toward her apartment. We walk up the stairs, and Dylan goes on and on, but I'm not even focusing on him. I'm focusing on the fact that I need to make sure Caroline is okay. When we get to the door and Dylan turns the knob, it's locked. I'm both happy and then worried. What if she got hurt somewhere and her phone is broken? The what-ifs are playing over in my head, so I don't even hear Dylan knock on the door nor do I hear the door unlock and open, but I do see her face, and I step back. "Mom," Dylan says, and she switches right away before my eyes.

"Hey, sweetheart," she says, wrapping her arms around his shoulders and kissing his head. "How was your day?"

"Good. Justin had a one-on-one with Ralph, and he won," he says to her, "and then I played basketball, and I scored a three-pointer."

She smiles down at him, and he doesn't see the redness in her eyes or on the tip of her nose. "Did you score all the points one after another?"

"No, Mom," he says, going to the fridge and opening it, his eyes going wide. "The fridge is full." And it's at that moment my heart sinks for her. This woman who puts on the bravest face is now having all of it in front of me. "Can I have a Yop?" he asks, wanting a yogurt drink.

"Yes," she says and then looks at me. "Was everything okay?"

"Yes." I want to take her in my arms and kiss her softly and hold her and be her rock. I'm about to bring up the fact that her phone was off and that I tried to call her when the front door suddenly opens, and I turn to see who it is. I don't have to guess for long when I hear Dylan yell.

"Dad!" he says, running to this guy standing there with dirty clothes and stringy hair. His arms are bare and skinny, and you can see the scabs on the inside creases of his arms.

Dylan wraps his arms around his waist, but the guy doesn't even notice because his gaze is fixated on me. I'm watching him, but more importantly, I feel Caroline stiffen beside me.

"Who is this?" the man finally asks. It's almost as if he's accusing us of something. I want to step in front of Caroline, but before I can do that, she speaks up.

"He's nobody, and he was just leaving." Her voice comes out strong and firm. I look at her. "Thank you for bringing Dylan home. We'll see you tomorrow." And just like that, my heart breaks for the woman who I thought was mine.

TWELVE

CAROLINE

$\mathcal{M}$Y DAY WENT from amazing to kick in the stomach yet again. And I'm suddenly reminded not to ever get my hopes up again. Every single time I think things are looking up, someone somewhere says "Not today."

I got my groceries for just under a hundred dollars. With the leftover food stamps that I had and shopping the sales, I was winning. Then I was about to cook dinner and thinking of doing something nice for Justin after everything he's done for me, but when I went to call him, I got sent to the collections department. Since it was my third time being late, they couldn't do anything unless I paid off the total due, which at this time was going to be impossible. I had just hung up the phone when I heard a knock on the door, and when I opened it, Justin stood there with a worried look on his face.

I avoided eye contact, knowing full well he could probably tell I've been crying again. But then everything happened so fast—the joy of Dylan finally seeing the old fridge full to the front door swinging open. Andrew's eyes went straight to Justin, and the only thing I could think of was to get him as far away from Andrew as I possibly could.

"He's nobody, and he was just leaving," I say in my firmest voice possible. Justin turns his head to look at me, and I see the hurt in his eyes, but it's better this way. "Thank you for bringing Dylan home. We'll see you tomorrow." He looks at me one last time before nodding and turning to walk out of the apartment. The sound of the door softly closing behind him is almost too much for me. Heading to the kitchen, I turn on the tap to get some water, and the whole time, I'm fighting the stinging of tears in my eyes.

"So is that a new boyfriend?" Andrew asks, and I don't turn to him. "Dylan, go to your room while your mom and me talk."

"But, Dad," he says but then just walks away. I wait for the door to close before I turn around and look at him.

"Get the fuck out," I say in a voice so soft it's like a whisper.

"Oh, what's the matter, Caroline? Sad that your boyfriend left with his tail between his legs." He taunts me. "I should remind you that we are still married."

"Really?" I say. "I should have reminded you about that when Dylan was six months old and you fucked the sorority girls, or when he was two and your girlfriend showed up in the middle of the night." I put up my hand. "No, it was when I walked in on you fucking our landlady when Dylan was three."

"That was a mistake!" he shouts, and I just shake my head.

"I don't even care," I say. "What are you doing here?"

"I need a place to crash until tomorrow," he says. He walks to the fridge, and I see his hands shake just a touch.

"No freaking way are you going to stay here while you're high," I say, shaking my head. "Not a chance in hell."

"I'm not high," he says. Grabbing the chocolate milk that I splurged on for Dylan, he opens the top and drinks straight out of the container. "I'm just a little shaky. I think I'm coming down with something."

"Yeah," I say, shaking my head. "I bet." I might have been in the dark at the beginning, but after all this time, I know the signs. He's coming down from his high, and if he doesn't get it soon, he's going to get all grumpy and then twitchy.

"Look, I just need a shower and a place to crash, and then I'll be gone," he says, and I keep telling myself it's the last time. I can't do this anymore, that next time it's going to be a no and get out. "You just have to tell your boyfriend to come back tomorrow," he says with a sneer before he walks into the bathroom and closes the door.

"Give me strength," I say under my breath, and the bedroom door opens and out comes Dylan.

"Where is Dad?" he asks, looking around, and then he hears the shower turn on. "Is Justin your boyfriend?"

"No," I say, shaking my head, "he's not." I ignore the way my chest feels. "What do you want to eat for dinner?" I ask, ignoring the singing from the shower.

"Do we have fish sticks?" he asks, hopeful that I picked up his favorite ones, and I just smile and nod my head. "Yes,"

111

he says, closing his fist and cocking it back.

I make dinner for the three of us, and Dylan tells him all about the hockey camp and all about his new skates. Then they sit down and watch hockey videos, or actually Dylan watches the videos while Andrew sleeps. I want to kick him to tell him to get the fuck up and get the fuck out. I look at the man I once loved, or at the very least liked a lot, and I decide this is the last time I let him come into my home. This is the last time I help him.

When it's time for bed, I close the door and slip in with Dylan. "Good night," I say to Dylan, and by the time I turn to face him, he is softly snoring. I don't know what time I fall asleep, but I hear the door open and then close, and I know that Andrew has gone. Walking out to the living room, I find the couch empty and go to the door and lock it behind him.

I don't sleep the rest of the night. I toss and turn, and when my alarm goes off the next morning, I drag myself out of bed. The thick air in the room is making it unbearable. "I'm going to take a shower," I tell Dylan, who just grumbles and turns to go back to sleep. I walk to the bathroom, not bothering to turn on the light and step under the cool water. With my eyes closed, I think about the only thing I have been thinking about all night. *Justin*. His face, the hurt in his eyes, the way my chest hurt when he walked away. I put up walls for this reason. I put up walls so I don't have this pain anymore.

I get out and dry myself off, ignoring the voices in my head telling me he's different. I know he is. He comes from a great family, and he is going to make some woman very, very happy. I slip my shorts back on, and when I open the door, I stop in my tracks when I find Dylan standing there with tears running down his face. "He took it," he says between sobs and hitched breaths. He's holding the hockey bag, and all the new equipment is gone. "He took it all."

A hand goes to my mouth as I watch my son's world shatter. "Honey, I'm sure he'll bring it back," I say, knowing full well that I am lying to him. It's gone; it's all gone. "Why don't you put on what you were wearing yesterday, and you can take your other equipment for the day? I'll drive around and see if I can find your dad."

"Justin gave me all that stuff," he says, sitting down now. "It was all new." I walk to him and sit next to him as he cries in my arms. I thought I hated Andrew before, but I was wrong. This right here is the last straw. I'm done trying to be the good person, and I'm done trying to pretend that everything is fine in front of Dylan. I never wanted him to know about his father and the demons that he had, but I can't hide him from it anymore. I can shield him as much as I can, but I refuse to have Dylan hurt this way again.

"I know, honey, and I'm going to get it back," I say, and if I can't, I'm going to beg, borrow, and steal to make sure that he has it tomorrow. "Go get your stuff on and have some breakfast. I bought you some Toaster Strudels."

"I'm not hungry," he says, getting up and going into the bedroom. I pop a couple of strudels into the toaster and pack them in a container, and when he comes out, he is carrying his old bag over his shoulder. His eyes are still red with tears.

"Ready?" I ask, and he just nods his head. I don't know if Justin is coming this morning. I don't know if he will be waiting, and I'm not going to let myself get my hopes up. Dylan's shoulders are slumped as we walk down the stairs, and I stop and take the bag from him, putting it over my shoulder.

We walk down the sidewalk, and I see Justin standing near his SUV, and I want to smile at him. I want to do so many things, but I don't have a chance because when he looks right past me and straight to Dylan, he steps forward to meet us. The whole time, his eyes never leave Dylan's, and when we are close enough, he asks right away with a panic in his voice. "What happened?" He gets down in front of Dylan, and my boy is trying so hard not to cry in front of him. He is trying so hard to be brave, but Justin just holds out his arms, and he walks into them. His arms wrap around his neck, and I look at him in his shorts and a T-shirt, and he's wearing a baseball hat today. "What's the matter?" he whispers to Dylan, and I want to tell him that he's fine, and that everything is okay.

"It's gone," he says softly, and then Justin looks at me, and I finally see his eyes. He looks as if he hasn't slept all night.

"What's gone?" he asks, and Dylan finally stands there, not making eye contact with Justin. I was wrong before. I hate Andrew even more now.

"All my new stuff," he says, and his voice is so low you can barely hear him. Justin puts his hand under Dylan's chin and raises it. "I'm sorry."

He looks at him. "Things happen," he says. "It's not your fault. You didn't do anything to it."

"No," Dylan says.

"Sometimes things happen, and it's not our fault, and we feel bad about it," Justin says. "Just like once when I took my brother's hockey card to school. I was so proud that it was signed, and then I handed it to my friend, and it fell out of his hands and into a puddle." Dylan looks at him with open eyes, and he wipes the tears away from his face. "I remember picking it up so fast and wiping it on my shirt, but the card was still soft, and it started to peel." He tells him the story, and my heart just explodes. "I remembered being so scared to tell my dad that I hid it from him for a year." Dylan gasps.

"Was your dad mad?" he asks, and Justin just shakes his head.

"Just like I'm not mad," he says, "but I am sad for you because I know how much you loved your new stuff."

"Yeah," he says and then looks at me. "But my mom said she's going to try to get the stuff back."

I'm waiting for Justin to look up at me, but he doesn't. He doesn't do anything but look at Dylan. "How about we get some breakfast before heading to the rink?"

"I'm starving," Dylan says, and now I'm the one about to gasp.

"Let's get going," he says, and Dylan just nods and walks toward the vehicle.

"Justin," I say his name almost in a whisper. "I'm so sorry."

"Yeah," he says, and the way he looks at me, I want to reach out and grab his hand. "We should get going."

"What?" I ask, surprised. After everything that I've done and said to this man, he still came out and helped us. He is still going to give me his SUV to get to work. "After everything that just went down, you are still going to go out of your way to help us?"

He stands now and shrugs. "I said I would help you, and I keep my word." He looks at Dylan, who is getting in the SUV as though he's always been doing it. "It's not my place to say anything, but he deserves better." He takes off his hat and scratches his head. "You both do."

THIRTEEN

JUSTIN

$\mathcal{I}$ KNOW I shouldn't want her, but I can't seem to change anything. I talked myself out of driving over here this morning. I gave myself a lecture in the car. Legit, I was having a conversation with myself.

But I couldn't not come. I couldn't do that to Dylan, and I couldn't do that to her. I sat on the couch all night in the dark looking out my window at the moon in the sky, thinking about what she was doing and wondering if he stayed the night. Wondering if she let him hold her hand or kiss her lips.

I repeatedly told myself that I have to just be her friend, that I was there helping her, but when I saw Dylan, and his eyes were puffy and red and he was clearly crying and upset, all thoughts and reasoning went out the window. Trying to keep my cool, I tried not to rush toward them and tried to stop my heart from beating so hard I thought it would come out of my chest. I wanted to hold him and protect him and make him feel safe.

He rushed into my arms, and I felt his tears on my neck as he silently and quietly told me that his father took his stuff. "Shh," I said, soothing him and then hugging him with both arms. "It's okay," I tried to tell him.

I have always been the chill one in the family, always been the voice of reason. I mean, Matthew is more than enough of a hothead for any family, but at that moment, if you were to put me in a ring with Dylan's dad, I wouldn't stop until he was bloody. I avoided looking at her, avoided the fact that I wanted to take them both in my arms and take them away from here and never have them come back, but she told me to go.

"It's going to be okay, buddy. Why don't we just put your stuff in the trunk? I promise it's going to be okay. It's not your fault," I whispered into his ear, and I knew that I was no one to him. So I did what I thought was the right thing. I took care of Dylan and hopefully made him see that what his father did were his actions and had no reflection on him. "You did nothing wrong." That was for his father to carry. "Now bring your bag to the SUV for me, yeah?" I was on my knees and trying to not lose it in front of him when I sent him to the vehicle and counted to ten.

I used to watch my father walk away and go into another room when he was upset with something that Matthew and Allison's biological father did. He would walk into an empty room and count to ten. We would literally hear him count out loud. I hear her voice, and I finally look up at her, and my breath hitches. She is so beautiful it hurts to look at her.

Especially knowing that I can't do anything to her.

"Justin." When she whispers my name, the hurt and crushing I felt yesterday is nothing like it is today. Today, it feels like an elephant is sitting on my chest, and I can't get up. "I'm so sorry."

"Yeah." I finally look into her eyes. "We should get going."

"What?" she asks, almost surprised that I'm actually going to continue helping her. "After everything that just went down, you are still going to go out of your way to help us?"

I stand now and shrug. "I said I would help you, and I keep my word." I turn to see Dylan getting into the back seat. Then I take a deep breath and say the words I wanted to tell her yesterday right before she sent me away. "It's not my place to say anything, but he deserves better." I take off my hat, scratching my head. "You both do."

I turn to walk away, not expecting her to say or do anything, but I feel her grab my wrist with her small delicate hand that has to juggle all the balls in the air without letting one fall. "Please," she says in a desperate plea, and I wonder how many times she's said that, only to come up with no answer. I don't shrug off her hand, but I turn, and she slowly slips her hand away from my wrist. My fingers graze hers, and I struggle not to grab it and keep it in mine, but I let it go. "I want you to know that before today, I have never, ever let him see what his father has done," she says. I see her eyes gloss over with tears, and I want to cup her cheek in my hand. "And I don't know that I wouldn't have lied for Andrew this morning if I'd found the bag first."

"Where is he?" I ask, not sure if it's the right thing for me to know right now.

"He's long gone," she says. "I heard the door open and close last night, and I just thought he was leaving. I never, ever …" she says, rubbing her hands over her face. "I never expected him to take his equipment. It's hockey equipment. The TV was a given. The iPad was like waving candy in front of a kid." My stomach burns as she says this, and my hands clench at my sides. "But this …" She shakes her head. "I never expected this."

"I have an extra bag of equipment at the rink," I say.

"I can't have you do that." She shakes her head. "This is not your problem."

"No, you're right, it isn't," I say, and I step closer to her, "but I can help, and I'm going to."

She shakes her head and bites her lower lip, looking off into the distance. "I never wanted him to see what his father was really like. I wanted to shield and protect him, and I knew deep down that eventually there would come a day when I'd have to answer his questions, but I never ever wanted him to find out like this."

"Are you two still together?" I ask, and I hold my breath waiting.

"God, no," she says without missing a beat. "We haven't been together since I walked in on him fucking our landlady when Dylan was three years old. And even before then."

I take a deep inhale and let it out and then put my hands on my hips. "We should really get going, or you'll be late to work," I say, and she looks down and then up.

"I got fired," she says, and I stand here with my mouth open. "Two days ago. But I got another job at the church two streets over."

"Why didn't you tell me?" I ask. "You went through all that alone."

"Not the first time," she says, and then mumbles, "and not going to be the last time."

"Justin!" Dylan yells from the back seat, and I look over my shoulder. "I'm starving."

Caroline laughs. "Not twenty minutes ago, he told me he wasn't hungry."

"Why don't we get breakfast, and then I can drop you off at work before we go to the rink?"

"I would like that," she says and then looks down. "I'd also really like to have a second to talk to you," she rambles. "I mean, I know we are talking now, but you need to know that I'm a good person. I'm a good mom. At the end of the day, I don't want him to suffer for my choices."

"I would never think you aren't a good person, let alone a good mom," I reassure her. "Now before he starts honking the horn, let's get some breakfast." I hold out my hand for her to walk in front of me, and she looks down and smiles. Her hair falls in her face, and she tucks it behind her ear. We walk side by side, and I open the door for her. She smiles shyly, and I can swear my heart skipped a beat.

Breakfast is different than it was a couple of days ago. I still see her eyes roam over the menu and take it upon myself to order for us all, and at the end of the meal, I'm happy to see that she actually ate.

"I can walk to work," she says when we walk to the truck. "It's two streets over, and you'll probably get stuck in traffic," she says and then grabs Dylan and hugs him. "Have a great day."

He hugs her and looks up at her, and I know that in a couple of years, he will tower over her. "I will."

"We should go out." My mouth opens before my brain can register what it's saying. "To celebrate the new job."

"I couldn't," she says at the same time Dylan says, "Yes! Can we go somewhere nice?"

"We can go anywhere you want," I say with a smile. "What is your favorite?"

"Pizza and spaghetti," he answers without thinking about it.

"I know a great place. I'll pick you up after the rink. I'll call you," I say, and I see her face fall.

"Um," she starts and then looks down and then up again. "I'll give you the number to my work." I look at her. "I can't have my phone at work, so use this one in case something happens."

I hand her my phone. "Put it in there for me." I turn and open the door. "Dylan, let's go."

"Bye, Mom," he says, getting into the back seat and buckling himself.

"I'll see you later," I say, hoping that she doesn't realize she is still holding my phone, but I don't have luck this morning. While she is typing, something must happen because she shoves the phone back at me.

"Here is your phone. I put the name under Caroline work," she says, and then she waves at Dylan and walks away. I watch her when my phone buzzes in my hand. I look down and see an unknown number, and the text.

Unknown: *Last night was everything.*

I look down at the phone and then up again and see that

she has disappeared around the block. Right then, another text comes in.

Unknown: Sorry wrong number.

"Fuck," I say under my breath, but before I can do anything about it, I hear Dylan yelling my name. I put the phone in my pocket and walk around to the driver's side and get to the rink in time to change and get on the ice.

The morning flies by with the classes on the ice. Dylan just keeps getting better and better. If he had the height, he could smash even the kids three years older than him.

At lunchtime, I walk outside and call her cell phone by accident, and I get the same generic message about the caller not being available. So I call her work number, and she answers right away.

"St. Vincent, Caroline speaking," she says, and I smile.

"Hey, it's me," I say. "Justin."

It's almost like I can see the way she changes. Her voice is curt. "Hi. Is everything okay?"

"Yeah," I say, and then I sit in the same spot I did yesterday when I called her. "I was just calling to see how your first day was going."

"Good," she says, answering with one word.

"It was a wrong number," I say, and she doesn't say anything else. "This morning, the text I got. It was a wrong number."

"Justin, there is no need to explain anything to me." Her voice is flat. "You're free to do what you want with who you want."

"Caroline," I say her name, and I really don't want to have this conversation on the phone.

"I really have to go," she says, and just like that, she hangs up, leaving me stuck looking down at the phone.

This woman is going to push me to be like Matthew, I think. Suddenly, everything that he's ever done makes so much sense.

FOURTEEN

CAROLINE

*H*E ISN'T YOURS, I tell myself the whole way to work. He isn't yours, and you aren't his. This is what you want for him. But the whole time, all I see are the words in my head.

Last night was everything.

No wonder he looked so tired this morning. He probably spent the whole night with someone. I force my mind to shut off when Father Rolly explains my duties. Luckily for me, Murielle left everything in order, so just picking up where she left off is a breeze.

By the time noon rolls around, I'm sitting at the desk with nothing else to do. Father Rolly went out to make a house call and will be back, so I turn the computer on and search for the pawn shops in the area.

I call ten of the ones that I know Andrew has been to, but none of them have anything like what I'm describing. I hang up the phone, and it rings right away, and when I answer it,

I'm smiling until I hear his voice.

I want to be mad that he was with someone, but I can't be. I give him one-word answers, and he knows within two minutes into the conversation—hell, within one minute into the conversation—that I'm not myself.

"It was a wrong number," he says, and the pen in my hand that I was tapping on the notepad stops. "This morning, the text I got. It was a wrong number."

"Justin, there is no need to explain anything to me." I pretend that I'm fine, and that everything is fine. "You're free to do what you want with who you want." I close my eyes, trying not to picture him with someone else.

"Caroline," he says, and my heart pulls to him. To tell him that I was jealous and angry. That I don't know what is going on, but I want to tell him everything, except I don't.

"I really have to go." I put the phone down and take a deep inhale and exhale.

"We are sometimes our own worst enemies." I look up at the woman who runs the Narcotics Anonymous meeting. "Sorry for eavesdropping. I'm Cheryl," she says. Her brown eyes look almost black, and her curly long brown hair is everywhere. "You must be Caroline. Father Rolly was telling me all about you last night." Her smile fills her face, and I watch as she sits down in the same chair I sat in just yesterday.

"I thought you were only coming in at one?" I ask. She smiles and crosses her leg, and I have to say she looks so graceful.

"I got finished early and figured I would come around and introduce myself." She puts her hands in her lap. "I should have thought this through and got coffee."

I laugh now. "No need." I put my pen down. "What you said before …?"

"About us being our worst enemies?" she says, and I nod. "It's things that we do when we've been around addicts."

"How do you move past it?" I look at her.

"My father was an addict, my mother an addict, and then my sister and brother both followed in their footsteps." She starts to share her story. "I was the one pretending everything was okay. The one covering for them." She shakes her head. "From the school, from their co-workers, from their bosses. Until I left them to fend for themselves."

"How did you do it?" I ask, and she looks at me, waiting for me to expand on the question. "When did you finally say fuck this and let them sink?"

"When I came home, and the lights were cut off," she says. "I had hidden the money for the electric bill in the bathroom in a plastic soap container that I put in a junk drawer that no one ever went in. I was wrong. When you are chasing your next fix, you search everywhere."

"My son's father stole his hockey equipment last night," I say. "I knew that he was low. I mean, he's stolen just about everything that I have of value."

"But you allow him to come into the home," she points out.

"I don't want my son to miss any time that he can have with him," I say.

"You mean you don't want to be the bitch who keeps a child from his parent?" She uses the same words that Andrew threw at me last year after he sold our third television set. "Oh, I've been called more than that by my own father."

"How do you do it?" I ask, waiting for the answer.

"I put myself ahead of them. Me." She smiles at me. "I was a teen mom at fifteen because I was looking for any type of love I could get, and just like that, I fell for an addict who destroyed himself at the end and took a piece of me when he left our child in the stroller while he went to get high in December." My hand goes to my mouth. "I've made peace with it. God has a plan for us, and I didn't know it then. I will never fully understand it, but ..." She wipes a tear away from her cheek.

"How?" I ask. "How do you do it?"

"I stopped being my own worst enemy and saw that no matter what I did or how I did it, I can't be blamed for other people's actions." The sound of the door slamming makes us both look toward the door, and we see a man coming in and sitting in one of the chairs. "I guess that's my cue." She gets up. "This was nice."

"It was," I say as she turns to walk out of the room.

"You know, the meetings are not just for the addicts but also for the ones living through this. If you ever feel like sitting with us."

"Thank you," I say. "I have a couple of things to finish before Father Rolly comes back."

"Well, the meeting is always open," she says with a smile, and then she turns to walk into the room, and I'm left with my head spinning. I get up and decide to update the filing system, and then when that is over, I see about maybe making all items digital. When Father Rolly walks in two hours later, I look up from the computer.

"Hey there, Father." I smile at him. "How was this morning?"

"As expected. Mrs. Rodriguez is not going to recover from losing her husband, but we can sit and talk for as long as she wants."

"It must be hard," I say, and he looks at the files in front of me. "I'm going to try a system," I say, and he just smiles.

"You young kids and your systems," he jokes.

"Just think of all the extra space we'll have if I get all these papers into this computer," I joke, and he smiles at me.

"You have a great night," he says and turns to walk up the stairs and, then I get bombarded with phone calls about baptisms and communions. When I finally hang up, the phone rings again, and I pick it right up.

"Hey, Mom," Dylan says, and I'm already halfway out of my chair.

"Dylan, are you okay?" I ask, frantic, and if this was a cordless phone, I would be outside already.

"He's fine." I hear Justin's voice, and I sit back down in my chair. "We are just letting you know that we are on our way, and we'll pick you up at work."

"But it's early?" I say, and then look at the clock on the wall and the computer to make sure they are both right.

"Yeah, the rink had a power outage, so we left early, and we got some ice cream. We're going to come and get you."

"But—" I start, and then Dylan cuts me off.

"Mom, I did a three-pointer again." I close my eyes.

"That's great," I say, and then the other line rings. "Okay, I have someone on the other line. I'll call you right back."

"No need," Justin says. "We'll be there in twenty minutes.

Come out when you finish," he says and then disconnects.

I press the button to switch to the other line. "Hey, this is Travis," he says. "You called earlier about hockey equipment for a kid."

"Yes," I say softly. "That's me."

"We got skates and a helmet," he says. "I can let both of them go for two hundred," he says, and I close my eyes.

"Thanks for letting me know." I hang up the phone and try to think of ways that I can pay for it, and I literally can't. There are so many things coming that I have to pay for, especially my phone.

After turning everything off and then tucking in the chair, I walk out into the daylight and hear Dylan laughing. I turn and see that Justin has him over his shoulder like he's a sack of potatoes while he tickles his stomach. "Okay, fine, fine, you're better than Matthew."

"You better say that," he says, and then he spots me. His eyes light up, and his smile gets so big. "There's your mom." Justin puts him down, and Dylan runs to me. I almost go back a step, but I hug his head, leaning down to kiss his wet head.

"Mom," he says. "Justin is a grasshopper."

I look up at Justin, who just groans. "He was in the car when my brother called, and he calls me grasshopper." He walks over to us and towers over me and leans down and kisses my cheek. "Did you have a good day?"

"Um ..." I say. My cheek's still tingling when he puts his arm around my shoulder and walks me to the SUV while Dylan hugs my waist. He goes on and on about what he did, talking a mile a minute, and I just want to savor it.

"I'm starving," he says right before climbing into the back seat, and Justin opens the passenger door for me. "Mom, can I have a whole pizza to myself?"

"No," I answer the same time Justin answers, "Sure."

"He's never going to eat the whole thing." I look at Justin, who shrugs.

"He can have it for a snack later," he says, and I climb up into the vehicle.

"What's going on right now?" I whisper as I watch Justin walk around the front and get in.

"We are going to get pizza and spaghetti," Dylan says from the back, and Justin looks over his shoulder.

"What did you say?" he asks, starting the SUV and putting his seat belt on.

"Mom was asking what is going on," he says, and Justin looks over at me. "Mom, I got new stuff." I look at Justin, who slips on his shades and makes his way out of the neighborhood and onto the highway.

"You didn't have to do that," I say softly, and he looks over at me.

"I know I didn't, but I wanted to," he says, and I just nod at him and look out the window.

I watch the city come into view, and when he turns down one of the richest streets in the city, all I can do is look at the skyscrapers. All of them are so tall, and the sun reflects off them, making them look like mirrors. He slows down when he gets to the tallest building and then pulls into the underground parking area. I look at Justin. "The restaurant is right across the street." I open the door, and he gets out, and Dylan is already getting out of his seat.

Justin walks a little ahead of us, and Dylan holds my hand while we follow him. I spot a sign that says for residents only, and I stop walking. "You can't park here," I say, pointing at the sign.

"I'm pretty sure I can since I live here," he says, and at that moment, I'm reminded of how so very different we are.

FIFTEEN

JUSTIN

I SEE HER face change when I say I live here as she looks down at her clothes and then looks up at me again. "Let's go," I say, walking back to her and putting my hand around her shoulders. I let my arm hang lightly even though I want to pull her into me.

"You live here?" Dylan says, smiling when we walk to the elevator, and I press the up button.

"I do," I say, and I'm praying like fuck that the elevator gets there before she bolts. I watch her every move as she tries not to make eye contact with me, and she looks around and sees all the brand-new cars. Thank fuck I didn't tell her that the four cars I parked next to are mine. The ding of the elevator makes her look forward, and I'm not sure this is better.

The inside walls of the elevator are all mirrors, and the floor is a light gray marble. Pressing the lobby button, I hold my breath as the doors open, and then I put my hand on her lower back to usher her out. She hasn't dropped Dylan's hand, and if she wasn't with Dylan, I wonder if she would try to make a run for it.

I watch as her eyes take in the room, and I wonder what she's thinking. Turning left when we get off the elevator, I walk past the security desk. He spots me and stands, showing you the uniform of a black jacket and white shirt. "Good evening, Mr. Stone."

"Hey, Bob." I smile at him. There are a total of six security agents who work during the week. "Nice day, isn't it?"

"It is," he says, and I just walk toward the glass door past the big round marble table that holds a vase of flowers with four chairs. It's the waiting area. You don't get past security if you are not on the list.

"Does that guy block people?" Dylan asks when we walk outside, and the heat hits me right away.

"Yeah," I say. "The restaurant is just on the corner," I say, turning to walk toward it.

"Why?" Dylan asks me.

"Why what?" We walk in sync, but I feel her stiffness next to me.

"Why does he block people from seeing you?" I love that he is so curious. He is always asking questions and always trying to figure out puzzles.

"Well, you know I play hockey, right?" I ask, and he nods. "Well, sometimes I don't play good, and then you have people who want to come tell me that. I don't mind if they tell me at the restaurant, but I don't want them coming to my door."

"And you don't want to hear it." He nods his head. "I would do the same."

"Yeah, that's it," I say. I don't tell him it's because people push their limits and just decide it's okay to knock on your door to get you to sign a shirt or a stick. It's amazing that I'm being paid to do what I love, but there are times and places for that, and my home isn't one of them. It's a piece of me that no one gets to see unless I want them in my space.

"Here we are," I say, pulling open the door, and the smell of pizza hits you right away.

A hostess stand is located right in front with a blonde and a brunette standing behind it. One of them notices me right away and perks up. "Hi there," I say. "A table for three in the back if possible."

"Sure thing," the blonde says and looks at her screen and talks to the brunette as they discuss where to sit us.

"It smells really, really good," Dylan says, and I look at him and smile and then look at Caroline who now has her hands folded in front of her stomach.

"Wait until you try the pizza," I tell Dylan, and then I hear my name being called.

"Look at this." I turn and see Lara, the owner, come over to me, and I lean down to kiss both her cheeks. "You look too skinny," she says, slapping my stomach. "We need to put some meat on those bones."

I laugh and then look to my side. "Lara," I say, smiling, "this is Dylan and Caroline. Guys, this is Lara. She owns this place."

"Nice to meet you two," she says and turns to the girls. "Give them the private room in the back."

"Will do, Mrs. Cicionni," the brunette says.

"What do you like to eat?" She looks at Dylan, smiling.

"Pizza and spaghetti," he says and then smiles, putting up his finger. "With meatballs."

Lara claps her hands together in joy. "Now this I can do," she jokes with him, getting the menus from the girls and then smiling at them. "I'll take them back there. Will you tell Tony that I need a special plate for Justin and his guests?"

"Sure thing," the blonde says and walks to the back of the kitchen.

"Come with me," she says. Dylan walks next to her, and I see Caroline shiver.

"Are you cold?" I ask, and she still doesn't look at me. Instead, she just nods. We walk past the dining area full of high-top tables with steel stools. The outer walls are all windows, and then the wooden wall inside has all the signed jerseys from the team.

"Are you taking us to a secret room?" Dylan asks, his eyes going wide when she nods her head. "Mom, we are going to a secret room."

She opens one of the doors in the hallway, and we are taken into one of the private dining rooms. This one has a round table in the middle set for eight people. "Sit," she says, putting the menus on the table. "And I'll be back with some wine and some juice?"

"Thank you," I say to her, and Dylan is already sitting in one of the chairs.

"Come and sit," I say, taking her hand in mine. It feels like ice. "You're freezing."

"Not really," she says, and then she shivers again. "I get

like this when I'm nervous."

"I'll be right back," I say and walk out of the room. Closing the door behind me, I come face-to-face with Lara, who is carrying a tray of drinks. "Hey, can you make sure she doesn't leave?" I say, and she smirks at me.

"Don't tell me we finally found someone who is immune to your charm?" she says, laughing, and I have to smile.

"Let's just say that I think if she could, she would have already hightailed it out of here."

"I'll keep her here." She winks at me and then goes to open the door. "Even if I have to throw myself down in front of her." She walks into the room.

Walking past the hostesses, who smile at me, I run back to my apartment. I rush past the security and take the elevator up to my condo, hurrying to my room and snatching the first sweater I see. I make it back to the restaurant in a matter of two minutes. The hostess smiles at me again, and I see that her shirt is down just a touch. I shake my head and jog back to the room, and when I walk in, I see Lara sitting at the table talking to Caroline.

"Hey," I say, my chest heaving as I walk in, and Lara now gets up and smiles at them.

"Dylan," Lara says, "would you like to come and help make your pizza?" He looks at Caroline, his eyes big.

"Mom," he says, pleading, "can I?"

"Sure," she says. He gets up, and they walk out of the room and close the door.

"Here," I say, handing her the blue sweater I ripped off my shelf. My hand stays outstretched, and she just looks at it. "It's just a sweater," I say, and I'm about to just put it on her

143

when she reaches out and takes it from me.

"Did you run home?' she asks softly as she puts on the sweater, and it's so big on her the shoulder lines are in the middle of her arm. I sit next to her and nod, grabbing a glass of water. "You didn't have to do that."

"You were cold," I say, and I put my arm on the back of her chair while I lean back. "So."

"You just solve everything," she says, and she looks down and then up again.

"If I can do it, I do it," I say, looking at her, and fuck, do I ever want to kiss her. If her son wasn't out there and she wasn't scared and nervous of this thing happening, I would lean over and devour her. "Why are you nervous?" She looks down and then up again and leans forward to grab her wine glass and takes a sip. "Is that called liquid courage?"

"I've never drank wine before," she says. "I like it."

"Have you ever been drunk before?" I ask, and she shakes her head and takes another sip.

"I think that's enough wine for now," I say. "I have experience with it."

"Oh, I bet you do," she mumbles under her breath, and I smirk.

"My sisters should open a winery with all the wine they consume," I say. "I don't give a shit if you drink the whole bottle. But are you ready to sleep over at my house?" She looks at me, and her mouth opens and then closes. She looks down at the glass in her hand and then up at me again and then down. "I don't mean with me," I say. "Although I wouldn't say no," I say softly, and she leans forward and puts the glass back on the table. "What's the matter, sweetheart? Don't want to sleep over?"

"Um ..." she starts to say.

I throw my head back and laugh. "Stop being nervous. It's just me."

"Yeah," she says, "but it's here at this really fancy restaurant." And I have to wonder if the wine is really working on her or if she's opening up to me. "And I'm not fancy, and the girls are all smiling at you, and then you have me"—she points at herself—"with my Walmart clothes and the whole closet of skeletons." She grabs the wine again. "I mean, how do I even compete with that?"

"Drink water," I say, reaching for her water and giving it to her. "If we are going to have this conversation on why I want to be with you, then I'm going to do it with you understanding and listening to what I have to say."

"I'm listening, Justin." She raises her fingers to her ears. "My listening ears are open."

"I want to kiss you," I say, waiting to see if she says or does anything, and when her eyes only widen, I continue. "I want to take you into my arms, put my hands on your face, and kiss the ever-loving shit out of you."

"Oh, my," she says, "I think I need water."

"I want to sit with you and learn everything about you. I don't care what you wear." I lean in, and her breath hitches, and her tongue pokes out to lick her lips. "Although I have to say that seeing you wear my clothes is putting me in a very difficult position." I look down at my cock that has been rock hard since I sat down next to her and she put my sweater on. Her eyes move down, and she must see my outline because she leans forward again.

"More water," she says, drinking. "Definitely need more water."

"We both have a past," I say. "How do you know I'm not ashamed of the shit I've done or what has happened to me? How do you know that we might have a bit more in common than you think?"

She puts her glass of water down and takes a deep breath. "My cell phone got cut off yesterday," she says and doesn't stop talking. "To top it all off, my scumbag of an ex stole my kid's hockey stuff and pawned it, and now they want two hundred dollars."

I don't think I can hear anything more without wanting to flip the table over and go hunt down her ex. "Tonight, you take my phone," I say, and she shakes her head.

"I'm not taking your phone," she huffs. "I'm just pointing out how different our lives are."

"What if you need to call 911?" I ask, and then I play dirty. "What if something happens to Dylan, and you can't call for help?" I take my own glass of water, and I'm surprised it doesn't shatter in my hand. I'm so angry about what she just told me. I take a sip of the ice-cold water, but it's hard to swallow. "And fuck the equipment. We got him a spare bag."

"But you shouldn't have to pay for that," she says.

"Neither should you," I say. She's about to argue with me when the door opens, and Dylan comes skipping back into the room.

"Mom, there is a guy, and he tosses the pizza into the sky." He mimics tossing a pizza in the air with his arms. "Then he catches it."

"Really?" she says, and he climbs into the chair next to

146

me.

"And Lara let me make my own pizza," he says. "I did a meat lover's because I need some meat on these bones." He slaps his stomach, and we both laugh. I look over at her and see her eyes glistening with tears, but for once, I don't think they're sad tears.

Sixteen

Caroline

*M*Y HEAD IS spinning for a couple of reasons. I'm sure the wine is playing a part in it, but his words are making it spin more. Dylan is going on and on about something with Justin, and the only thing I can hear in my head is I want to kiss you. It doesn't help that his smell is all around me because of his ginormous sweater. I had to roll the sleeves just to get them over my hands.

I pick up my wine by accident and take a sip, putting it down and then looking over at Justin who just smirks. "If you really want to sleep over, sweetheart ..."

"It was an accident," I say and then pick up the glass of water and finish the whole thing. "I need more water."

"Do you now?" He smiles, and Lara comes in with a tray and places it in the middle of the table.

"This are just little samples," she says. I look at the tray of what she calls "little samples," and it's enough food to last a week. "Little meatballs, garlic bread, calamari, bruschetta, sausage and rapini and arugula salad." She smiles and puts down a stack of white plates in front of me.

"I want meatballs," Dylan says. "And the sausage." He looks at Justin and scrunches his nose. "No green stuff."

Lara throws her head back and laughs. "Is there anything specific you want to eat for the main?"

"The main?" I ask, and then look at Justin, leaning in. "What does she mean by that?"

"I think a couple of pizzas and maybe a penne vodka and a spaghetti would be good," he tells her, and she smiles and nods at us.

"Did you just order more food?" I ask Justin, who is already filling a plate for Dylan and then putting a bit of everything on one for me.

He puts the plate down in front of me and the smell of garlic and tomatoes hits my nose right away, making my mouth water. "Eat, sweetheart," he says softly, and my stomach feels like it just did a wave. No one has ever called me that.

I look over at Dylan who has just destroyed the meatball and is asking Justin for another one. His mouth is covered in sauce. "So how many sisters did you say you had again?" I ask him as I take my first bite of the meatball, and it has to be the best thing I've ever tasted in my life.

"Three," he says, chewing. "Allison is the oldest girl." He smiles. "Then the twins, Zara and Zoe." His eyes light up when he talks about his family.

"So you're the baby?" I ask him again, this time eating a piece of the calamari. It melts in my mouth.

"Matthew is the oldest," he says, looking at Dylan. "The guy who called me when I was driving." Dylan couldn't care less what he is saying as he eats his food.

"How much older?" I ask him.

"Eighteen years," he says, and my eyes open wide. "Were you an oops?"

He throws his head back and laughs. "Matthew and Allison are from my mom's first marriage."

"So your half brother and sister?" I say, and he shakes his head.

"Not to us," he says. "My dad is their dad; doesn't matter what blood they have." I put my hand on his arm. "Their father cheated on my mother, and she caught him. I've never met the man, but I've been told he's a tool."

"Do they still keep in touch with him?" My hand remains on his arm.

"Nope. He stopped coming around when my dad came into the picture. He tried to get my mother back, but my father, well, let's just say he squashed that idea right away," he says, and his face lights up again. "It took one look from my dad, and he was a goner. I mean that, and my mother told him to take a hike, which made Dad want her even more."

"Love at first sight." I smile now and take my hand off his arm and eat another meatball. "Are your siblings married?"

"Yeah, all of them. Matthew is married to Karrie, and they have four kids." My eyes go big. "He's a caveman. If he could carry her around over his shoulder and pound his chest while screaming she's mine, he probably would." I laugh. "Allison is married to Max, and they have two kids. He is also Matthew's ex-enemy."

"Holy crap," I say, mesmerized by the family.

"Oh, yeah, not only did they get married"—he starts to laugh—"but they eloped, and Matthew found out watching *SportsCenter*." I put my hand to my mouth.

"One more meatball," Dylan says, and Justin looks at me for approval.

"You sure? There is pizza and pasta coming," I say, and he nods his head.

"So tell me more," I ask, wanting to hear more.

"Zara was the first twin to get married to Evan Richards," he says, then waits for my reaction after he says his name, and when I just shrug, he looks at Dylan. "Evan Richards."

"He's the best. He won a Stanley Cup," he says, wiping his mouth. "Not as good as Justin, though."

"Wait," Justin says. He takes out his phone, and suddenly, he's FaceTiming someone, and the man who fills the screen is hot. "Yo," Justin says, and the man speaks up.

"Hey," he says, and then I hear a woman's voice yelling in the background.

"Why the hell is Justin calling you?" She now stands next to the guy, and I don't think I've ever seen a prettier woman in my life.

"He likes me better than you," the man says.

"Okay, listen," Justin says. "I want you to hear what I just heard."

The woman snatches the phone. "Oh my God, is this gossip?" she says with a squeal. "I love gossip. What is it about? Is it about Allison? Did you notice her weight gain, too? You think she's pregnant?"

"What?" Justin asks, shocked. "I need Evan."

"I'm here," he says, and he comes to stand next to who must be his wife, Justin's sister Zara.

"Dylan," he says, pressing the button to turn the camera around. "What did you say about Evan Richards?" Dylan smiles and becomes shy. "It's okay, buddy. He knows," Justin says.

"I said he's good," Dylan says, almost hiding his smile.

"And ..." Justin says.

"But you're better," he says.

Zara starts laughing, and Evan yells, "Bullshit!" Loudly.

"There is a kid in the room," Zara says, and now Evan grabs the phone from her.

"I want to speak to Dylan," he says, and Justin hands Dylan the phone.

"How old are you?" he asks Dylan.

"Eight," Dylan says.

"What level do you play?" Evan asks him.

Zara is in the background. "Would you stop harassing the child, Evan?"

"I play forward," Dylan says proudly.

"When I'm down in two weeks, how about we play one-on-one?" Evan says, and I hear dogs barking in the background.

"You just threw down to a child," Zara admonishes.

"It's on," Dylan says, and I shake my head as he hands phone back to Justin.

"Okay, just thought I would share that with you," Justin says when he gets the phone back.

"I'm sure you did." He laughs. "Where are you?"

"We are at Cicionni," Justin says.

"Who is *we*, Justin?" Zara asks, and I see Justin give the same smile he did when he was talking about his family.

"Dylan and Caroline," he says and comes closer to me. "Caroline, say hi to my bratty number one." He turns the phone on me, and I try not to panic, but I swear my hands start shaking, and I have the sudden need to drink another gulp of wine.

"Oh, shit," Evan says in the background and comes closer to the phone. "It's about to be real."

"Hi," I say, and Zara's eyes open wide.

"Hi," she says, "it's so nice to meet you."

"You, too," I say, and I don't know what else to say so Justin takes over.

"Okay, squirt, call you later," he says.

"I'm so telling everyone," Zara says, and he laughs, then he hangs up. Before I can ask him what she means, the door opens, and Lara comes back with another waiter, both of them carrying trays.

"I hope you guys are hungry," she says, and I don't say anything else because two pizzas and two huge plates of pasta are set down on the table.

Dylan digs into the spaghetti and then eats a slice of pizza, and the only thing that I can fit in my stomach is two slices of pizza. But Justin eats us both under the table, and when I look at him, he just winks at me.

When Lara comes back in, she takes the remainder of the food and offers to box it up for us. "I'm stuffed," Justin says, stretching backward and then putting his arm around my chair to pull me closer to him.

"Did you eat enough?" he asks, and I look over at him

and nod.

"Okay, you two," Lara says, coming back in with a tray. "I made this special tiramisu and then a Nutella cheesecake this morning," she says, putting the dessert in the middle of the table.

"If I eat anything else, I'm going to explode," I whisper, but Justin sits up and takes a spoon and then cuts a piece of tiramisu and brings the spoon to my mouth.

"Taste it," he says, holding the spoon to my lips. I open my mouth, and the cool of the cake hits my tongue, and then the sweetness follows. "Good, right?" he says and takes another piece and eats from the same spoon.

Dylan is eating his own piece, and I swear the kid has a hole in his stomach sometimes. "Dylan, don't make yourself sick."

"Mom, it's so good," he says, finishing the whole piece.

"Here, taste this," Justin says, holding the spoon to my mouth.

"I can't," I say, trying to duck from him, but he doesn't let up.

"Just taste a bite," he says, and I open and take the spoon, and I swear I will never taste anything as good again. "Good, right?" I nod my head.

I watch the two of them finish the dessert, and then Justin stands. "Let's go, sweetheart," he says again. I look at him, and he just smirks at me. Then he turns to Dylan. "Ready, champ?"

"Yup," Dylan says and gets up, and Justin grabs the bag with the takeout. I follow Justin out of the room and expect him to walk ahead of me, but he doesn't. He waits for me and then puts his arm around my shoulder. When we walk past the hostess stand, he doesn't even look their way.

"Thank you for coming," the two women say, and all he does is nod. We are almost out of the door when a couple of fans come over and ask for pictures. He is very polite to them, and they pose for pictures.

"It's so cool," Dylan says next to me, and I have to agree that it really is. When he finishes, he comes to us, and we walk back into the lobby.

"Let's get you guys home," he says as we walk through the lobby and to the elevator. I try not to look around too much, and when we get into the garage, I follow him to the SUV.

"Look at that red car," Dylan says, pointing at the sleek red car next to the SUV.

"You like that one?" Justin asks, opening the passenger door for me and then the back door for Dylan.

"I bet it goes fast, fast," he says, sitting in the car seat.

"I'll take you out in it this weekend," he says to Dylan, and Dylan squeals while I just stand here looking at him. He slams the back door and turns to me. "You ready?"

"That's your car?" I ask him, looking at the red car. I don't know what it is, but it just looks expensive.

"Um, yeah," he says. "That one also." He points at a truck and then the sleek black BMW next to it. "That one also."

"You have four cars?" I ask him, and he puts his hand on my back and ushers me to get in the SUV.

"Does it matter?" he asks, and I want to say yes, it does, but he just continues. "It's a car."

"Yes," I say. "Four. You own four cars."

"Well, five," he says. "I keep one at my parents' house for when I visit."

He smiles. "Now, let's get Dylan home. He must be tired."

"Smooth," I say. "Very smooth."

He looks at me and winks, and my stomach literally flutters. "Oh, you ain't seen nothing yet, sweetheart," he says, closing the door.

"Mom," Dylan calls from the back seat, and I turn around. "I really like him."

"Yeah, baby," I say, looking back to the front. "Me, too," I say quietly under my breath.

SEVENTEEN

JUSTIN

"*F*OUR." I HEAR her mumbling from beside me. She turns her back to the door and looks at me. "Four cars."

As I look over at her, she's still wearing my sweater even though it's like a dress but she folds her arms over her chest. "I mean, five," I joke with her, and she rolls her eyes.

"Sorry," she says. "Five, you have five cars." She shakes her head. "You see, right?"

I look in the rearview mirror and see that Dylan is slowly losing the battle to stay awake. "I'm not sure what you're asking me right now."

"I'm saying that we are literally night and day," she says, but I interrupt her.

"We are two people who met and like each other. What does it matter how many cars I have?"

"You having all those cars is not the issue," she says.

"So why are we still talking about this?" I wink at her. "If I had zero cars, would you like me more?"

"Well, no," she says, and I laugh.

"That's a step in the right direction." I glance over at her, and she looks confused. "You admitted you like me."

"That's what you got from that?" she asks, then lowers her voice and checks to see that Dylan is now sleeping with his head to the side. "Out of everything I said, that is what you focus on?"

"Yup," I say. When I hear her huff, I reach over and take her hand in mine. "Shh, you'll wake him," I say as I link my fingers with hers. I take in that she let me, and I also take in that she holds my hand back while she just looks outside for the rest of the drive.

When we pull up to her apartment complex, she shows me where to go, and I park in her parking spot. "You grab the food. I'm going to grab Dylan," I say before she gets out. It looks like she is going to argue with me, but she doesn't. She gets the food, and I slowly unbuckle Dylan and carry him in, following her. "He's out cold."

She opens the door and walks in and puts the bag of food on the table and then rushes into the bedroom. The house is literally a sauna. "I'm going to open the windows and get a breeze going," she says, opening the windows, and I notice there is no breeze even when she does that.

I lay him on the bed, and he curls into the fetal position, but I take off his shoes and socks. "Will he be okay?" I ask, and she nods her head and takes off my sweater that she is wearing.

"Yeah, he'll probably be out until tomorrow," she whispers, and I walk out of the room, and she follows me.

"Do you want something to drink?" she asks me, and I nod my head. She goes to the fridge and opens the freezer to get some ice cubes out.

I turn to sit on the futon and wait for her. She walks back into the room holding two glasses and hands one to me. "Here you are."

"Thank you," I say and take a sip and then wait for her to sit down. "Tonight was fun." I start the conversation, and I watch her as I talk. "I don't know what the deal is with your parents or your siblings, and I didn't want to ask about them in front of Dylan, but I want to know everything."

"There really isn't much to say," she says, taking a gulp of water and then looking down at the glass that is already forming condensation on the outside. "My parents were ..." she says and then corrects herself. "They are religious people, and they didn't like the fact that their only daughter got knocked up at seventeen." My heart sinks for her. "So when I told them I was pregnant, they gave me two options. One, give the baby up for adoption, which I was never going to do, or two, move out."

"But ..." I start to say, but when she shakes her head, I want to pull her to me.

"I refused to give him away. I wasn't even two months pregnant, and I loved him with everything I had," she says softly. "So I packed my stuff and moved in with Andrew and his family. His parents were not much more understanding, but he was eighteen. They weren't going to have their grandson living on the street, so they took me in. He was the star quarterback, and his name was on everyone's lips as the next big thing. He got a scholarship, and I followed him here. The only way for us to have housing was for us to be married, so one day, we went to city hall and made it official. It was my happy ending," she says, and her eyes then look down.

"But then I gave birth to Dylan, and he started to spend more and more time away from home. He would complain that he couldn't focus with Dylan crying all the time. I was with a newborn who had colic and only slept two hours a night. A day would turn two and then close to the end, he would be gone for a whole week. I just didn't get it. Dylan was such a beautiful baby, and every single time he smiled, it just made me love him more." She smiles now, and I notice every time she talks abut him, there is this look she gets in her eyes. The look that I see every single time I look in my mother's eyes or my father's.

"I just tried to be understanding. He had all this stress on him, so the least I could do was take care of Dylan. When he was home, he was angry and stressed. He used to get pissed off that there were too many toys around, and he was constantly stepping on them." She wipes away a tear. "Of course I would go to some games, but even then, I felt like I was intruding in his life. He had this whole other life without us in it. I suspected that he wasn't faithful to me, and when I found out the first time, he promised me it was a mistake. Promised me it wouldn't happen again. I knew it was stupid to believe him. Maybe that was my clue to get out, but I wanted Dylan to have a family. I wanted him to have a mother and father together. But then it came knocking on my door again at two in the morning looking for him. It was the day before Dylan turned two years old. I had these little gifts wrapped for him when he got up, and Andrew got so pissed when I asked who she was that he threw one of them at the wall, smashing the gift." She takes a deep breath, and I want to go to her and hold her while she tells this story. I want to give her the strength from inside me.

"Junior year, he got sacked so hard he tore his ACL." I look down at my own hands that are now folded into fists, the rage coming out of me, and right then, I think about when I was drafted first overall. It was a dream come true. "Well, he was put on painkillers after his surgery, and he somehow got addicted," she says softly and now wipes another tear off her cheek. "You have to know that I had no idea. Not even one that he was so addicted." She looks at me, and I want her to stop telling me all this.

"It was not your fault," I say. My hand goes to her cheek, and my thumb catches the tear that escapes her eyes.

"When I found out he was addicted, I went to his parents," she says. Her voice makes my stomach start to burn, and my heart speeds up faster and faster, and my neck suddenly becomes hotter. "They actually blamed me." She laughs bitterly, but it comes out more like a sob. "Said I pushed him in that direction, and that if it wasn't for me and Dylan, he would be okay. That having a child put extra strain on him." The sobs rip out of her, and I pull her to me. She cries in my chest, her tears soaking straight through my shirt. "I never once put pressure on him."

"It was not your fault," I say, hugging her, and I kiss her head.

"When I found out that he had wasted all his scholarship money, I ..." She gets up now and starts to pace in front of me. "I was so pissed and angry, and to top it all off, we got kicked out of the house." I sit here now and rage tears through my body, making my legs start to move up and down. "He promised me everything would be okay. We moved into a one-bedroom studio that was horrible. There were roaches everywhere, and I was afraid that I'd wake up, and they'd be all over Dylan. He didn't pay rent, and one day I caught him fucking the landlady on our couch. I got tested right after that, and I never touched him again."

"Stop," I say, my heart sinking, my stomach burning. "I don't know if I can take much more."

"This is me." She stands there with her arms out to her sides. "You wanted this. You asked for it. I told you that we shouldn't go there. We are so different." She looks down, and I see a single tear roll down her cheek. "There were drug dealers breaking down my door to get him. There were times I came home, and the money that I had set aside to buy food with was in a syringe and his eyes closed on the couch. We ate bread for a month with peanut butter. I went to the church and asked for help with food, and we got food stamps. It took me over a year to finally save enough to escape him." She looks up now, her shoulders square.

"But before I left, he gave me one last gift." I wait for it, holding my breath. If he hurt her or put his hands on her, I'll kill him. "He gave me the credit cards he had opened in my name. I was in debt to the tune of fifty-seven thousand dollars. I had a three-year-old, and I was making seven fifty an hour." She puts her hands together. "So when I said you and I are night and day, I was not lying. I have worked hard to get myself where I am today, and every single hurdle that is thrown at me, I have somehow climbed over it." She smirks.

"Yes, I have bumps and bruises and scrapes, and I have nothing in my retirement fund, and the only thing I can afford is the bare minimum, but"—she takes a deep breath—"I will never let Dylan live one day thinking that any of this is his fault. He asked about his grandparents once, and I said they lived too far. When he's old enough, I'll tell him the truth, but hopefully, his life is going to be filled with so much love in his heart that he won't even care."

I get up now and walk to her and take her beautiful face in my hands. "He won't ever need them because he has you. He has all the love in the world he'll ever need," I say softly and then put my forehead to hers. "I really want to kiss you right now," I say, almost as if I'm asking her for permission. "In my whole life, I've never wanted anything so badly."

She puts her hands around my wrists, her fingers not touching, and she takes the one step closer to me. "After everything I've been through, I think this is what my reward should be. If only for one kiss," she whispers. She gets on her tippy toes just a bit, and it's like a magnetic pull. My hands move from her face to the bottom of her neck, and her hair slips between my fingers. My heart is beating so fast and so loud that I wonder if she'll hear it. My fingers are trembling right before I tilt my head and kiss her gently. Her soft lips are on mine, and she whimpers just a bit. I'm about to let her go when she opens her mouth, and her tongue slides with mine. My other arm pulls her closer to me, and I get lost in her taste, lost in her touch, lost in her.

"Mom!" Dylan yells, and she jumps back as if my touch

burned her. "I'm so hot," he says, and she looks at me and then walks to the bedroom. I look up at the ceiling, and for the first time in my life, I pray that in the end we both get what we need and what we want.

EIGHTEEN

CAROLINE

*W*HEN I HEARD Dylan's voice, it was as if ice water was dumped on me. I jumped so fast away from Justin that I'm surprised I didn't fall. Spilling everything I had inside me and reliving everything that I went through was exhausting. I don't know why I did it or how but something about Justin Stone just made me want to share with him.

"I'm so hot," Dylan says when I get to the bedroom. I didn't want to say anything before but walking into the room was like entering a sauna. I need to get a box fan or two or maybe three. He pulls his shirt over his head, and I see that his hair is matted to his head.

"Do you want to take a cool shower?" I ask, and he just shakes his head and lies back down and falls asleep. I know that by the time I wake up in the morning, he'll be in just his boxers.

I turn and walk back out of the room and see Justin

standing there looking at me. His eyes never leaving mine. "Is he okay?"

"Yeah, just hot," I say. I'm suddenly embarrassed and feel silly about how I practically threw myself at him.

"I should get going," he says, and I just nod. When I walk him to the door, he turns and takes me in his arms. Before I can say anything, he wraps his arm around my waist and picks me up off my feet, then kisses me on the lips. "Lock up, sweetheart."

He gives me one more small kiss when he sets me down and then walks out of the apartment. I close the door after him and quietly turn the lock. My forehead hits the door, and I close my eyes, my lips still tingling from his kiss. I swear I smell him all around me.

"Don't go down that path, Caroline," I tell myself. Pushing off from the door, I take a deep breath, but it's the wrong thing to do since his smell is still all over me. His sweater is on the table, so I sniff my T-shirt and realize his smell is all over me. My hands, my bare arms, everything around me smells like him. I walk to the bathroom and undress after turning on the shower and adjusting the temperature to cold. It never really gets cool, or maybe my body is scorching hot just thinking about him. I stand under the water, letting it cascade all around me. The whole time, I'm having this conversation with myself about how stupid it would be to get involved with him. How he is so out of my league and there is nothing I can do to catch up to him.

I use the white towel hanging on the towel rack to dry off and then slip into my shorts and a tank top. When I open the door, it's still not cooler. I open the windows a touch more, but there isn't even a breeze outside tonight. It's just stale hot air. The sounds of crickets in the distance and someone arguing somewhere. I look out at the courtyard and see a group of guys hanging by the front door. Off to the side, some teenage kids are shooting basketball.

I don't know how long I stand here when the ringing starts. I turn to look around, confused as to where it's coming from, when I finally find it under Justin's sweater on the kitchen table. I turn it over and see it's his cell phone, and that someone is calling him. I look down at the phone not sure what to do and then the ringing stops. I don't have time to think again when the phone starts ringing again, and this time, I slide the button right and answer it. "Hello," I say, my voice low.

"Hey there," Justin says.

"Justin?" I say, confused. "I think you forgot your phone here."

He laughs now, and I hear him walking around. "I guess you can say I forgot it."

"You didn't forget it." I walk to the futon and sit down, folding my legs under me. "You left it here."

"I did," he says. I hear covers in the background and wonder if he's sliding into his bed. I wonder what his house looks like. I know from just the lobby that it must be gorgeous and also worth a fortune.

"Why?" I ask. Getting up, I walk to the table to get his sweater and bring it back to the futon with me, putting it beside me.

"Would you have taken it if I had handed it to you?" he asks, and I don't have to answer. "Exactly."

171

"So you just left your phone here?" I ask, shaking my head.

"Yup, the passcode is one, two, three, four," he says without skipping a beat. "I want to have you and Dylan over at my house."

"What?" I whisper.

"I want you and Dylan to come and hang out here tomorrow after work," he says. "I can throw a couple of steaks on the grill, and we can watch a movie." My stomach does this weird thing where it feels like it's sinking but then flutters. "Or we can go out. It's up to you."

"Justin, I—" I start to form the words.

"Caroline, there is something here," he says softly. "You can pretend it's not, but tonight when I kissed you." His voice goes even lower. "It was everything."

"I just don't think …" All these reasons are there, practically written on the wall, yet nothing comes out of my mouth.

"Stop thinking," he says. "Tomorrow, I'll come get you guys. We can go out for breakfast before work, and then you let me spoil you by making you dinner and taking care of you for once. Come over and sit down. I'll get you some wine if that will help," he says, chuckling, and I laugh also just a little. "Come on, sweetheart, say yes," he whispers. "Take a chance on me. I promise you won't regret it."

I want to say no. I should say no, but I close my eyes, and whisper, "Yes."

"Thank you," he gushes. "Thank you. Now, go to sleep, and I'll be there in the morning."

"Good night, Justin," I say and hang up the phone and look down at the lock screen. A phone is so personal. He has everything in this phone, and he just left it to me. The Facebook app has a red number with ninety-nine, and then next to it is the Instagram app with the same number. I don't open any of the apps, but I do check what he has and find Gmail, TSN, NHL, Zara's Closet, and the Horton Foundation. There are a couple of others, but I don't touch any of it. I will admit that I'm almost tempted to go through his pictures and see if there are any pictures of his family or even ones of him with other women.

The thought makes me sick, so I lie on the futon with his sweater in my arms. Slowly, my eyes close, and I dream of him and his smile.

When the alarm goes off, I groan out loud. Opening one eye, I see that it's still dark but I can hear the birds chirping outside, so I look at Justin's phone. Since it's only four a.m., I set another alarm for six and then quickly fall back asleep. This time when the alarm goes off, it's followed by a knock on the door. Groaning, I get up and walk to the door. "Who is it?" I ask.

"It's me," Justin says, and I open the door. "Good morning," he says cheerfully. Walking into the apartment, he has his hands filled with coffee and doughnut boxes. He stops next to me and bends to kiss my lips. "You smell like me," he says, and I shake my head and close the door. "You look tired."

"Yeah, well, your alarm went off at four a.m.," I say, and he takes a white cup of coffee and brings it to me. "Why do you get up at four a.m.?"

He hands me the coffee, and I take a sip while he walks back to the table to grab his own coffee. "I work out from four to five thirty."

"In the morning?" I ask, shocked. "Why?"

"I usually work out after the rink, but I like the morning better," he says, and I have to wonder if he does it because he's stuck driving us home.

"You do that for us?" I ask, and he just looks at me and sits down at the table. Today, he's wearing blue shorts and a white polo with his signature black and white Nikes.

"I need a shower," Dylan says from behind me as he walks to the bathroom, ignoring or maybe not seeing Justin. He closes the bathroom door.

"I'm going to go get dressed." I look at Justin who is just staring at me.

"That would be a good idea," he says and adjusts himself, and I roll my lips. My hair is probably sticking up all over the place, my shorts are big on me, and the tank top has bleach stains on it, yet he's sitting there getting aroused by me.

"I'll be right back," I say, turning to go into the bedroom. I open the closet, and of the ten hangers, seven are empty. I have the bare minimum of two pairs of jeans, two pairs of shorts, and seven tops. Same with shoes; I have sneakers and then ballerina shoes. If there is extra money, it goes to Dylan and his clothes since he's growing like a weed.

I grab the summer dress that I use for church and slip it over my head. The short sleeves ruffle just a bit at the end, so I smooth them down. Looking down at the green dress with white flowers, I wonder if this is silly, and if I should just wear the jeans I wore yesterday. I don't have time to think about it before there is a knock on the door. "Come in."

The door opens, and Dylan comes in with a doughnut in his hand. "Justin brought doughnuts," he says, standing there in his boxers as he gets the shorts and matching shirt he wore yesterday. He opens his drawer to take out a pair of clean socks and then puts on his new blue and white Nikes. "How many can I have?"

"One and then I want you to eat something nutritious." I turn and walk out of the room, seeing Justin on his phone. He looks up, and the smile on his face fades as he eyes me from top to bottom. I look down at my dress and wonder if it's not good enough. "I'll be ready soon." I avoid eye contact with him and walk into the bathroom, closing the door.

I wash my face with cold water, hoping that it'll make the sting of tears go away. "It's just temporary," I say to myself while I dab my face with the towel. "Soon enough, he'll move on." I have to prepare myself for it, but my heart, my heart is left unprotected for the first time.

NINETEEN

JUSTIN

$\mathcal{I}$'M SCROLLING INSTAGRAM trying to get my hard-on down when Dylan comes out of the bathroom in his boxers. "Oh, hey," he says, going to the fridge. "I didn't see you there."

"I got here when you went into the shower," I say and get up to help him open the orange juice that is in his hand. I open the cupboards and find it bare with just two of everything and nothing more. My heart breaks for her. And hearing her story made me fall for her even more. If there is anyone who should give up and wave the white flag, it's Caroline, but no. She just dusts herself off and gets ready for more.

"Did you bring food?" he asks me while I pour the orange juice, and I nod. He turns to look at the table. "Doughnuts!" he says, grabbing the glass of juice I hold out for him. He walks over to the table, and after I put the juice back into the fridge, I go sit down at the table while he decides which doughnut he wants. "Is this one filled with jelly?" he asks about the white powdered one, and I nod. "That's Mom's favorite," he says and chooses another one. After taking a bite of it, he sits down on the chair.

"Now go get dressed," I say when he's finished, and Dylan nods, getting up and knocking on the bedroom door before going in. I put my head back and close my eyes, the pit of my stomach burning. They share a bedroom. I grab my phone again and scroll through my private Instagram, which is mostly just my family. I see that Viktor and Zoe are on the last leg of their vacation, and my niece looks more and more like Zoe.

The door opens, and the smile I have on my face fades when I see her. The dress just makes her more angelic, and I'm almost afraid to touch her. The best part is that she has no idea just how beautiful she is. The dress doesn't show any of her curves that I know are under there. My cock springs to action again when I look her up and down, and the smiles fades as I panic about having a hard-on and Dylan coming into the room. She looks down and escapes the room before I say anything.

My heart pounds in my chest. "I can't have another one. Mom is going to be mad if I have another one," Dylan says, but my eyes are on the closed bathroom door. I watch while he finishes the orange juice that I poured him, then takes the glass to the sink, rinses it out, and then leaves it there.

"Did she say that?" I ask, one ear listening for his mother while he tells me he needs to eat breakfast first. "As soon as your mom is done, we can leave."

When the bathroom door opens, and she comes out,

well, I have no words anymore. "Are you ready?" Dylan asks, and she nods at him.

"Close the windows and I'll make sure nothing is in the sink," she says, and he gets up to close the windows.

"Can I have one more doughnut before we leave?" he asks Caroline, and I look at him. "We never get fresh dough- nuts, and I promise I'll eat my breakfast." I want to just make him eat all the doughnuts.

"Why don't we bring the doughnuts with us, and you can have one after breakfast?" I tell him, and his eyes go big.

"I want eggs and pancakes," he says, going to the door. I watch Caroline walk to the sink, making sure everything is clean. She grabs her purse, slipping it around her. "Mom, are we going to church? You're wearing your church dress."

"Not today," she says softly. "Not for two days," she says, and I wait for her to walk out and lock the door. Dylan walks ahead of us, and I walk with her. The sun hits right us right away, and I look up, seeing not one cloud in the sky. "It's going to be a hot one."

We walk down the sidewalk toward the car. Our hands graze each other and finally my pinky grabs hers, and I hold it there in mine, her eyes going straight to our joined hands. "What's wrong?" I ask quietly, and she just shakes her head. I stop walking, and because I'm holding her hand, she stops also. She turns to look at me and then she looks away at Dylan, who is getting to the vehicle. "You look beautiful," I say, and she turns again to look at me, but the sun is in her face, so she squints, closing one eye. "Every single day, I don't think you can look more beautiful." I close in on her, and now my frame blocks the sun from her face. "But every day I'm wrong." I lean in and kiss her lips softly.

"Mom!" Dylan shouts. "Justin, I'm starving, and it's hot."

"I really have to check and see if there is a hole in his stomach," she says while I laugh, and finally, I see her smile. "I'm not kidding."

"He's a growing boy," I say when we get to the SUV, and I open the door for her. "It just gets worse."

"Great," she mumbles, climbing into the passenger side.

When I pull into the same diner we ate at yesterday, Dylan already knows what he's going to order. I wait to see if Caroline orders for herself, but she looks at the menu and then just orders a bowl of fruit. I order more than I'm going to eat, and I'm happy when she takes a bit of the eggs and a sausage. When I pay the bill, she starts to go through her purse. "Don't even think about it."

"You've paid for breakfast this whole week," she says. "Seriously, I can pay for breakfast."

"Yeah," I say, draining the juice from my glass. "Good to know. You're not going to but still good to know."

I slide out of the booth, and Dylan follows me and walks ahead of me. I wait for Caroline to slide out, and the dress has risen a bit, showing off her long legs. "Next time, I'm not going to order anything."

I shrug and grab her hand in mine. "It's okay. I'll order for both of us."

"I won't eat." She thinks she can one-up me.

"I'm sure I can force-feed you." I wink at her, and now I put my hand over her shoulder and pull her to me as she groans. "Eventually, you'll eat."

She doesn't say anything. Instead, we just walk to the

SUV, and Dylan opens the back door. "I'm going to walk from here," she says, and I look down at her. "It's two blocks."

"It'll take me thirty seconds," I say, and she just shakes her head.

"Give me a kiss," she says to Dylan, who leans over and kisses her. "Have a good day at camp."

"It's free Friday," he says, and she looks over at me.

"They can do whatever activity they want all day long," I fill her in. "If he wants to stay on the ice the whole day, that's okay. If he wants to stay in the gym and then go on the ice, that's okay, too."

"I'm going to do whatever Justin does," Dylan says to her.

"That sounds like a great day." She smiles at him and then closes the door. "Have a good day, you two."

I walk to her, and I'm not sure I'm okay with Dylan watching us kiss, so I lean in and kiss her cheek. "Call me when you get to work."

"I'll be fine," she says when I walk around the front.

"Either you call me or I drive you?" I give her the option. Everyone likes options, right?

"Or I walk to work and start my day and see you tonight." She crosses her arms over her chest.

"Yeah, those options are both negative." I look at her. "I can always carry you over my shoulder, put you in the vehicle, and then drive you there." I smile now as she puts her hand up to shield the sun from her face. "Not going to lie to you. The latter is my preferred."

I can't see her eyes with the sun. "I'll call you when I get there."

"See, that was easy," I say, smirking, and she just shakes

her head and turns to walk away. I watch her for way too long, until she disappears around the corner, and I want to jump into the SUV and follow her, but I know she'll just close up again.

Instead, I start the vehicle and make my way to the rink. After five minutes, I'm about to turn back around when my phone rings. "Hello," I answer the Bluetooth.

"I'm here," she says, and I smile.

"See, was that so hard?" I ask, waiting for her answer.

"Yes," she huffs out. "Now I have to go."

"Have a great day at work, sweetheart," I say, and she doesn't answer me; she just hangs up, and I laugh. Dylan just looks out the window while I drive to the rink. I park in my usual spot, and I'm getting him out of the truck when my phone rings, and I see it's Allison.

"Hey," I say, putting the phone to my ear and grabbing Dylan's hand.

"Don't hey me," she starts, her tone angry. "Why would you tell Zara you think I'm getting fat?"

"What?" I ask, confused, and we walk in. "Go get changed," I say, and he runs off.

"Zara just called," she says. "I'm not getting fat. I just weighed myself, and I'm the same I was the last time you saw me."

"I never said you were getting fat." I laugh. "Not once."

"You better not," she says. "So I heard something."

"And there it is," I say. My sisters are like the newspaper. If one gets a morsel of a story, then it's only a matter of minutes before all three of them know and then also Karrie and her best friend Vivienne. "Spit it out."

"You're dating a single mother," she comes right out and tries not to screech, but she fails. "Justin, you really think that's a good idea?"

"I think it's a great idea," I say, waving at a couple of parents and going into the changing room.

"You know it's not just her," she says softly. "You can't just dip and go."

"Dip and go?" I close my eyes.

"It's slang," she says. "Mini Cooper taught me." She mentions Matthew's son, who is now almost fifteen. "Means you go in, do what you need to do, and then bounce."

"I know what it means." I laugh. "Does Max know you use that 'slang'?"

"Um, no," she says and then calls Max's name. "Babe, I'm going to dip and go."

"What the fuck?" I hear Max in the background. "You aren't dipping anywhere. Don't say that."

"Told you." I laugh.

"Anyway," Allison says, "how serious is this?"

"Very," I reply, not skipping a beat. "I just need to convince her of this."

"I don't think this is a good idea." Her voice goes low again. "When you break up with her, you are going to be breaking up with her son."

"Who said anything about breaking anything?" I say, and she gasps out.

"But," she says, "you don't really do relationships."

"I didn't," I admit. "But Caroline is different. There is just something there." I try to find the words, but I can't. "I can't explain it, but it's different."

"Shit," she says. "This isn't just a fling."

"No."

"Fuck, I owe Zara five hundred dollars," she says. "I told her she was crazy. There was no way you would go there."

"I'm there, and if everything goes my way …" I look at the door, seeing Dylan walk by in full gear. "We are all going to be there."

"I can't wait to meet her," she says, and I grumble.

"What?"

"You didn't think that you would find someone, and us not come and see what is going on?" She laughs. "You silly, silly boy. We are all coming up in two weeks."

"What do you mean by all?"

"I mean, all of us." She laughs. "Stone family vacation is coming straight to you, Justin." Her laughing never stops. "Hope she's ready for us."

I don't bother answering her because I really hope she is ready for what my family brings to the table.

TWENTY

CAROLINE

I HANG UP the phone as soon as Father Rolly walks into the room. "Good morning, Caroline." He smiles at me.

"Good morning, Father," I say, and the door opens, and we hear footsteps coming down.

"Good morning," Cheryl cheerfully sings. "You will not believe what just happened."

We both look at her, waiting. "We got a whole U-Haul full of secondhand clothes." Her smile fills her face. "We just need help sorting through it."

"Count us in," Father Rolly says. "I have a couple of people to see today"—he smiles and then looks at me—"but Caroline can help all day."

"Are you sure?" I ask, and he nods.

"Well, the perk of helping us is you get to take your first pick," she says. "And you get fifty percent off."

"Wow," I say, anxious now to dig through the bags.

"Where do you want to start?"

I follow her out, and she looks around as two guys bring in garbage bag after garbage bag, putting them all in the center of the room. She explains how to sort through the clothes. I start with my first bag and start to separate it, finding some of the articles still have the tags on them. I don't know how long we do it for, but when I roll my neck and look over at the clock, I see it's almost three.

"I can't believe we did so much," Cheryl says, looking around the room and seeing that there is only one bag left.

"How about we pick out a couple of outfits for you?"

"I couldn't do that. It doesn't seem right," I tell her, and she smiles at me.

"You did more than I did," she says, "and we didn't even stop and eat."

"I'm okay," I say. "I usually skip lunch."

"I usually just grab an apple," Cheryl says. "Now, let's get you a couple of outfits." She goes over to the pile and grabs the shirt I was looking at before and then a couple more and puts them in a bag. I walk over to the jeans and go through them to see if they have my size. "Any big plans for the weekend?"

"I work tomorrow," I say, finding my size and smiling when I see they are almost new.

"Where?"

"Motel Carpe," I say. "I do housekeeping on Saturday."

"That's a nice little place," she says. "I stayed there once when I first got to town."

"It really is," I say, thinking about the other motel in town that rents rooms by the hour. I lasted two weeks before my stomach gave out when I went to clean a room, and there was so much lube and blood on one bed that it had seeped into the mattress.

"Where does Dylan stay when you clean?" she asks, and I look over at her.

"I bring him with me. He usually watches videos or goes to the park next door," I say. The door opens, and I hear his voice, so I turn to see Dylan and Justin walking into the room.

"See, I told you that she was here," Dylan says, and Justin just looks at me with a huge smile on his face.

"Hey there," he says, looking at me and then nodding at Cheryl who sits there with her mouth hanging open.

"What are you two doing here?" I ask, looking back at the clock to make sure it's working.

"We got out a bit early," Justin says. "We can go wait in the SUV."

"No," Cheryl says, recovering from the shock of either Justin or that he is so good looking. "She's done anyway."

"I still have this bag to finish, and then I have to help sort them." I look at Justin and Dylan, who is now standing like Justin.

"Oh, no," Cheryl says. "I have to go in twenty minutes, so I'm leaving all this here and we can work on it on Monday."

"Are you sure?" I ask, looking around at the heaping piles of clothes.

"Oh, yeah," she says, smiling. "Your boys are waiting for you."

"Okay," I say, getting up and ignoring the way my stomach flipped when she said my boys.

"Can we get ice cream?" Dylan says. "Justin says only if you said yes."

I look at him, and he just shrugs. "I said I was okay only if you were okay with it."

"So can we?" Dylan asks.

"We'll see," I say, grabbing my purse and then waving to Cheryl. I walk out, and the heat hits me right away. "It's so hot."

"Yeah, and it's only going to get hotter," Justin says, walking next to me. His fingers graze mine, and he finally wraps his fingers around mine. "They are calling for a heatwave for the next two weeks."

"So can we have ice cream?" Dylan asks, and I nod my head.

"Only if Justin lets me pay for it," I say, and Justin stops walking and looks at me and glares.

"Justin, will you let Mommy pay for the ice cream?"

Justin looks at me, and I'm all excited because I finally got the upper hand. "Sure," he says, and I'm just happy I won until the rest comes out. "But my dad taught me that it's rude to let a girl pay for ice cream if you like them." Dylan just looks at me. "And I really like your mom, so if she pays for it …"

"Mom," Dylan says, "it's rude if you pay, so you have to let Justin pay."

"Yeah," Justin says. "It's rude for you to let the girls pay. Besides, girls should be treated like princesses, and we all know that no princess pays."

"Yeah, because the king or the prince pays," Dylan agrees. "So let's go get ice cream, and Justin is going to pay because he likes you, and it's rude if you pay."

"That sounds like a great idea," Justin says, and I can't glare at him enough.

I cross my arms over my chest the whole ride there, and then I don't even talk to him. We walk to the window, and he orders Dylan's and then looks at me, and I just shake my head. "Dylan, what is your mom's favorite?"

"She likes the two colors," he says. "Vanilla and chocolate."

"Traitor," I say. Justin just throws his head back and laughs and then comes over and takes me in his arms. He puts one arm around my shoulder and then pulls me to the window.

"Sweetheart, just order your ice cream," he says quietly. "And the next time you pull a stunt like that," he says, leaning in just a touch more, "I'll really throw you over my shoulder." I should push him away from me. I should tell him that I'll kick him in the balls if he even so much as tries it, but instead, I stand here while my heart skips a beat, and my stomach flips with butterflies. Even my body is a traitor.

He orders me a vanilla and chocolate swirl and hands it to me. "Here you go, sweetheart."

"Yeah, right," I say, grabbing it and bringing it to my lips while I look over at Dylan who has his own vanilla cone.

"Do you want to sit over there?" Justin points at the picnic table beside the ice cream place. Dylan walks over, and Justin sits with his legs on each side of the bench. I sit beside him, but he scoots over, and it's almost as if I'm sitting between his legs. Dylan sits in front of us, and he tells me all about his day and how he scored on Justin when they played one-on-one.

"He did try to trip me," Justin mumbles, and I look over at him, laughing. He just leans forward and kisses me on the lips as if he's been doing it forever. I look over at Dylan to see if he saw, and he is just licking away at his ice cream.

"You're beautiful," he whispers, his face close to mine. All I can do is smile at him, and he kisses me again. "Everyday even more."

"I have sticky hands," Dylan says. We both look at him and see that the ice cream has leaked over the cone and onto his hands.

"We'll go wash them," Justin says, getting up and waiting for Dylan. "There is a bathroom over there." He points at a Starbucks. "You want something to drink?" he asks me, and I just shake my head. "Let's go, buddy." I watch them walk into the Starbucks for Dylan to wash his hands.

Sitting at that table, I can't recall a time Andrew ever did such a thing. Not even in the beginning. He would just look at me and expect me to know how to make him stop crying. As if I held a magical switch that would automatically get him to stop, and when the colic started, it was even worse. He would go away for days at a time, and I thought he was just staying with a friend so he could get the sleep he needed for school. What I didn't know was that he was off getting high.

I spot Justin walking out of Starbucks with Dylan by his side, and they are laughing at something when Justin holds up his hand, and Dylan jumps and gives him a high-five. Then he holds his hand and walks across the street, his eyes making sure that he's okay, but then looking at me.

"Ready?" he asks when he finally comes to me, and I

have to blink away some tears. He must see it because he comes over to me. "You okay?"

"Yeah," I say with a smile. He puts his arm around my shoulders, pulling me to him, and for the first time, I put my arm around his waist as he leads me to the SUV.

"We should have a movie night," Dylan says, getting into the back seat, and I look at him.

"You've never had a movie night," I say.

"I know, but Justin told me about it," he says, and I look over at Justin, who just stands there. "I thought it would be fun. We each get to choose a movie every week."

"Is that so?" I ask, and he nods his head.

"And we get to eat pizza and make popcorn and even sleep on the couch," he says, all amazed. "Sometimes all night." His eyes go bigger.

"We should do it tomorrow," Justin says. I don't say anything as I get into the passenger seat. He makes his way over to his house, and I'm suddenly nervous. He parks his vehicle in the same place he did yesterday, and this time, he presses the button for the top floor. I look down, not sure what I'm expecting.

My palms are sweaty, my knees are a bit weak, and when he puts his hand in mine, I don't look up. He walks to his door and slips the gold key into it to open it. "Welcome to my home," he says. When I look at him, he even looks nervous.

He opens the door, and the sunlight hits the hallway right away. "Wow," Dylan says as he walks in first, and then Justin waits for me to walk in. Looking down at the floor, I see it's a light beige marble. "It's huge."

193

"It's not that big," Justin tries to say, and I just look at him, and he shrugs.

"Let's start right here," he says, walking straight and coming to the open room. I look around in awe. The whole front and one wall on the side are completely windows. "This is what my mother calls the family room." I look around and see the huge table at the front of the room with eight chairs around it. When he steps farther into the room, I see the L-shaped kitchen behind the wall. The cupboards are a shiny beige that almost match the floor. The huge stainless-steel fridge fills almost a whole wall. Against the wall is the sink, and the stove is right next to it. My eyes fly to the island that sits in the middle with four white stools. A huge vase filled with flowers decorates the middle.

"Look at this TV," Dylan says, and I turn to look. I love how the kitchen opens to the dining room, and right after that is the living room. The TV hangs above the fireplace. Two massive beige couches are on either side with a square wooden table in the middle with more flowers on it. The fluffy throw pillows on the couches make you just want to curl up into a ball and take a nap. "Wow, look at this," Dylan says, running to the window.

"Don't touch anything," I say, and he stops in his tracks.

"What?" Justin says from beside me.

"I don't want him to get his fingerprints on the windows," I say. I don't want him to touch anything in this house with the fear he might get it dirty, and I can pretty much bet with everything I have, which isn't much, that I can't afford to replace anything.

"You can touch whatever you want," he tells Dylan. "Let's

go see outside."

He walks past me, grabbing my hand and pulling me to the door. We walk out on the terrace that wraps all the way around. "You can see so many boats," Dylan says, going to the railing and pointing. "Can we eat outside?"

"Sure. It's a little hot, but if it's okay with your mom, I'm good," Justin says, and I look at him and I shrug, not sure what the good answer is. Even his outdoor furniture looks like it's from a magazine.

"Can we see the rest of the house?" Dylan asks, and Justin smiles at him.

"You are going to flip out," he tells Dylan and walks back into the apartment. "I'll show you my room first," he says. I follow him out of the room and toward the door, but he walks straight to the end of the hall and opens his door. "This is my bedroom," he says, walking into the room. He flips a switch that I think is for the lights, but the curtains slowly open, and the far wall is also a wall of windows. I try to look at the view, but instead, I look at the unmade bed. The huge king-size bed is in the middle of the room with a wooden wall behind the beige and brown headboard. The side tables look like they are floating on both sides of the bed with lights hanging over them.

"Wow, your bed is huge. Who do you share your bed with?" Dylan asks, and I close my eyes.

"Just me," he says softly, and Dylan looks at him. I want to say so much, but I don't. "Now, let's go check out the best room in the house."

Dylan follows him out of the room with me right behind as he walks toward the other end of the apartment. "This is a spare bedroom," Justin says and opens the door to show me a king-size bed with a light gray headboard. Two light gray chairs and a round table are arranged at the side of the room with a long mirror dresser against the wall.

"This is a girl's room," Dylan says with disdain, and then Justin nods his head.

"It's where my mom and sisters stay when they visit," he says. "Now come and see the man room," he says, and Dylan's eyes light up.

We walk down a long hallway, and the walls are lined full of pictures. There are pictures of Justin on the ice celebrating and then another of him with what looks like his whole family around the Stanley Cup. Three huge sweaty guys in jerseys with Matthew standing in the back wearing a suit with a huge smile on his face. Then a couple of a huge family in front of a Christmas tree. One when he got drafted, and he looks like a little boy. "This is the man's room," he says. Opening the door, he turns on the light, and Dylan gasps.

The whole back wall is a television. A white chest sits under it with all the game consoles you can think of. Three bean bags are on the floor in front of it but then behind the bean bags is the most massive U-shaped couch I have ever seen in my life. With over twenty throw cushions, I was wrong before. This is where you want to sit and take a nap. "Does this TV play movies?" Dylan asks, and Justin nods. "I want to do movie night in here."

"Sounds like a plan," Justin says, and I'm at a loss for words.

"What do you want to watch?" Justin asks Dylan.

"I don't know," Dylan says, and Justin hands him the remote.

"Here, find something while your mom and I go talk about dinner," he says, and Dylan grabs the remote and goes to sit on one of the bean bags.

"Don't touch anything," I whisper, and he ignores me while he watches the huge television. I follow Justin out to the family room.

"It's time to have a talk," he says. Looking at me, he takes his baseball hat off and tosses it onto the big wooden table. "Are you going to sit?" he asks, and I just shake my head. Right before he starts to talk, the doorbell rings.

TWENTY ONE

JUSTIN

$\mathcal{S}$HE STANDS IN the middle of the room not moving. Ever since we walked into the room, she hasn't touched anything, and when Dylan was going to touch the window, I thought she was going to throw up. I toss my hat on the middle of the table, hoping for her to see I don't care about all this stuff.

"Don't move," I say to her when the doorbell rings.

"I'm not going to move," she mumbles under her breath. I go to the door and open it to find Raul, one of the security guys.

"Hey," he says, handing me a brown box. "This just came for you."

"Thank you," I say, closing the door and walking back into the living room. So help me God, I don't even think she was breathing while I was gone. Putting the box on the island, I walk over to her and grab her hand, bringing her to the couch with me.

I sit down, and she lightly sits down next to me, her ass almost off the edge of the couch. "You know I live here, right?"

"I know," she says, looking down at her fingers and then up again. "It's beautiful."

"Yeah, it is. Except I make a mess, too, and the cleaning lady comes in and makes it clean," I say, taking her hands in mine. "You have to also know that my nieces and nephews sometime come and visit." She just looks at me. "They are kids, and they touch things. Sometimes, more than once, they have broken little knickknacks here and there." I take a deep breath. "I also didn't care as long as they weren't hurt. I live here, but it's not a museum. I don't want you to walk on eggshells when you're here." I smile at her. "Hopefully, you'll want to be here a lot."

"It's just that …" she starts, and I hold up my hand.

"They're just things," I say. "Things that are pretty but can be replaced. But you here, sitting on that couch eating chips …" I smile, pushing her hair behind her ear. "I would buy ten couches just to see that."

"Is the food almost done?" Dylan asks, coming into the room. "I'm starving."

I laugh when Caroline smiles. "Take off your shoes, curl up on the couch, and turn on the TV." I kiss her lips. "I'm going to cook."

"I want to help you," she says to me. "We can do it together."

"That sounds even better than just me cooking," I say, taking her hand in mine and going to the kitchen.

Dylan climbs on a stool. "Is this a present?" he asks, picking it up and shaking the box.

"Yeah," I say. "It's your mom's."

His eyes open wide as Caroline stops walking and looks at him. "Mom, you have a present. Can I open it?"

"It's not mine," she says, but Dylan is already ripping the tape open and reaching in and pulling out the small white box.

"It's a phone," he says, handing it to Caroline who stares at the box.

"You bought me a phone?" She looks at me. "I have a phone."

"Yeah, but yours is always not working," Dylan says, and she just turns to him.

"That's enough," she says, and he just shrugs.

"I'm not taking this phone," she says, handing it back to me.

"Fine," I say, putting it down. "I'll give it to Dylan then."

"You will not," she huffs out. "I don't want the phone."

"Okay," I say, making her think she's winning this, but if I have to plant it on her without her knowing every single day, then that is what I'm going to do. "I was thinking steak and some salad."

"Oh, yeah, steak," Dylan says, throwing his hands in the air.

"You've never had steak," Caroline tells him. "Go watch television so I can talk to Justin for a minute."

He gets off the stool and looks at me as if I'm in trouble. She waits for him to walk out of the room before turning to me.

"I don't need you buying me stuff," she says. "I can take care of myself."

"I'm sorry," I say, leaning against the counter. "When did I ever say you can't take care of yourself?"

"This," she says, picking up the phone. "This isn't the first time my phone service has been cut off."

"Well, it's going to be the last because it's not safe for you and Dylan to be without a phone."

"And that …" she says, pointing at me. "You can't keep doing that either. I'm a good mom." She points at herself.

"No," I say, and her hand falls as tears well in her eyes, "you aren't a good mom."

"What?" she whispers.

"You're a great mom," I say. "The best mom." I walk to her. "But you're also my woman, and I'm going to take care of you."

"Your woman?" she asks.

"Yeah, I know." I smile. "I admit that Matthew used to walk around all the time claiming Karrie as his woman, and I never understood it. I mean, my father loves my mother with everything he has. He literally won't eat if she's not at the table beside him." She looks at me. "Let me help you. You have all these balls in the air, and it's okay if you let me catch them."

"I've been doing this all by myself for the past eight years," she says. "I just …" She looks down, and I put my hand under her chin and lift her face so I can see her eyes. "I just don't know how to let anyone in."

"How about we start with baby steps?" I suggest. "Take the phone, and when the other one gets turned back on, you can give it back to me."

"That won't be for another two weeks," she says, and I suddenly fill with rage. She was planning to go two weeks without a phone. There could be so many situations that come up, and she wouldn't have any lifeline.

"Then it's two weeks," I say. "It doesn't make you a weaker person if you accept help. You know that."

"I do," she says, letting out a deep sigh. "It's just that I don't want to depend on anyone. I want to do this on my own."

"And you have been, but if there is a helping hand"—I lean in and kiss her lips—"accept it. I won't bite." I smirk now. "I mean, unless you want me to."

Her cheeks turn a bright pink, and her eyes turn just a touch darker. "Are you guys done now?" Dylan asks, and we both laugh quietly. "I'm starving. Can I have a snack?"

"No," Caroline says. "No snack."

"Fine, but how long until dinner?" he asks as if he didn't just have ice cream thirty minutes ago.

"About thirty minutes," I say, walking to the fridge and taking out the steak that my cleaning lady bought.

"If you cook, I have to clean," Caroline says, finally taking off her purse and placing it gently on one of the stools. "Those are the rules. It's universal."

"How about we both cook, and then we both clean up?" I ask, and she just looks at me. "It gives me more time to spend with you, and if your hands are in the water, I can kiss you, and you can't push me away."

"I've been letting you kiss me," she says, laughing. "What do you want to make with the steak?"

"Normally, I would make baked potatoes," I say, and her eyes light up. "We can pop them in the microwave for ten minutes," I say, and she nods. "Is this you saying you want baked potatoes?"

"This is me saying that I don't mind, and it's totally up to you." She smirks at me. "I'm a guest."

I roll my eyes. "Touché," I say. Grabbing the steaks, I open the butcher paper, then walk to the stove and open a drawer where I keep the spices.

"What can I do to help?" she asks, coming into the kitchen.

"I'm marinating the steak, and then I was going to do the potatoes," I say. "Do you want to start the salad?"

"Yes," she says. "Can I go in the fridge?" She looks at me.

"From this moment on, you can go in the fridge, the pantry, or the bathroom. You can go take a nap in my bedroom. Please do whatever you want to do. I want you to feel at home." I want to shake her, but more than anything, I want her to smile more. I want her to laugh more. I want her to do all these things, and I want to be the reason she does.

"I mean, I don't think I'm going to nap in your bedroom, but that couch in the man cave has potential," she jokes, walking to the fridge and then opening it. She opens the drawers and takes out what she wants for the salad. "I'd ask you where the bowls are, but I'm going to guess, and you can say hot or cold." I laugh at her and shrug, watching her open the cupboards and talking to herself. "If I was a salad bowl, where would I be?" She opens four before she finds it. "Found it."

She walks beside me and looks at me. "What?"

"I need a knife and a cutting board," she says, and I point at the drawer and then move my hand to under the stove. "Thank you," she says.

"Let's get to know each other," I suggest, and she looks at me. "Favorite food?"

"I like mostly everything," she says, and I just look at her.

"If there was one food you had to eat for the rest of your life, what would it be?"

"I don't know," she says. "I guess Italian, you?"

"That's not a food; it's a food group." I laugh at her, and she rolls her eyes. "Toss up between burgers and steak," I say. "I mean, more toward steak but …" She smiles at me. "What?"

"If there was one food …" She starts to mimic me, and I shake my head.

"That mouth is going to get you in trouble," I say, and her eyes fly to mine. "Favorite drink."

"Coffee," she answers without hesitation. "Actually, before I had Dylan, I hated the taste, then when he went through his eight months of crying for twenty-three hours a day, coffee was my lifeline."

"Just regular?" I ask.

"If there is milk, that is even better, but I can drink it black," she says. "Sometimes, I used to splurge and buy the flavored creamer." She cuts up the salad. "You?"

"Water," I say, and she looks up. "What? I like water." She shakes her head. "Favorite holiday."

"Usually, I would pick Christmas," she says, "but as he gets older, and the gifts get harder and harder to buy, I'm going to go with Halloween." My heart sinks, but I don't show her nor do I make eye contact with her. "You?"

"Christmas," I answer. "Hands down for me, it's Christmas and not for the gifts. My family couldn't care less what was under the tree. The thing that I love is being with my family. I don't even know how many there are of us anymore, but just hanging out with them and being with them for four days." I look at her, and she just looks at me. "It's just everything."

"What do you guys usually do?" she asks.

"We usually have it at my parents' house since it's a touch bigger than everyone else's," I say. "My mother usually does the cooking, or they cater, but more often than not, it's my mom who cooks. On Christmas Eve, we just get together. Everyone comes over, and we watch movies, or the kids play games, but it's just us. We usually all stay at my parents'. Well, we did before. Now with so many kids and since they all live a block away, they usually just go home and come back at the ass crack of dawn." I laugh. "We open the gifts in our pjs, and then we make a huge breakfast."

"That sounds like exactly what Christmas should be about," she says. I don't add in that she is going to experience it for herself this year because I'm afraid she'll close up again.

"Favorite color?" I ask, and this time, she answers without thinking twice.

"Pink or purple. What about you?"

"I would say blue." I don't add that guys don't usually have a favorite color. "Favorite movie."

"Gosh," she says, cutting and adding to the bowl of salad. "The last movie I saw was *Beauty and the Beast*." She laughs.

"I mean, we watched it on my phone, so you can imagine the size of it." She looks at me. "You?"

"Anything but *Frozen*," I say. "Like literally anything but that movie."

"Should I ask why?" She laughs.

"My niece went through a phase. And by phase, I mean every single time it finished, she watched it again. At first, it was okay, but by day two, I wanted to snap the Wi-Fi wire."

"So no *Frozen* for movie night?" She smiles at me, and I walk over to her, leaning down and kissing her, and she kisses me back this time.

"I'm going to start the grill, and then I'm going to make the potatoes," I say, and she nods. This time, she leans up and kisses me first. I want to run around with my hands over my head and cheer out victory, but I don't. After I walk outside to start the grill, the door opens, and Dylan comes out.

"Is it almost ready?" he asks, and I have to laugh at him.

"In about fifteen minutes," I say and go inside. The salad is now done, and she's waiting for me. "What's up?"

"I wanted to start the potatoes," she says, "but I don't know how to work your microwave." She points at my microwave. "That has way too many options. Mine has a dial that you turn to the amount of time you want." I walk over and show her how it works.

"Do you want to eat inside or outside?" I ask, and she shrugs. "Sweetheart, just pick."

"It doesn't matter to me," she says, looking at me. "Either one is fine."

"Dylan." I call his name, and he comes running in. "Inside or outside?" I ask, and he chooses outside.

"What do we need to set the table outside?" she asks, and now it's my turn to shrug. "Do you have place mats? A pitcher so I can bring some water out?"

I show her where everything is, and she sets the table while I check the steaks. When I walk out with a plate, I look over at the table and stop. She has set it with place mats and napkins. She has brought out the glasses and a pitcher of ice water that will slowly melt before we sit at the table. "It's ready," I say, bringing the steaks to the table, and Dylan comes out, sitting on one of the chairs. "Sit. I'll go get the rest," I say, and she, of course, doesn't listen to me. She follows me inside, and when we get into the kitchen, I turn around and grab her face in my hands. "Thank you," I say right before I lean in for a kiss. "For having dinner with me."

TWENTY TWO

CAROLINE

*H*IS VOICE IS so soft that if he wasn't so close, I wouldn't have heard it. "Thank you for having dinner with me," he whispers right before his lips crash down on mine, and I open my mouth for him. I wrap my arms around his neck, for the first time admitting that I want this kiss more than anything. I also admit I really like this guy. I also push away the thoughts of what is going to be left of me when he moves on.

His hands move from my face to my neck and then to my waist, pulling me to him. His tongue dances with mine softly at first, and then the kiss deepens, and I feel him against my stomach. I moan, and it's swallowed by his kiss, making his hands slip down to my hips, and he pushes me into the wall. My hands move up into his hair, the hair I itch to touch all the time. "Fuck," he hisses, moving from my lips to my neck, and I move my head to the side to give him better access.

"When you two are done kissing, can I eat?" When I hear Dylan, my hands drop so fast, but Justin just keeps his hands on my hips, and he laughs in my neck.

"Yeah, buddy," Justin says, turning to look at him. "We're coming right out."

Dylan nods and skips away to the door going outside. "Oh my God," I say, and Justin looks at me. "I can't believe he caught us making out."

"I'm planning on making out with you a lot, so the chances of him catching us again are very high," he says and kisses my neck, but his hands fall. "Assuming you are okay with making out with me?"

"I mean …" I start to say, and he looks at me. "I like kissing you, but I also don't want him to think that …" I try to find the words. "That I'm, you know."

"I don't know." He looks at me and then puts his hands on his hips. "I think that he will see us kissing and know that when you like someone a lot, it's okay to show them you like them."

"He's never seen me kiss anyone," I say. "And I mean anyone. Not even his father."

"There is so much that needs to be said right now, but I don't think Dylan is going to give us another minute before he just says fuck it and eats the steaks. So for now, I'm tabling this, but I'm not going to shy away from kissing you nor will I sugarcoat it."

"I don't even know what that means," I mumble under my breath and go to grab the bowl of salad that I made and seasoned with the olive oil and balsamic I found in his pantry. A pantry that was overflowing with food.

"Give me enough time, and you are going to know what that means," he says, and I have to wonder if he's telling me or asking me. Either way, I walk outside and sit at the table. After placing salad on Dylan's plate, he also opts to have a loaded baked potato.

"Now you dig in," Justin tells him, cutting his steak for him. "But be careful because it's hot." I don't want to think about how Andrew has never once fed our child, not even a bottle when he was younger. He used to use the excuse that Dylan wanted me instead. He never cut his food or even cooked for him.

"Mom, can we have baked potatoes tomorrow?" he asks, and I have to laugh.

"I have no idea," I say, cutting a piece of steak and eating it. It melts in my mouth. "I have to work tomorrow, so we will see when we get home."

He groans and takes another bite. "Do I have to come?"

I look at him. "Yes," I say. "We go over this every single time."

"But it's so boring." He groans between bites, his eyes never leaving the plate as he does it.

"Why doesn't he stay with me?" Justin says, and I look over at him. I fixed the table with most of the stuff he showed me, and although I didn't want to touch the glass pitcher, I did anyway because it looked beautiful and I've never had one. "I'm home all day tomorrow, and I kind of have an assignment I need to do, and he can help me with it."

"An assignment?" I ask, taking another piece of steak.

"Well, I'm going to be on the cover of the next NHL video

game," he says, chewing his own piece of steak.

"WHAT?" Dylan shrieks, throwing his fork down. "On the cover?" The look of pure joy covers his face.

Justin just nods. "And they just sent me over the game, and I have to check it out and play it."

"So your assignment is to play a video game?" I ask, my foot moving back and forth as he glares at me.

"There is a lot more than just playing a video game, sweetheart," he says, and I shake my head and take a piece of salad, hoping the conversation ends.

"Mom, there is so much more to playing the game." Dylan copies Justin's words. "That is so cool."

"This steak is so tender," I say, changing the subject and hoping that Dylan forgets.

"It's the best," he says, chewing on his last piece. "So can I stay with Justin?"

"Dylan, I don't think …" I start to say and look for Justin to help me out, but he just leans back in his chair and puts his hands on the arms of the chair, making his shirt go tight across his chest.

"Why?" he asks, and I sit in the chair and look at him. "Why don't you guys sleep here?"

"Um, no," I say the same time that Dylan says, "Yes!"

"Hear me out," he says, and I want to hurt him, but then I want to kiss him again.

"You guys sleep here tonight," he says, and I shake my head. "Then tomorrow, I can stay with Dylan, and you can go to work, and then we can have movie night."

"That," Dylan says. "Let's do that, Mom. Please," he begs, then he turns to Justin. "Can I have more steak?"

"Sure, buddy," he says, taking a steak and cutting it on his plate.

"We can't just stay here," I tell them.

"Why not?" Dylan asks, eating a piece of steak.

"Yeah, why not?" I glare at Justin's question.

"Well, for one, we don't have any clothes." I start with the obvious.

"I can lend you something to sleep in," Justin says.

"Well, I need clothes for work tomorrow," I say.

"I can lend you something, and you can swing by your place before work," Justin says, and I want to tell him no.

"The bus ride alone is going to be …" I start saying, and he shuts it down.

"You aren't taking the bus. You can take the SUV," he says, and I want to hit the table and tell him to stop it.

"I don't think it's a good idea," I say softly.

"Why?" he asks. "I have two extra bedrooms. You can each take a room."

"Justin," I say, and he looks at me, trying not to smile.

"Besides, I want Dylan to help me with my game," he says softly, and I look at the man who has taken my son under his wing and has included him in every single direction we are going. It's overwhelming, and I put my napkin down and get up.

"Excuse me," I say, trying to walk away so he doesn't see the tears in my eyes. I walk inside, and I'm looking for the bathroom when I accidentally walk into his room. I turn to walk back out and face-plant in his chest.

"Are you okay?" he asks, his hands holding my arms. I look up, and it's the wrong thing to do because he makes me want to take all the leaps. He makes me want to do all these things I said I would never do. He makes me want all the tomorrows. He makes me want it all, and I know that even if I guard myself, I'll fall for him, and I'm not sure I can survive him leaving.

"No," I say, moving out of his touch. "I'm not okay."

"Why?" he asks, and I lift my arms up as if he should know.

"Us staying here," I say. "Dylan falling in love with you."

He waits for me to finish. "It's just … it's not just me I have to worry about."

"I will never ever hurt him," he says softly. "Never. You never have to worry about that." And I know by his tone that he would never hurt him.

"Let me in."

"Letting you in isn't what I'm worried about anymore," I say, and it's the truth. "It's about surviving after."

"You'll never know unless you take that chance," he says, and I have to avert my eyes. "I've never had anyone in my house before." I look at him with shock all over my face. "I mean, don't get me wrong, I've dated. But here"—he points at the floor—"this is mine, and I wasn't about to bring any-one in here that I didn't think deserved to be here."

"You've known me a week," I say.

"And I would have brought you here the day I met you," he says and then comes to me. "I want to date you, and that means you coming over."

"What else does dating entail?" I place my hands on his chest, the feel of his heart beating under my palms.

"It entails doing stuff for each other," he says.

"You don't need me for anything," I say.

"That's not true," he says. "If I asked you to do something for me, would you say no?" I roll my eyes, and he laughs. Arm around me, he pulls me in for a hug, and my hands go around his waist. "How about you stay here tonight? Tomorrow, you can get up, go to your place to change, and then pack a bag."

"Pack a bag?" I repeat.

"Well, we are going to have movie night. You can't just leave during movie night."

"Oh my God," I say, and he leans down.

"Nope, not God, just me, Justin," he says and kisses me softly. "Now if we don't get back out there, Dylan is going to eat my food."

He lets me go and grabs my hand. "We haven't even talked about things."

"Later," he says, and for the first time, I live in the moment and go with it.

TWENTY THREE

JUSTIN

"*H*ERE," I SAY, walking back into the kitchen and seeing her wiping her hands. After she agreed to stay, we ate what Dylan left us, which was not that much, and when we cleared the table, he helped, but then he went to watch television.

"What is that?" she asks, looking at the clothes in my hand as she takes them.

"It's stuff to sleep in," I say. "I mean, unless you want to sleep in your dress," I point out.

"Oh, I was just going to sleep naked," she says. My cock springs to action, and then she throws her head back and laughs. "I'm kidding."

"I would not say no," I say, "but Dylan is here, and if you're going to be naked, I can't be trusted."

She pushes my shoulder, thinking I'm joking. "You would never," she says, and I look at her.

"I would never what?" I lean my hip on the counter. "Climb into your bed while you're naked and kiss you until you beg me for more?" She crosses her arms over her chest. "Maybe."

"I need to take a shower," she says, "and so does Dylan."

"He can take one in the game room," I say. "You take one in either my bathroom or the bathroom in the spare room."

"I'm going to use the one in the spare room," she says and then looks down at the clothes. "Thank you," she says and leans up to kiss my chin. I turn my face, and she kisses my lips.

"We are so going to make out tonight," I say, and she laughs. "Me, you, and the couch, it's on."

"Wow, I was thinking maybe a bed, but if you want to do the making out on the couch …" She shrugs and walks off. The door to the guest room closes softly, and I try not to think of her in the bathroom naked.

It doesn't work, so I walk down the hall to the game room and poke my head in to see that Dylan is on one of the bean bags. "Buddy, shower," I say to him, and he gets up and yawns.

"I'm hungry." I swear this kid is never not hungry. "Can I have a snack?"

"Yup," I say, "after you shower." I walk over to the closet in the room and take out some of mini Cooper's clothes that he left here last time. "You can wear these."

He grabs them and goes to the shower, and I walk back out, heading to my own shower. I close the door behind me and start the water, but my cock has other ideas. I palm my cock in my hand and close my eyes, and her face is all I can think about. Her calling my name, her moaning out my name, and in record time, I'm whispering her name while I come all over myself.

After I get out and towel off, I slip on my boxers and then shorts and walk out to the kitchen and see that they are both there. "You don't go in the pantry unless you ask." I hear her hiss at Dylan.

"But," he says as I walk in, "Justin said I could have a snack."

"Everything okay?" I ask. She turns around, and I have to take a second to take her in. Her wet hair is piled on her head, she is wearing my shirt which fits her like a dress, and the shorts that I gave her go way past her knees. It's swallowing her up, yet it's the sexiest thing I've ever seen her wear.

"It's fine," she says. "Go sit and have your snack." She points at the box of cookies he took out of the pantry. "Um …" she says softly. "Are you going to get dressed?" she asks, and then her eyes fly to Dylan to see if he's listening or looking, and the kid couldn't care less.

I look down. "I'm wearing shorts," I say, and she looks again down and then up, and she avoids looking at me.

"But a shirt?" she says, and I have to say knowing that she's a bit turned on by this makes me want to puff my chest out even more.

"Nah, I'm good like this," I say, and she just nods. Dylan eats his snack and then drinks a glass of milk.

"I'm going to bed," he says, and I walk with him to the back room and set him up with covers and pillow. I pull off the big pillows on the back, and it's now the size of a queen-size bed. I hand him a huge king-size white duvet blanket and three pillows. "Thanks, Justin," he says and turns around.

"If you need anything, call my name," I say and walk out of the room. I find her in the kitchen putting the dishes away.

"He's out," I say, and she looks over at me.

"What do you mean he's out?" she asks.

"He's gone to bed," I say. "I set up the bed for him, and he climbed under the covers and said good night."

"But he didn't even say good night to me," she says. She walks into the back room and sticks her head in, and the sound of him softly snoring fills the room.

"He works hard during camp," I say from behind her. "Harder than any other kid on the ice and it shows."

She walks to him and kisses his cheek and then comes back out of the room. "He's out." She smiles. "Not even pizza would wake him."

"I don't know about that. He's probably getting energy to eat again," I say, and then I turn to walk back to the kitchen, and she stands there. "What do you want to do, Caroline?"

"Um …" she says. I see her playing with her fingers, and I know that she does that when she's nervous.

"Would you be mad if I said I wanted to go lie in bed?" she asks softly, and I just shake my head.

"Not at all," I say and then walk to her, and I kiss her lips. "Good night, sweetheart."

"Good night, Justin," she says, and she walks away, going to her bedroom, but this time, I don't hear the soft close of the door because she leaves it open.

I grab my phone and walk to my own room. Slipping

under the sheets, I turn on the television and put it on *SportsCenter*. I listen for any noises, and when it finally hits eleven, I turn off my light and fall asleep in record time.

I don't know how long I sleep, but when I finally open my eyes, I see that my door is closed, and I hear voices coming from the kitchen.

I get up and go to the bathroom and brush my teeth, giving my cock enough time to get presentable. "Morning," I mumble and look at them. She's in the kitchen cooking while Dylan sits at the island eating.

"Did we wake you?" she asks, worried. I just shake my head and go over to her and bend to kiss her. "I made coffee," she says, and I look around.

"What time did you wake up?" I ask, spotting all the food. There are pancakes and scrambled eggs, bacon and sausage, and some toast.

"I woke up at around six, and after lying in bed for about twenty minutes, I got up and decided I was going to cook breakfast before I left."

"How did you sleep?" I ask, and she grabs her cup of coffee and tries to hide her smile with it.

"Like I was floating on a cloud," she says. "It was awful."

"I slept like a king," Dylan says. "There are no lumps in his couch."

I try not to laugh and grab the coffee. "With that said, I have to leave or I'm going to be late," she says. "Do you mind if I take these clothes home and then bring them back tonight?"

"Nope," I say, and she smiles, grabbing her purse and going over to Dylan.

"Be good." She kisses his cheek, and I grab the keys.

"Buddy, I'm going to go walk your mom to the car," I say. "Don't touch anything unless it's food."

He just nods, and I walk out, following Caroline, who's waiting for me. "You aren't going out like that," she says. "Go put a shirt on." She points at my door. "I'll wait here while you go get dressed."

I look down. "I am dressed."

"No, you're half-dressed," she points out. "Now go put the rest of your clothes on, and I'll wait here."

"But …" I start to say, and she hands me her purse.

"Here, hold this," she says, and I look at her. "I'll just give you back this shirt that I'm wearing, and then we can go." She now leans down and tries to pull up her shirt.

"I'm going," I say, handing her back her purse and walking back into the house.

"Did you go out naked?" Dylan asks me while he chews and pours more syrup on his pancake.

"Apparently," I say, jogging back to my room and grabbing the first shirt I see. I pull it over my head, then stop in the kitchen. Picking up the syrup, I look at him. "You need some more pancakes for all that syrup."

He just shrugs, and I grab the box and go into the hallway. "There you are," she says, smiling, and I hand her the box with the phone.

"You forgot something," I say and then walk to the elevator.

"I don't need it. I'm going to be in the car," she says.

"What happens if you have a flat tire or get into an accident?" I ask, pressing the button, and she just sighs. "That is what I thought."

"Annoying," she says, walking into the elevator when it opens. I follow her, but instead of going over, I pull my arms around her shoulder and pull her to me in a hug. I lean down to kiss her, and I smell myself on her.

"You smell like me." I smile and smell her cheek and then her neck, rubbing my nose on her the whole time. "I like it."

She moves her neck to the side, giving me access to the other side. "It was the only soap in the shower," she whispers, and I kiss her. My tongue slides into her mouth, and the sweetness of the syrup hits my tongue right away, and my cock springs into action. I push her against the wall, and her hands roam all over the front of my shirt. When the ding of the elevator fills the small space, I almost curse.

"Call me when you get there to let me know you got there okay," I say when we get to the vehicle. "Then you call me when you are coming home."

"I'm going to be fine," she says and takes the key from me. "You call me if you have any questions with Dylan."

"I got him covered," I say. She leans up, and I lean down, and we kiss goodbye.

"Maybe tonight we can work on that making out on the couch," she says, climbing into the driver's seat and smiling at me as she starts the SUV. I watch her back out and make her way out of the garage before I make my way back upstairs.

I slam the door and go to the kitchen first. "I'm back," I say, grabbing an empty plate and filling it with food.

"Why did you walk Mom out?" Dylan asks, getting up and rinsing off his plate.

225

"When it's a girl, you always walk her to the car and make sure she leaves safely," I say. "And you always open the door for her."

"Do girls walk you to your car?" he asks, and I shake my head.

"It's a guy thing," I point out to him. "It makes them know you like them."

"But what if I don't like the girl?" he says and then leaves the plate in the sink.

"You still walk her to her car and make sure she leaves," I say.

"You always, always take care of the girls."

He shrugs at me. "Can I go play?"

"Wash your hands with soap and then fold the covers," I say. He walks back to the sink and washes his hands with more soap.

"We can't leave the food out," he says. "Or else the bugs come, and once they come, they never leave."

"What?" I ask him.

"Once, I left a plate in the sink, and I didn't rinse it off. The cockroaches came, and it took forever for them to leave. They were everywhere." I look at him. "She said it wasn't my fault, but I knew it was," he says quietly. "She used to be up all night sometimes cleaning and doing these homemade tricks."

"Your mom is great at taking care of stuff," I say, trying not to think about her running herself at both ends. "How about you go fold the covers, and then we can hit the gym a bit before we work on the video game?"

He skips to the back room, and I finish eating, and then

I put the leftover food on the stove with plastic wrap over it. "I'm done!" Dylan yells and comes back into the kitchen. "Can I have a snack?"

"You can have a banana or some peanut butter," I say, going to the bedroom and grabbing my sneakers. "Ready?" I ask him when I come back and see him finishing off a banana. He nods and follows me out to the next apartment that I have. An apartment I didn't tell Caroline about. It holds my home gym, and it also has extra bedrooms for when my family visits. I run on the treadmill while I set Dylan up with two-pound weights, and for the next hour, we work out side by side. "You did good, buddy," I say while he drinks water. I look at my phone and see that she hasn't called yet.

"Let's go back and take a shower, and then we can get started on the game," I say. When he gets into his shower, I call the number, but she doesn't answer. I don't want to worry, but I do anyway, and when I'm about to dial her again, I get a text.

Caroline: I'm fine. I got to work five minutes ago, and I'm late. I'll explain later. Is everything okay?

Me: Everything is fine. Just worried.

She doesn't answer me, and when I finally shower and get out, Dylan is waiting for me in the kitchen. "I had a snack," he says. I laugh and make a protein shake, then I make him a fruit smoothie.

We spend the afternoon playing the game, and at the end of three hours, he has schooled me in seven games. "Okay, buddy," I say, turning it off. "Let's go."

"Where are we going?" he asks, getting up and placing the remote next to mine.

227

"We are going to go pick up things for dinner and then get your mom some flowers," I say. He holds my hand as we go downstairs, and I take out the BMW.

"What are we going to eat?" he asks, and I look at him in the back seat.

"Your mom said she likes Italian, so let's get stuff to make spaghetti," I say, and he nods eagerly.

We make it to the grocery store, and I've already googled a recipe, so we walk in and grab a cart. He walks next to me as I tell him what we need, and he picks up the items and puts them in the basket. He holds back at first, and when I tell him to go pick out dessert, I see him looking at the prices. "Whatcha doing?" I ask, standing next to him.

"That's ten dollars," he says, pointing at the fruit pie. "That's a lot of money for a pie."

I try not to grab all the pies and show him that he doesn't have to worry about it. "It is," I tell him, "but I'm lucky I have a really good job, and it's not that much money for me."

"Really?" he asks, almost shocked. "I want to do that job then." He picks up the pie and puts it in the basket. By the time we leave, we have enough food for three weeks. I get him in the car and then look over at him. "Where are we going now?"

"To get flowers," I say.

"For Mom?" he asks. "Because you like her?" I nod. "But it's not her birthday."

"That makes it even more special," I say. "You always give them flowers just because."

"But why?" he asks.

"So they know you are thinking about them," I say. "So

they know how special they are to you."

"I want to buy Mom flowers," he says. "Will you lend me the money?"

I want to laugh out loud. "You got it," I say. When we enter the flower shop twenty minutes later, he walks straight to the woman. "I want some flowers for my mom," he tells the lady, who smiles at him and looks at me. "Her favorite color is purple."

"Is this for a special occasion?" the lady asks.

"No, it's just to tell her that I love her," he says, and I could swear I hear her swoon.

"Why, aren't you the cutest?" she says and then looks at me. "You got yourself a special little boy there," she says, and I suddenly beam with pride.

"He's one of a kind," I say, putting my hands on his shoulders and squeezing them.

TWENTYFOUR

CAROLINE

"*I*'M SO SORRY I'm late," I puff out, almost running into the reception area, my hands still shaking from when I walked into my apartment.

"It's fine," Tamara, the daytime receptionist, says. "You have ten rooms to get done by three," she says, handing me a clipboard with the room numbers. "I marked off the rooms that have already checked out."

"Thank you," I say, trying to get my heart to settle, but it's not going to happen anytime soon.

"I'll keep you informed on the rooms as they check out," she says, handing me the walkie-talkie. I take it and walk out of the reception area, and the phone rings in my purse. I pick it up and see that it's Justin, and I know that if I hear his voice right now, I'm going to start crying, and there is no time for that. When I don't answer, he calls again, and this time, I just send him a text.

Me: I'm fine. I got to work five minutes ago, and I'm late. I'll explain later. Is everything okay?

I walk into the employee room and store my purse in my locker and change into the uniform. I slip on my running shoes when the phone beeps, and I look down.

Justin: Everything is fine. Just worried.

I tuck the phone into my pocket and walk up the outside stairs to the third floor. I walk down the pathway while the hot air sticks to me. A man opening one of the doors and pushing his luggage out smiles at me and then walks toward the stairs. I grab the cart and make my way to the closest room. After parking it right in front of the room, I look over the railing and take in the parking lot when a car backfires. I open the first room, and the cool air hits me right away. I put the wooden stopper under the door and go to turn off the A/C. I walk back to the cart and put on the rubber gloves and then go into the room and start stripping the bed.

Closing off my mind for the next six hours, I finish the last room five minutes after three. I park my cart back in the supply room and load it for the person tomorrow. I walk back into the employee room, and my mind starts to wander even more now.

"Here you are," I say, handing Tamara the clipboard with all the rooms checked off. "All of them are done."

"Thank you," she says. "I'll let you know about next week." I nod at her and turn to walk to the SUV, getting in and starting it. I make my way back to Justin's apartment with a heavy lump in my stomach like a pound of coal.

I call him right before I get there. "Hello." He answers

right away, and he sounds like he's doing something.

"Hey, it's me," I say. "I'm going to be at your place in five minutes. I just don't know how to open the garage door."

"The code to get in is 7-4-2-3," he says. "See you soon." He hangs up, and I just look down at the phone that is now on the locked screen. When I get there, I put in the code. It opens right away, and I make my way to the parking spot.

Grabbing my purse and the little plastic bag that holds our clothes for tomorrow, I walk to the elevator. When I enter it, another man also steps into it, and he presses his own number. He just looks over at me and nods. I look down at the floor the whole time, waiting for him to ask me what I'm doing here.

When he gets out, all he says is, "Have a great night." I look up and smile as the doors close and take me up to Justin's floor. When I get to his floor, I'm expecting to see the door closed, but instead, they are both standing there waiting for me.

I try not to let the tears come, but they come anyway, and the look on Justin's face goes from a smile to a worried look. He looks at me, his eyes never leaving mine.

"Mom, we got you something!" Dylan says, and I wipe the tears away and pretend to smile. He's so excited about this surprise that he has for me that he doesn't realize I was crying. He takes my hand in his and pulls me to the kitchen where two huge bouquets sit.

"This one is from me," he says, pointing at the massive bouquet of purple flowers. "It's just to tell you that I love you," he says. I look at the flowers and realize it's more flowers than I've ever seen in my whole life.

"Oh my God," I whisper. The tear escapes, and I wipe it away. "This is the most beautiful," I say to him, hugging him and trying not to sob.

"Mine is bigger than Justin's," he says with happiness in his voice.

"I'm trying to explain to him that size doesn't matter," Justin says, and I close my eyes. "It's not working." I let go of Dylan and see the bouquet next to his filled with colorful flowers in a glass vase with a lilac bow.

"Dylan, you can go play the game now while I talk to your mom."

"Okay," he says and is about to run out of the room. "Can I have a snack?"

"Yeah, there's fruit on the table." He points at the fruit bowl, and Dylan just hops and skips over, taking a green apple and then going away.

I avoid Justin's eyes, knowing that I'm on the edge of a cliff and about to jump off. "Mind telling me why you are crying?"

I look down at my finger, and I feel him coming close to me. His hand covers mine, and with just his touch, I break down and put my other hand in front of my mouth and sob. He turns me around and takes me in his arms, and I swear he smells like home. "Sweetheart," he says softly, and I start to shake. "I'm trying really hard right now not to freak out."

He rubs my back and kisses the top of my head. "But I've been a nervous wreck all day, and I've wanted to call you, no lie, maybe a million times to find out if you were okay."

Listening to his heartbeat, I avoid looking at him when I say the next words. "My apartment was vandalized." I close my eyes when his body goes rock solid.

"Let me check on Dylan real quick," he says, walking out and leaving me here. I just stand here in this room that smells like a flower shop. I turn my head when I see him in the entryway of the room. "He's fine. I gave him another snack." I look at him. "I need you to tell me what happened," he says.

I take a deep breath and relive the morning that is now burned in my memory. "I went home, and the minute I put the key in the lock, I knew something was off," I say, and he puts up his hand.

"And you went in anyway?" he asks, his voice tight. I nod at him, and he puts his head back and looks at the ceiling.

"Well, when the door opened, I saw it right away," I say, his hands going into fists. "The food was all over the floor. The drawers were pulled out and dumped on the floor. The plates smashed all around the room as if someone just tossed them like Frisbees." I try to get it all out once and for all. "The bedroom was the worst." I take a deep breath. "They tossed everything on the floor and cut through the mattress."

"Motherfucker," he hisses out and charges to me, grabbing me by my hand and pulling me to his bedroom, then closing the door behind us. He walks to the bed and sits down and pulls me down next to him, but my leg starts to shake, and I have to get up and walk, so I pace in front of him. "What did the police say?"

"The police?" I laugh bitterly. "The last time this happened, I called and all they did was take a report. They did nothing," I say, recalling when it happened the first time. The minute I mentioned Andrew and that he was on drugs, it was like I was wasting their time. They took the report because that is their job, but I doubt they did anything else with it. "I don't know what they were looking for, but there was nothing there for them," I start to say. "The futon was also slashed to the point where there is no way it can be salvaged, and the wooden frame looks like someone kicked in every single slat. They even put holes in the walls, and now I'm going to have to patch them up before the landlord sees it and evicts me for good this time." I walk back and forth. "The bathroom was the only thing not touched."

"Are you done?" he asks, and I look at him.

"What?" I whisper.

"You could have been home last night," he says, his voice almost in a whisper, but anger is clearly radiating off him. "You could have been in the middle of that, you and Dylan, and it might have had a different outcome."

"I mean," I say, "I didn't think of that."

"Of course you didn't," he says, and my head snaps back.

"What does that mean?" I say.

"It means that you could have been there. It means that the person could have come inside the house and beat and raped you while Dylan watched," he says, his voice trembling. "I don't want you to go back there. I don't want you in that place."

"Justin," I say. Walking to him, I step in the middle of his legs and he wraps his hands around my legs. "I would never put myself in that position."

"They came into your house. Do you think they knocked before coming in?" he says, and my hands come up to hold his face in my hands.

"I can't just pick up and leave," I tell him as much as I would love to.

"You can get another place," he says, and I smile at him. I smile for the first time today. "A place where Andrew doesn't know where you're at." He blinks. "A place where you can have peace of mind and not worry about someone coming to hurt you or get information from you because of Andrew."

"I just …" I start and then decide to bare my soul to him. "I would love nothing more. If I ever get a chance to move, I would do it in a heartbeat. I would leave this crappy fucking town behind me and never look back."

"Will you let me help you?" he asks. "I mean, not leave this crappy fucking town because I really want you here with me." He blinks away the tears. "Let me help you find someplace that is safe for you and for Dylan."

"Justin, I can't let you do that," I say. "I can't let you just …"

"Let me be the one who protects you for once." His hands rub the backs of my legs. "Let me be the one who holds your hand for once."

"You really are that perfect person," I say, leaning down to kiss his lips.

"Not even close," he whispers, "but with you, I want to be as perfect as I can be."

"Where is everybody?" We hear Dylan yell. "Mom," he calls my name. "Justin."

"In here, buddy," Justin says, and the door opens, and he stands there looking at us.

"Is the food almost ready?" he asks, and I look at him. "We made food."

"What?" I ask, looking at him and then Justin.

"Justin said after a long day at work, it's good to come home to a home-cooked meal so you know we missed you."

"Is that so?" I ask, and he just nods.

"Why don't you go take a bath?" Justin says. "And I can get dinner ready."

"What?" I step back.

"We can talk about all this after," he says, and then Dylan's eyes go big.

"Yeah, Mom, we have another surprise," he says, and this time, he jumps up and down. "Can we show her? Can we show her?"

"Sure," Justin says, and I have to stop smiling so much because my face hurts.

"Come see, Mom," he says, turning and running away.

"Do I want to know?" I ask Justin, and he just shrugs.

"Mom," Dylan sings my name. "Come on, come on." I walk out of the room and go to the game room, and Dylan is jumping up and down. "Close your eyes," he says, and I close my eyes. He takes my hand, and I walk blindly into the room. "Surprise," he says, and I open my eyes, and I stare at the room in shock.

"What …" I start to say, "is this?" I look around.

"It's a fort for movie night," Dylan says excitedly, still jumping up and down. Sheets are tied up to the ceiling and hang down to look like the top of a tent, all around the couch. "Come see inside," he says, crawling inside, and pillows are everywhere and covers along with snacks are on the table. "Look, it's a fort."

"How did you guys do this?" I ask, peeking in.

"We did it after we got home from working out, Mom," he says so matter-of-factly.

"You guys were just busy as bees today," I say, and he nods.

"Okay, buddy," Justin says. "Time to go finish dinner so we can eat."

Dylan nods at him and walks out of the room.

I watch him with awe. "You …" I say, shaking my head. "You really are."

"I really am," he says and grabs my hand, pulling me back into his room and through to the bathroom. I stop dead in my tracks.

"Mother of God," I say, looking at his bathroom. I don't know what I was expecting—obviously, it had to be amazing—but I wasn't expecting it to be so big. Double vanity sinks with marble counters and deep gray drawers under it. But the best is the floor-to-ceiling window with a deep white tub facing it. Right in front of a huge walk-in shower.

"Just take your time," he says, bending to kiss my cheek. "And we'll be ready whenever you get out."

"But …" I start to say.

"I'll give him a snack," he says, and I laugh when he walks out of the room. I sit down on the edge of the tub and rub my face. The beginning of the day, I thought I was done, that there was no light at the end of my tunnel. Yet I'm sitting in a room that is all light and no darkness. I don't know what else is going to come, but I'm suddenly not afraid of the dark.

TWENTY FIVE

JUSTIN

*C*LOSING THE DOOR to the bathroom, I go into the kitchen and see that Dylan is sitting on one of the stools waiting. "You can go play a bit," I say. "Mom is going to take a shower." Before he moans that he's starving, I tell him, "Get a cheese stick."

He walks over to the fridge and grabs two and then runs back to the room. I grab my phone and dial Matthew.

"This has to be a record," he says, answering the phone with a laugh, and I hear people talking all around him.

"Yeah," I whisper and then look to make sure I'm alone. "I need your help."

"Shit," he hisses, and all of a sudden, the background gets quiet, and I hear a door close. "What happened?"

"I have a …" I say, pinching my nose. "Let's say Karrie was living in an apartment."

"Negative," he says right away, and I groan. "Okay, okay,

fine. Let's play pretend."

"She lives in this apartment, and it gets vandalized," I say the word, and I could swear Matthew stops breathing altogether. "When she wasn't there."

"Justin." He says my name. "I have to say I'm done playing pretend. What the fuck have you gotten yourself into?" I close my eyes. "I don't think this is a good idea."

"What, would you just leave Karrie?" I ask him.

"I love her," Matthew says, then stops. "Wait."

"Yeah, whatever," I say, not addressing the question.

"Dude, you have to just move her shit into your house," he says. "Just don't even tell her."

"What?" I whisper, looking back again.

"Just don't tell her and move all her things in," he says, and I look at the phone. "Or I mean, this worked once ..." he says. "Just handcuff her to the bed and don't let her out until she agrees."

"How are you even married?" I ask, and he laughs.

"She never stood a chance," he says. "But seriously, Justin, I don't know what's going on, but I'm assuming if you are this in, then you are all in?"

"Yeah," I say softly. "I'm all in."

"I'll see you next week," he says. "Things just got pushed up."

"There is a lot I haven't told you," I start to say. "Dylan's dad"—I sigh—"um, he's not really involved, and when he is, let's just say it's not good." I wonder if by telling him this, I'm breaking her trust.

"What?" he whispers.

"I swear, Matthew, the kid is the best," I say. "He is hands down the best kid I've ever met."

"Then that's all I need to know," he says. "Get your woman ready for us."

"There is not enough time in the year to get anyone ready for my family," I say with a smile.

"We aren't that bad," he says, laughing. "See you next week."

"Can't wait," I say, and I hang up the phone. After setting it on the counter, I sit down on one of the stools. I put my head in my hands, and I hear her voice in my head. My heart is in my throat when I think about the fact that she could have been there alone with Dylan.

"Hey." I hear her soft voice next to me, and I look up at her. She's wearing what she was wearing last night. She looks so beautiful I just want to hold her and protect her. "What's the matter?"

"Nothing," I say and move to get up.

"If I have to be honest, then you have to be honest," she says, and I turn around.

"Fine," I say, putting my hands on my hips. "I was thinking about the fact that I could have lost you and Dylan." The way my chest rises and falls, I have to put my hand to it and press down. "That just like that, you could have been hurt, and there was nothing that I could have done."

"But I'm not," she says, coming to me. "I'm fine."

"He brought that danger to your front door, and he doesn't even care," I say, my voice getting louder. "He left his child to face those guys," I say, running my hands through my hair. "Like who the fuck does that?"

"He's a coward," she says, looking down again, then

243

looking up. "He's always been a coward and inattentive."

"You could have been so hurt. Dylan, fuck Dylan, who has this heart of fucking gold, he could have been …" My voice trembles.

"Justin," she says, stepping closer to me.

My hands go to her face, and I kiss her with everything that I have. I kiss her, knowing it could have been the last time. I kiss her, promising her everything that I have to give. I kiss her as a vow to protect and treat her like she should be treated.

"Oh, God," Dylan says, "you guys are always kissing. I'm starving."

And just like that, we both laugh, but I don't let her go. "I'm starting the pasta now."

"Good," he says, coming into the kitchen and climbing on the stool. "Mom, we made the sauce."

"Did you?" Caroline says, and I let her go as I go into the kitchen and turn the water on.

"Yeah, but Justin had to call his mom, and she laughed at him."

"Dylan, bro code," I say, smiling, and he just looks at me.

"So what else did you do today?" she asks, sitting down on the stool next to him.

"Justin has a special place where he goes to work out," Dylan tells her. "It's down the hall."

"It's a gym," Caroline tells him.

"No, it's an apartment," he says. "He keeps it for his family when they come visit."

"Really," she says, smiling at him. "Did you work out?"

"I did," he says. "Feel, I pumped iron." He puts his arm in a curl. "And he made me a protein shake."

"Without protein," I say. "It was basically a fruit smoothie."

"Then we went to the grocery store," Dylan says. "And he bought you all the milk." I put my head back and groan.

"Not all the milk," I say and then look at her. "I just didn't know which you liked, so I bought you a couple of choices," I say, and Dylan laughs.

"It fills the whole door," he says, getting down and going over to open it. Her mouth drops open.

"What?" I shrug. "It's just a little something." Then I look at Dylan. "Remember what I said. You buy little things to make her happy and to let her know you think about her all the time."

"Yeah, and then we bought flowers," Dylan says. "Mine are bigger."

"They are both beautiful," Caroline says. "I've never gotten flowers." She leans over and smells the roses.

"What do you mean?" I ask. She got married; she had a baby.

"I mean, no one has ever bought me flowers," she says as if it's fine when it's not. I make a note to buy her flowers every fucking week.

I finish making the pasta, and we eat inside at the counter in the kitchen side by side. I even make garlic bread, which burns a touch but still tastes good. When she gets up to clean, I tell her to sit down.

"You know the rules," she says, and I look at her.

"You worked all day. I got the dishes. Why don't you and Dylan go and choose a movie?" I say, and she doesn't get a chance to answer because Dylan pulls her down to the bedroom.

I have most everything cleaned and put away the leftovers when she comes back into the kitchen. "Are you almost done?"

"Yes," I say.

"You did a lot today," she says, and I smile. "Dylan told me you said lots of bad words also when you were hanging the fort." She rolls her lips.

"I did." I laugh. "There were a couple of colorful words, but I told him that you aren't allowed to say them until you're forty."

"You aren't even forty." She laughs, and the sound fills the room.

"You're beautiful when you laugh," I say, and she blushes. "You should do it more."

"Something says that with you around, I'll be doing a lot of smiling," she flirts with me.

"Is that so?" I grab her hips and pull her to me, and she laughs.

"I found the movie," Dylan says, and I look at her.

"When my family comes, my brother is going to babysit him for a whole weekend," I say, and she stops laughing.

"When is your family coming?" she asks me, and I see the nerves set in.

"You'll get to meet them next weekend," I say, and the horror sets in.

"I don't think it's a good idea," she starts to say, but I don't let her continue.

"Well, I told them about you, so if you don't, my mom will think you don't like her." I totally play the low card, but I have no choice.

She stands there with her mouth open, and then closes it, and then opens it again. "But …"

"Then my sisters will want to know where you are, and I'll have to say you don't want to meet them." I walk over to the freezer and take out the ice cream.

"You wouldn't do that," she whispers.

"Dylan, come get ice cream!" I shout for him and get the ice cream cones.

"I chose the ice cream," Dylan says. "I want a big scoop."

We get the ice cream, and she glares at me as I give her a cone. We walk to the fort, and I press play, and I about groan when I see that it's *Frozen*. "Why?" I ask him.

"I wanted to know why you don't like this," Dylan says, hiding his laughter while he licks the ice cream. We start watching, and twenty minutes in, Dylan is all into it, and I lean over and pull Caroline to me.

"Will you lay with me?" I ask, and she leans down and kisses my lips, her lips all sweet.

"Yes," she says softly. I wrap my arms around her, and she lays on my chest. With her head on my chest, her hand on my chest, her in my arms, and Dylan beside me, I know this is where I was always meant to be. I don't even give a shit that he's playing the movie I hate most in the world or that he laughs when I groan.

After *Frozen*, he puts on *Tangled,* and I swear he's doing it to punish me for kissing his mother. I turn to the side, and Caroline drapes her arm over my stomach and looks up at me. "This has to be the best night I've had since I gave birth to Dylan," she says softly. "Thank you for giving us this."

"For you two," I say. "Anything."

Twenty Six

Caroline

"SWEETHEART," JUSTIN WHISPERS from beside me, and I open my eyes. He's got me wrapped in his arms since we laid down. I was going in and out of sleep, trying to keep my eyes open. "Do you want me to carry you to bed, or are you okay with sleeping here?"

"What time is it?" I ask, looking up at him.

"Almost ten," he says, and I bury my face in his chest, laughing. "Thank God, he fell asleep before the last credits. I think he would have chosen *Beauty and the Beast* next, and I think I would have put my foot down."

"You lie," I joke with him. "He has you wrapped around his finger."

"I can be mean," he says, and I look up at him and see that his hair is everywhere.

My hand moves up to play with his hair. "Yeah?" I ask him, trying not to laugh at him. The whole night was a dream.

Coming home after this morning, I didn't think I would be able to think of anything else. But here with Justin, he made me look at things differently.

"Yeah," he hisses and then leans down and kisses me. At first, it starts with just a peck, and then the peck gets longer, and he leans down, this time, lingering even longer. The next time he comes back, I slide my tongue out and slip it into his mouth. I push myself into him, and he rolls us to the side and takes the kiss deeper. His tongue invades my mouth, and his kisses leave me itching for more. Wanting more. He leaves my mouth and slowly moves down to my neck, and I give him access and close my eyes, his smell all over me. He rolls me to my back, and his arms on either side of my head hold him up. My legs open for him, and I wrap my legs around his waist. His mouth comes back to me, and he kisses me again, and then he stops suddenly. "I really, really don't want to stop," he says. I suddenly get a rush of embarrassment, and I lose eye contact with him. "Hold on tight, sweetheart," he says, and I look at him confused. "We're going to do this, just not next to Dylan." He motions his head to the side where Dylan is on his back passed out. "I'm getting up now," he says, and he wraps one of his arms around my waist and picks me up. My arms and legs tighten around him, and he walks out of the fort.

I bury my face in his neck and rub my nose against him back and forth, giving him little soft butterfly kisses. He walks us to his room and puts his knee on the bed and slowly lowers me. My hands loosen their hold of him, and just like that, his lips are on mine again. The kisses are everything you dream of. When you're a little girl and you read all the fairy tales about the handsome prince coming to save you, this is what you dream the kisses are. This is what you dream would happen.

My hands roam from his neck to his shoulders softly down his back, and then I take the biggest step. I raise his shirt, and I finally touch him where I've wanted to touch him since I saw him without his shirt. My hands roam to the front of his shirt, and I slowly move them up over his abs and one hand rests on his chest right where I feel his heart beating under my hand. "Justin," I say breathlessly when he leaves my lips and slowly kisses me from my cheek to my jaw and then slowly kisses me down to my neck and right behind my ear.

"Everything," he says, and my eyes close at the sound of his soft voice. "Everything about you is perfect." I shiver at his words. His mouth is on mine again, and this time, I'm the aggressive one. I can't get enough of him. I want to touch all of him. Whatever the future holds, all I want is this moment right here. It's a moment that when I'm seventy and talking to my grandkids, I'll tell them about this man who became my prince for a short while.

"Justin," I say his name over and over again as he kisses, licks, and nips his way down. His hand goes under my shirt, and I arch my back, itching for him to touch me more. Itching to feel his skin on mine. "Take it off," I say as soon as he cups my bare breast.

"Fuck," he hisses, and I move my hips up just a bit so I'm lined up with his covered cock. "I need to close and lock the door," he says and gets up, walking to the door and shutting it. "I don't think I can face Dylan if he comes in here, and I'm trying to get busy with his mother," he jokes, and I hide my face and laugh. "Don't do that." His voice comes out again, and I look at him as he takes his shirt off. My stomach flips, and my heart speeds up. "Don't hide from me."

"I'm not hiding from you," I say, getting on my elbows. "I'm just shy."

"Don't," he says, coming back to the bed and standing at the edge. "Don't ever be shy in front of me."

"But ..." I start to say. "I just ...." I try to find the words, and I know this could totally change the course of tonight. "I've been with one man my whole life."

"What?" he whispers.

"I mean, you knew I wasn't a virgin," I joke, and he just shakes his head. "But Andrew was the only one I've been with, and I know ..." I try to not make eye contact. "I can guess you've had your share of women."

"Wow," he says. "This is not something I thought we would be talking about before I tried to get you naked."

"I don't know about naked," I joke with him, "but you were for sure going to reach second base."

He puts his hand to his chest. "Can we use hockey terms?" he asks.

"I don't even know what second base means in baseball. I just said it for, you know, the meaning."

"How about I'm skating into the zone," he says, and I sit up now, laughing.

"Okay, you were going to be skating in the zone," I say, "but before the zone, I wanted you to know." I take a deep inhale. "Here goes nothing," I say and peel the shirt over my head, and just like that, I'm topless in the middle of his bed.

He doesn't say anything to me. He just stares at me, and I suddenly want to take it back. I grab the shirt at the same time as I cover myself, but he pulls the shirt from my hand.

"I'm so skating in the zone," he says, and he falls forward on me, and just like that, the awkward moment is gone, and in its place is the need that was there before. His mouth crashes on mine while my legs circle his waist, and he holds himself up from crushing me with one arm as he cups my breast. "Jesus," he hisses when I feel his hardness under me and move my hips.

"Nope," I say breathlessly, waiting for his mouth on any part of me. "Just Caroline." I try to joke with him, but he goes one up, and his mouth sucks in one of my nipples, and I close my eyes and put my head back.

He nips the nipple before sucking it in his mouth again. I'm lost to his touch, lost to his mouth and his tongue. I'm reduced to panting, my hands are all over his chest, and it's just not enough. He rotates from one breast to the other and then comes back up to kiss me, his tongue hot and needy. My hands go to the side of his head as we get lost in the deep, wet kiss, then they roam from his chest to his back to his ass. I press him deeper into me, and his cock is right on top of my clit.

The clothes between us are almost like a shield, and I move my hips once. He must wait for the second time because the minute I move again, he pinches my nipple, sending me into another orbit. "God," I say, and I swear I might orgasm, and he's only touched my tits.

"Justin," he mumbles, and I want to have a sassy comeback, but with his hands literally all over me, I have nothing to say. My hand moves from his ass to his front, and I cup his covered cock. "Caroline." He now says my name. I slowly open my eyes, but my eyelids feel like they are a thousand pounds. "We are slowly skating toward the goalie."

"What?" I ask him.

"You are skating toward the goalie, and he's leaving the net empty," he hisses, and he doesn't move as he watches me not understand. "I'm going to go off in your hand."

"Oh," I say, smiling that I put him to the point that one touch, and he will go off. "Is that a bad thing?"

"Trust me, I really want to score." He kisses me. "But I want to do it when we have the whole night."

"The whole night?" I repeat.

"The whole night," he says. "Maybe even some of the next day, too."

"That's a long time," I say. "Are you …?" I try to ask him. "Can you go that long?"

"I'll just have to show you," he says, and it's like he threw down the challenge. "Better to show you."

"I mean, there are things we can do before then …" I try to think, but my hand on his cock and his fingers playing with my nipple are not helping. "Before we …" His mouth covers mine. "Before we pull the goalie."

"You are so hot when you talk hockey," he says and makes his way down, kissing my ribs. His cock is gone from my hand as he trails kisses to my stomach, and then he looks at me as I watch him. My elbows hold me up as he kisses my stomach and sucks in a bit, then goes to the waistband of his shorts that he leant me. I don't know how he is going to react to the fact I'm not wearing panties. He looks at me, and right before he's about to go lower, we both hear Dylan scream out crying.

He's off me in a blink of an eye and already out of the door. I grab his shirt and put it on, then run out into the hall, and my heart stops in my chest. He's standing there in the middle of the hallway with my son in his arms as Dylan cries.

"It was just a bad dream," Justin whispers to him while his face is buried in his neck. "It's probably that movie," he says and looks at me, the worry all over his face.

"What happened?" I say, walking up to them and rubbing my son's back.

"He had a bad dream that we left him," Justin fills me in. "And he couldn't find us, and when he woke up, he was all alone."

"Oh, baby," I say, rubbing his head, and he turns to look at me. My son who never had anyone but me to comfort him before is locked up in Justin's arms, and nothing will pry him from them.

TwentySeven

Justin

*H*EARING HIM SCREAM and then cry stopped my heart literally. I thought my heart was not beating while I ran to him standing there in the middle of my dark hallway, looking panicked and scared. He tried to wipe the tears off his face before I got to him, but the minute I held open my arms, he jumped into them. Wrapping his arms around me, he buried his face in my neck, trying not to cry. "I dreamed that you left me," he says, "and I couldn't find Mom."

I hold him to me tightly, whispering, "Never." I look up at Caroline who is now coming out of the room wearing the shirt I was just wearing. "We would never leave you," I say. Holding on to him, I feel Caroline beside me.

"What happened?" she whispers, and I look at her, expecting him to jump into her arms, but he doesn't. I kiss his shoulder and walk with him to the couch, sitting down with him on my lap.

Caroline comes over and sits next to me, and a few seconds later, he is snoring softly on my shoulder. "You can put him down," she says, rubbing his cheek softly.

"Not yet," I say, making sure I hold him tighter. "I bet it was that fucking movie." I look over at her and see she is trying not to laugh. "Or waking in the fort where it's so dark."

"I think it's just a bad dream," she says.

"Whatever. He's not going to sleep in that room," I say, getting up and walking to the bedroom she slept in the night before. She walks ahead of me and pulls down the covers, and I place him gently down and wait for him to wake up, but he just turns to the side, and Caroline covers him. "Let's leave the hall light on in case he wakes up again."

"He's going to be fine," Caroline says, walking to the other side of the bed and pulling down the covers. "I'll be right here."

"Um, no, you won't." I put my hand on my hip. "You'll be sleeping," I say, "but in that bed." I point in the direction of my room.

"What?" she says, and I put my finger to my lips.

"Let's talk about this in bed so we don't wake him," I say. Walking to where she is, I take her hand and pull her with me out of the room. After looking over my shoulder ten times, I leave the door open just a bit and turn the light on in the hallway.

"Justin," she whispers, and I stop by the fridge to grab a bottle of water. "Can we talk?"

"Yes," I say. Walking into my bedroom, I turn off the light and then walk to the bed. I remove the top cover and just about push her onto it, then go to the other side and get in.

258

Pulling her to me, I wrap myself around her. "Now we can talk."

"Justin," she says, turning in my arms, and I lean in and kiss her lips. "You can't …" God, her kisses are everything. I go back in again for another kiss. My cock gets harder than it was before, and let me tell you, it was fucking rock solid.

"I'm not going to win this," she says breathlessly between kisses, and she hikes her leg over my hip. If we weren't wearing any clothes, I would slip inside her.

"Good night, sweetheart," I say, and she just cuddles closer to me, putting one hand between us and wrapping the other one over me.

She leans up and kisses the underside of my jaw. "Good night, Justin," she says softly, and with her in my arms, I fall asleep. I don't think I move all night.

"Justin." I hear my name whispered, and open one eye first, seeing it's Dylan. "I'm hungry. Can I have cereal?"

"Yeah, buddy," I say and then turn back to gather Caroline in my arms. "Go ahead. I'm getting up in a second, and I'll make pancakes," I say, and he hops and skips out of the room.

"Why didn't you just get up?" Caroline says from beside me.

"Because he would have seen my morning wood, and that isn't a conversation I want to have with him right now," I say and kiss the top of her head. She looks up at me, her eyes still heavy with sleep. "Did you sleep well, sweetheart?" I ask, and she nods.

I turn over, and she slips out of my arms. I walk to the bathroom, and when I come back, she's already gone from bed. When I join them in the kitchen, she already has the coffee going. "Are you sure you're okay?" I hear her ask him, and he just nods while he fills his mouth with a spoonful of cereal.

"You okay, buddy?" I say, going to him and rubbing his hair, and he nods.

"What do you want for breakfast?" Caroline asks, and I look at her.

"Mom, are we going to church?" he asks, and she looks at me.

"Would you mind if we went?" she asks, and I shake my head. "I just don't have anything for Dylan to wear, so maybe we can stop at Walmart before."

"Yeah," I say. "We can do that."

"Perfect." She smiles at me and fills two cups of coffee. Going to the fridge, she then looks at me. "You really did buy all the milk."

"I didn't know which one you drank, so it was a safe bet to get them all," I say and sit next to Dylan, grabbing the box of cereal and popping some into my mouth.

"We have all the milk that they have in the store." He shrugs. "It's like we are the store."

"We have thirty minutes before we have to leave," she says, and I nod at her. "Dylan, you need to shower," she groans. "And so do I."

"Use my bathroom," I say, and she just looks at me. "Pick your battles, sweetheart."

She takes her cup of coffee, stopping at Dylan's stool first and kissing him and then coming to mine. "I have a feeling every battle I pick I'll lose."

"You're learning," I say and lean forward to kiss her lips, tasting the sweetness of her hazelnut creamer.

"Thirty minutes, people." She walks away from us, and I give Dylan a couple more minutes until I push him to go take a shower.

"Put your stuff from yesterday on, and you'll change in the car when we stop at the store," I say, taking the last sip of my coffee. When he goes to the bathroom to take a shower, I walk into my room. The bed is already made, and the shower has just turned off. She walks out of the bathroom dressed in last night's clothes with a towel around her head and the coffee cup in her hand.

"I'm going to take a shower." I kiss her, and she smiles at me. I don't know how long I take in the shower, but when I come out, my bedroom door is closed, and I don't hear any noise. I walk to my walk-in closet and put on a pair of boxers, grabbing a pair of blue pants, my brown belt, and a white button-down. I tuck in my shirt and slip on my brown dress shoes. I walk out of the room and roll up my sleeve, finding Caroline in the kitchen wearing her green dress. Her hair is dry now, and the ends are curled.

"Hey," I say, and she looks over, but her mouth opens.

"Is this okay?" I ask, looking down at my outfit. "I can always change."

"You ..." she starts to say and then closes her mouth again. "You." She points. "You're hot."

I throw my head back and laugh. "Thank you," I say, folding the other sleeve. "I think."

"Like wow," she says, and I shake my head.

I look around the kitchen and the living room and see

that Dylan isn't here. "Listen, I was thinking that after church we could swing by your place and you can go up and grab clothes for you two," I say, and her face goes white as though she's seen a ghost. "What's wrong?" Then I walk to her. "If it's too much for you, I can go up."

"No," she says almost like she's shouting, and she walks to the sink, grabs a glass, and drinks some water. She turns to look at me. "There is something I didn't tell you." Just the way she says it makes my heart sink. "I was going to, but it was just too much." She looks at me. "There are no clothes."

"Go on." I don't trust myself to say much more.

"All the clothes were slashed and destroyed. I think I have one shirt left that I had in the laundry basket," she says, playing with her hands again, and I want to shake something. "Tomorrow, I'm going to hit up the thrift shop and even the church shop and get us some things to hold us over." Her voice goes soft. "I'm going to take care of it." Her eyes fill with tears, and I don't want her to cry. I don't want her to shed another fucking tear for the rest of her life.

"Mom, I'm ready," Dylan says, but her eyes never leave mine. "Mom?" he calls her again. "Are we leaving?"

"Yeah," she says, grabbing her purse. "It's okay if you don't feel up to it."

"Justin, you aren't coming?" he asks.

"Of course, I'm coming," I say and then look down to see him wearing the same stuff he wore for two days. "We have to stop and get you some clothes." I grab my phone and my keys. "Let's go."

"Justin," she says my name softly.

"I hate this for you," I say softly. "Hate it."

She shrugs. "It's just another speed bump in the road." I look at her and wonder what road she is on because there

262

are craters in her road, and I suddenly want to pave them all. I grab her hand in mine and bring it to my lips when we walk out of the apartment. The elevator comes right away, and the three of us ride it to the garage. "We can take the BMW today," I say, and she looks at me, smirking.

"You know it's Sunday," she jokes, and I put my arm around her. "Sunday is for BMW and church."

"That mouth is going to get you into a lot of trouble," I whisper into her ear. When we get to the car, I unlock the doors, and Dylan climbs in. I kiss her lips. "Big trouble."

"Yeah," she says, getting into the car, and I get into the car also. "Will I end up in the penalty box?" she asks.

"You only go to the box when you do something bad, Mom," Dylan says, and I wink at her before putting on my sunglasses.

"Where to?" I ask, and she looks at me.

"The closest Walmart," she says, and I nod at her and punch it in the GPS. We get there, and she gets out of the car and opens the back door for Dylan.

"Are you coming with us?" Dylan asks, and I look at him.

"No, buddy, I have to make a phone call," I say. He jumps out of the car, and they walk into the busy Walmart.

I pick up my phone and dial the one person I know who can help me. "Well, well, well." She answers on the first ring.

"Hey," I say, looking to make sure they haven't come out. "I need a favor."

"It's going to cost you," she says, and my eyes never leave the glass door.

"Whatever it is," I say and put my plan into motion.

TWENTYEIGHT

CAROLINE

I WALK INTO Walmart, and the stale air hits me right away. My hands are clammy, and my knees are shaking. It's surreal; this whole week has been surreal.

I spent extra time on my hair today and curled it with the wand that he had in his bathroom. I tried not to think about who it belonged to, and when I went into the kitchen to clean up, my stomach was fluttering as if I was going to prom. He walked out, and I don't know what I expected, but I didn't expect him to be so, just. Hot. Then my mouth couldn't stop talking, but then when he told me we could stop to grab the rest of my clothes from home, I thought I was going to throw up and ruin the only clothing I had.

I didn't know how he would react, but I had to tell him the truth. I vowed never to lie to him, and I'm not going to. Besides,

watching him last night with Dylan was just the cherry

on the cake. The way he held him and refused to let him go. I was waiting for him to fight with me about the clothing, but he didn't, and when we step into Walmart, I head for the kids department and grab a pair of blue shorts that are on sale for nine dollars and a white T-shirt that is on liquidation for four ninety-nine. "Can I wear my sneakers?" he asks, and I nod.

"It's fine," I say and go to the register and slip a folded twenty that I keep in the back of my wallet in a secret compartment that I cut into it.

We walk out of the store, and I see Justin on the phone with someone. When Dylan opens the door, I hear him say. "Okay, I got to go. Make it happen."

"Did you find anything?" he asks, looking in the back at Dylan who just nods his head. I sit in the car next to Justin, and I realize that his whole outfit probably cost what I make in six months.

"Do you want to stop somewhere so he can change?" he asks, and I just shake my head.

"He can change in the car," I say, and he looks at me. We make it to church, and when I get out, I'm looking around to make sure no one is there watching me.

"You okay?" Justin asks, and I just nod.

"I'm just nervous," I say the truth. "I'm waiting for Andrew to show up and blame me for keeping him away from Dylan."

"Gotta say, sweetheart. I'm not sure I'll be able to hold myself back if that happens," he says, and just the way he says it, I know that he means it, but the last thing I want is for Justin to be in trouble because of us.

"I changed," Dylan says, coming out of the back seat

wearing his new clothes. I walk over to him and twist his shorts so they are straight. "Mom," he groans, and I grab his hand.

"Let's go before we don't have any seats," I say, and we walk into the church. I see more than one head turn to look our way. It's not hard to see why. I even hear a couple of whispers, but I ignore them and walk up to Father Rolly. "Hey there," I say, and he smiles at me and then looks at Dylan.

"Did you grow?" He asks him the same question every Sunday. "You are almost going to pass me."

"Father," I say. "This is Justin, a friend of ours."

"Father," Justin says, extending his hand. "Nice to meet you."

"The pleasure is mine," he says. "Now go sit."

"Do you need anything?"

"You did what you needed to do on Friday." He smiles at me. "And it was perfect."

"Thank you," I say and turn to walk down the aisle to sit in one of the pews.

We sit in the middle of the church. I wait for Dylan to go in, and then Justin waits for me to sit, and then he takes the seat next to me at the end of the pew. The service is just under an hour, and when it's done, we walk out of the church, and I walk to the car with my head high for once.

Justin must sense it because he puts Dylan in the car, and we take off. "Are we going to our house now?" Dylan asks, and I'm about to turn around when Justin speaks up.

"I was thinking we could go grab some pizza for lunch," he suggests, and Dylan quickly changes his mind.

"Yeah, let's do that," he says. We drive back to Justin's, then park the car and walk to the restaurant.

"Oh, can we take it home and watch another movie?" Dylan says, and I look at Justin.

"I like that plan a lot," he says. "What do you say, sweetheart? Want to take it to go?"

"A movie and pizza," I say to them both. "Yes, please."

We order the food, and they tell us it's going to be about thirty to forty-five minutes, and they will bring it over. We walk back to the apartment and make our way back to his place.

"Okay, it's my turn to pick a movie," Justin says when we walk into the apartment, and Dylan groans. "You chose two yesterday."

"But one was Mom's pick," he says, going to the fridge and grabbing a bottle of water as if he lived there.

Justin goes to the fridge, grabbing his own water, and then hands me one. "Thank you," I mumble and try to ignore whatever is going on inside me. "I'm going to go change," I tell them both and escape to the room, grabbing the clothes I had on yesterday and go to the bathroom.

I splash water on my face and look at myself in the mirror. "You have to stop this. Nothing good is going to come from this," I tell myself. I slip out of the dress and look at myself in the basic white cotton bra that I've had for four years now, the cups are not even there anymore and the wires that went under the bra were tossed away somewhere a long time ago. The white cotton panties that I have. The same four pair that I wash and rewash. "Stupid," I tell myself. "Stupid to believe this can go anywhere."

Tomorrow, tomorrow I'm going to get my ass in gear and look for another place.

I slip on the shorts and shirt and walk out of the room and see Justin sitting on the bed. "What's going on?"

"Nothing," I say, not making eye contact as I place my folded dress on the top of the dresser. "I'm just …"

"Look at me," he says, and I do. "What's going on?"

"It's just …" I say. "Dylan is acting like he lives here. He is coming and going to the fridge."

"Good," Justin says. "I want him to be comfortable here."

"But it's temporary," I say. "Eventually, we will have to get our new place."

He's about to say something when the doorbell rings, and Dylan comes into the room. "Pizza is here," he says, and I watch Justin get up and walk out with him.

"Thank you so much." I hear Justin say. "Just put everything over there."

I walk over and see two men bringing in bags and then more bags and then more bags. "What's going on?"

"It's not pizza," Dylan says from the fridge, eating another cheese stick.

"There are about fifty bags," one of them jokes with Justin.

"Fifty in this trip. There are still a couple more downstairs," the other one says.

"Take your time," Justin says to the two men, and I sit on the stool watching.

"Justin, you bought so much stuff," Dylan says, coming to sit on the stool next to me. "Is it your birthday?" he asks, and my head swings to Justin, and my heart sinks. What if today was his birthday, and I didn't know?

"Not my birthday." He smiles, and the men come in again.

"This is all of it," he says and smiles at us and then walks out.

"What is it?" Dylan asks, and then Justin looks down at the floor and then looks up again. I can tell he's nervous, and I have no idea why.

"So I know that you haven't been able to get your stuff from your place. And I know how cool your old stuff was," he says, and I have a sinking feeling I know where this is going. "And well, since I forgot to take you to pick up any things." He looks at me, his eyes pleading with me. "I called my sister, who is a professional shopper."

"You bought us new things?" Dylan asks, getting up and checking in the bags.

"Just a couple of things," he says, looking at Dylan and putting his hand on Dylan's shoulder. "It's just to hold you over until I can take you back to your house to get your things."

"Cool," he says, and then Justin looks at me.

"I got you a couple of things also," he says, and I look from him to the bags and then back to him again.

"A couple?" I look at the bags.

"I mean, I told her to get you a couple of things." He smiles. "This"—he points at everything—"is the exaggeration that is my family."

"Oh, cool, look," Dylan says and takes out a pair of new shoes.

"You can return some of it," I say. "Or most of it."

"What?" Dylan shrieks. "Why? Look at all these new

clothes."

He starts taking stuff out of the bags—shorts, shirts, bathing suit. "Can we go to the pool?"

"Yeah, after we eat, we can hit it up," Justin says and walks over to me. "Please don't be mad," he says softly, and I look up at him. "I swear I told her to only get you a couple of things."

"I'm even afraid to look in the bags," I say the truth. "I don't need all that."

"I know," he says and pushing my hair away from my face, his hands coming up to cup my face, and his thumb moves up and down. "You can keep whatever you want, and then if you want, you can donate the rest."

"Donate?" I ask, shocked. "How about you return it?"

He scrunches his nose. "No," he says. "Final sale." He winks at me.

"Mom, open this one. It's for you. It's bras," Dylan says, coming over with the light pink bag. "And underwear."

He hands me the bag, and it's a tad heavy for a bra, and I look in and see the pink tissue paper on the top, and inside, I spot maybe ten bras. "This whole bag is full."

"I can help you decide which one to wear." He winks at me. "Here, let me put this in my room." He grabs the bag and walks away.

"You got a bathing suit, too," Dylan says, coming to me and putting the thing in my hand.

"Dylan, don't open all the bags," I say, but he's already elbow deep into another one when the doorbell rings. Getting up, I walk to it and open it, spotting a woman standing there. She is dressed in jeans and a top and stilettos. Her blond hair is fixed perfectly, and her makeup is a tad too dark for morning. Let's not even discuss the heavy lip gloss. I can probably see myself in the reflection.

"Oh, hi," she says, "you must be the maid." She smiles. "Is Justin home?"

"Um …" I start to talk, but Justin is behind me.

"Not the maid, Gloria," he says, almost hissing. "What can I do for you?"

"We are just letting you know that we are going away, and that our daughter might be coming by." She now ignores me. "She was hoping you could show her around."

"Yeah," Justin says, "not likely." He puts his hand on my shoulder. "You should let security know that you're leaving," he says. The elevator pings, and the same security guy from before is coming up with the food. "Just in time. Gloria is leaving, and she needs someone to show her daughter around." He reaches out and grabs the food. "Have a great night," he says and closes the door in Gloria's shocked face.

"Do I want to ask if you know her daughter?" I ask him, and then I want to kick myself for even asking.

"Never met her," he says, "but if she is anything like her mother …" He shudders. "I'm not interested in the least." He turns to walk into the house and calls Dylan.

"Well then," I say and walk into the house with him, and I stop in my tracks. Not only does it look like a bomb exploded, but all the bags are empty. "What is all this?" I ask Dylan, and he points at the clothes.

"That's all yours," he says, pointing at mountain one. "Those are mine." He points at mountain two. "Can I go eat?"

"Um …" I start to say.

"We are going to eat, and then you're going to clean up that mess," Justin says, getting plates out. "And you are going to fold all the clothes and put them away."

"Put them away where?" Dylan asks, going to the stool.

"In your room," he says, and my head snaps to him. I wait for Dylan to say something, but he just asks for pizza.

"After that, can we go to the pool?" Dylan asks, and Justin nods his head.

"Sweetheart, come and eat," he says, and I look over at him. His eyes fly from the pizza to mine, and he smiles at me. At first, it starts off as a smirk and then his whole face lights up. I take it into my memory, and I know that I'll remember this moment for years to come.

TwentyNine

JUSTIN

"*I*'M NOT FOLDING Mom's clothes," Dylan says, taking his last bite of his spaghetti. "She has to do her own chores."

"It wouldn't be a chore if you hadn't emptied the bags," I say, and he just shrugs. When the bags arrived, I knew that Zara overdid it. I can't say I was surprised or that I even cared. But I was worried about what Caroline would say, and although she looked like she was going to murder me, having Dylan there protected me.

"Go wash your hands," Caroline says when Dylan slips off the stool, bringing his plate to the sink and rinsing it, then putting it in the dishwasher. Crooked but at least he did it. He hops and skips over to the couch that holds his pile of clothes. When he starts to fold them, I want to get up and go help him. "Sit down," she says. I look over, and she tries to hide her smile behind her glass of water, but her eyes are lit up.

"I wasn't going to do anything," I say and lean in to kiss her lips. "Okay, fine, I was going to do yours at the same time."

"Sit," she says. "He made the mess, so he gets to clean it."

"Fine." I get off the stool and take my plate and hers to the dishwasher. "Go fold your clothes."

"I can make piles of things you can donate," she says, and I stop and look up to glare at her, and she laughs. Sitting on the edge of the couch, she starts to fold her mountain.

I clean up the kitchen when my phone rings, and I look and see it's Zara on FaceTime. "What did you not understand with my instructions?" I say and look over to see Caroline look at me while Zara just laughs her head off.

"I may have gone a tad overboard," she says when she finally stops laughing. "Hey, it's like when you walk into a sports shop, and you come out with seven sticks."

"Yeah," I say, shaking my head. "I want to say I was surprised, but …"

"Do they fit?" Zara asks, and I look over at Caroline.

"She got me twelve pairs of jeans," she whispers and then motions with her fingers the one and the two.

"She hasn't tried anything on," I tell Zara.

"I chose all the guy things," Evan says, and he comes into view. "Tell Dylan I did that."

"Thank you!" Dylan yells and then smiles. "You're still better than him," he whispers to me, and I laugh.

"We arrive on Friday," Zara says. "I think Mom and Dad are coming in on Thursday."

"Cool," I tell them and look over to see that Caroline is looking down and folding clothes, and I can see her leg moving. "When is everyone else coming down?"

"I think Friday," Zara says.

"Mark is actually going to arrive on Saturday," Evan says. "In the morning."

"We should have a big family dinner on Saturday," Zara says.

"Can't," I say. "I'm taking Caroline out." Looking over at her, I see her head come up. "I already made plans."

"Oh, look at you, being all romantic," Zara teases me. "We can watch Dylan."

"Yeah, that sounds good. He can teach Evan some new tricks on the Xbox," I joke with her, and Dylan just smirks.

"Actually, I'm going to come down on Thursday. I want to get on the ice Friday," Evan says, then looks at Zara. "Beautiful, can we go down on Thursday?"

"I guess," she says. "Okay, I have to go now as I have to up my planning."

"Take care," I tell them. "See you Thursday."

"Family dinner Friday night!" Evan yells, and I nod my head right before they disconnect.

"Okay, are you two almost done with the mess?" I look over at them, and Dylan points at his pile of clothes.

"Can you help me carry them to my room?" he asks, and I nod my head, but I stop in front of Caroline first and give her a small kiss, then surprise her with another kiss.

"Why don't you get changed to go to the pool, and we can head down?" I ask, and she just nods her head.

"I'm going to finish folding the clothes first," she says and then looks at me. "I don't know what to do with all these clothes."

"Wear them," Dylan says as if it's a no-brainer.

"She bought me two cocktail dresses," she says, picking one up that is white. "And high heels." She picks up the white strappy heels that go with the dress. "I've never worn high heels."

"Well, you can wear it Saturday," I say, and she looks at me with her mouth open. "Let's get these clothes put away so we can hit the pool."

"Smooth," she says, putting the dress and the heels aside. "How did she know my size?"

"She's a magician when it comes to this stuff." I wink at her and take a pile of clothes to the spare bedroom. "Let's put this in the drawers," I say, opening the first two and then Caroline walks in the room with her clothes.

"What are you doing?" she asks me and Dylan, confused.

"I'm putting away my clothes so I can go in the pool," Dylan answers her. I want to laugh, but I try not to.

"But why here?" She looks at me.

"You can put your stuff with mine." I motion with my head. "There are some empty drawers."

"But that's …" she starts to say.

"Mom, can we go to the pool?" Dylan asks, and I have to say I owe him one.

"Yeah, go get changed so we can go to the pool," I say, and she puts the clothes on the bed and turns to walk out of the room. I finish with Dylan and hand him his blue swimming trunks, and he runs to change. I grab her clothes from the bed, trying to scoop them all up in my arms but dropping a couple of pieces on the way to my bedroom. I walk in and dump them all on the bed, knowing they all have to be fixed now. I'm picking up one when the door opens, and she walks out and I have to sit down.

"I think she got this one right," Caroline says. I look at her, and there are no words coming out of my mouth.

She stands there in a bikini. "That's going back," I say, and she laughs. It's a green color, and the top molds her breasts, and I see the string holding up the two triangles that look a bit too small for her tits. "Or maybe it's perfect for later, but it's not okay to go to the pool."

"What?" she asks, looking down at herself. "It's perfect." She adjusts one of the triangles, but there isn't that much more material.

"I'm ready." Dylan comes running into the room showing off his blue shorts. "Do we have to bring towels?"

"Um, no," I say, putting my hand on my knee. "Why don't we watch a movie?" Caroline laughs.

"Go get changed," she says, and I look at the bikini bottom, and I swear it's too small. If she goes into the water, it might ride up. Her long legs look even longer. She turns around, and I jump off the bed, taking off my shirt and wrapping it around her. "What are you doing?" she asks, confused.

"You're naked," I say, turning to see if Dylan saw her.

"I'm not naked. It's cheeky." She laughs. "At least that is what was written on the tag."

"It's called not in this fucking lifetime," I say. "Put on shorts."

"I'm not putting on shorts, Justin," she says, trying to push me away laughing. "Go get changed. Dylan is waiting, and I think he looks like he is going to cry." I drop my hands in fear that he's crying and turn to look at him as he stands there unamused by whatever is going on with us.

"Can we go?" he says. "Please."

"Go change," she says and then she spots the clothes on the bed. "What are those doing here?"

"I'm helping you put away your stuff," I say. "I have to go change," I say, walking into the closet and grabbing my blue shorts. I walk to the bathroom to change, and when I come out, the clothes are gone. "Caroline," I call her name, and I see them both on the couch waiting for me, but she at least put on a cover-up. Her hair is almost now braided on the side.

"Finally," Dylan says, getting up, and I see he's wearing a new pair of flip-flops.

"Let's go," I say to him and then grab Caroline's hand while we walk out. "Where are your clothes?"

"Away," she says, teasing me. "I put them away."

"I'm just going to move them," I say, and I swear I sound like a child throwing a tantrum.

We walk all the way to the end of the hall, and I press the button leading us outside to the pool. I guess no one is here; it's a community pool, but no one actually uses it.

"Look at how big the pool is, Mom," Dylan says, going to one of the five cabanas and taking off his flip-flops.

"You need sunscreen," I say. Walking into the cabana, I open one of the cupboards and take out a basket of sunscreen. I walk back to him and spray some on him and then rub it in. "Now you can go," I say, and he runs all the way to the pool, I'm about to tell him not to run when he yells.

"Cannonball!" Holding his legs up, he jumps in.

"You think he's excited?" Caroline says from beside me as she slips off her cover-up. "I don't think we've ever just sat near the pool. We used to go to the public pool every day when he was five."

"You need sunscreen," I say as I look at her pale skin, and my hands itch to rub it on her.

"Do I?" she says, and I pull her into my arms and turn her around so Dylan doesn't see my hands going straight to her ass. "I definitely need sunscreen on my ass."

My cock springs to action and is ready to go, and she feels it, so I bend and kiss her. Her hands wrap around my neck, and I swear I wish I could pick her up and carry her over to one of the chairs and lay her down and get lost in her. "Justin," she whispers my name when I leave her lips and make my way down to her neck. "Don't start something you can't finish."

"Oh, I can finish," I say, looking at her, "but you are going to have to walk out before me." Looking down at my cock, I say, "Give me a minute."

She throws her head back and laughs. "I'll give you a minute," she says and walks away on her tippy toes, her perfect ass on display, and I know that after she takes that bikini off, its disappearance will be a mystery. She walks to the steps of the pool and slowly walks in as Dylan gets out and then jumps back in. I walk to the pool, using the stairs, too, but I sit on one of the steps, and she walks over to me in the waist-high water. "You still need a minute?" she jokes with me.

"Very funny." I reach out and pull her to me. She sits on my lap, and we spend the time laughing while we watch

Dylan jump into the pool over and over again. The only time my arms aren't around her is when Dylan and I both do cannonballs, but then I swing to her and bring her with me.

"I'm being an old man," Dylan says, lifting his hand out of the water.

"You've been in the water for three hours," I say from the side. For the past three hours, the three of us have gotten to know each other better. I found out that Caroline is two years and two days older than me. I found out that Dylan hates math in school, which I can get. I found out that Caroline loves to read and has read everything the library has to offer. I found out that her eyes sparkle when she's really not thinking about anything and is in the moment. They tease me when I tell them I'm afraid of spiders. I kiss Caroline and then look back at Dylan.

"Let's get going." I get out of the water and walk over to the cabana and grab two towels. Caroline comes out first, and if I didn't hate the bikini before, I hate it now. Her nipples are hard and almost poking out. "Cover yourself." I wrap her in a towel, locking her arms inside. I hold her towel up while I hand Dylan his, and she laughs.

"I can't move," she says, and I loosen my grip just enough for her to reach out of the towel and hold it up herself.

"Okay, let's go," I say. "Bring the towels. I'll return them later."

"What's for supper?" Dylan asks, and I shrug. "Can we have the rest of the pizza?"

"Works for me," I say, thinking of the leftovers I was going to throw out.

"I want three slices," he says when we walk back into the apartment. I put the pizza in the oven to warm up and then look at Dylan.

"Go grab a shower," I say, and he nods, stopping to get an apple on his way to the shower.

"Do you want to shower before or after me?" Caroline asks me.

"Truthfully," I say, and she looks at me. "I want to shower with you."

She looks down and then shyly looks back up. "But I can go after you."

She walks to me and gets on her tippy toes. Her hands go on my waist. "I want to shower with you, too." She kisses the side of my lips and then walks away from me to my bedroom and then the shower. I make sure everything is set, and when Dylan comes out, I see he's wearing some of the new clothes I bought him.

"It'll be ready by the time I get out of the shower," I say, and he nods.

"Okay, I'm going to go watch television." He smiles at me. "I had fun today."

"Me, too, buddy," I say, and he stops.

"Mom never has fun," he says softly and then makes sure that his mom is not around. "She cries a lot at night." I want to tell him to stop, but he doesn't. "And I know that my dad took my stuff and sold it."

"You don't know that," I say to him, trying to defend his father.

"He takes anything that we have, which is why we don't have anything," he says. "He says he's going to get better."

"One day," I say. He just shrugs and walks away, and my heart breaks for the kid who wants his father, who knows his mother cries, and who just shared with me a secret that I won't be able to tell his mother.

THIRTY

CAROLINE

I LOOK AT the pile of clothes I now have, but I separate them into one pile of the clothes I'll wear, and the other of the clothes he will eventually return. Today with him and Dylan by the pool playing games, talking and getting to know him was everything.

Having not to think or worry or even care was something I don't think I've ever felt. I flip through the clothes, not even trying to imagine how much it cost him. Or that he actually called his sister and she did it, no questions asked. I try to ignore the fact that his family is going to be coming this weekend and I want to be out of his hair.

I slip on what has to be the soften cotton pants I've ever worn in my whole life with the matching shirt. I open the pink bag, and my hand pulls out one of the bras, and it's so delicate I'm afraid to touch it. "Are you done in the shower?" I hear Justin say from behind me, and I nod at him. "Dylan is watching television before we eat."

"Okay," I say, and he walks by me but then turns around and comes back to give me a kiss.

"You smell like me again," he says, and I am not going to tell him that I did it on purpose, taking his soap and lathering myself with it. He runs his nose along my neck. "You think he would notice if we took a shower together?"

"There is food involved," I say, and he laughs. "I'll get everything ready while you shower."

"Okay, sweetheart," he says and goes into the bathroom and closes the door. I don't even realize I'm smiling, and that it feels good.

I walk to the kitchen and look at the pizza in the oven, seeing it's almost done and seeing that there isn't that much. Which suits me just fine. I get the toaster out and then get the loaf of fresh white bread he has. "Is Justin done yet?" Dylan asks, coming into the kitchen, and I open my arms for him to give me a hug.

"You grew," I say, kissing his head and smelling the fresh scent he has now. "Soon you're going to be taller than me."

"Yeah, and then I can take care of you," he says, putting his head back. "And you won't have to worry anymore."

I push his hair back and try not to cry. "The only thing I worry about is you being happy," I say. "Nothing else matters."

"I like Justin," he says. "A lot."

"Yeah, he's pretty awesome," I whisper.

"Is it okay if I love him?" he asks in a soft, scared voice.

"Just because I love him doesn't mean I love my dad less."

"Baby," I say, and I blink away the tears, but one comes out. "The good thing about the heart is that it just grows with all the love you have."

"So it's okay if I love them both?" he asks, almost relieved.

"Yeah, it's more than okay if you love them both," I say, bending and kissing his nose.

"Okay, get the pizza ready." We both laugh when we hear Justin yelling as he walks into the kitchen and spots us.

"Are you guys that hungry?" He puts his hands on his hips. "That you are waiting in front of the oven."

I laugh at him, and Dylan drops his hand from me and shakes his head. I grab the oven mitt and take the pizza out of the oven, putting it on the square so I don't burn the counter. "Dig in, boys," I tell them and turn around to go slip two slices of bread in the toaster.

"What are you doing?" Justin asks me.

"I'm making myself dinner." I look over at him and open the pantry door and find my favorite, taking it out.

"You're eating toast for dinner?" He throws down his pizza and glares at me.

"No, I'm not eating toast for dinner," I say. "I'm eating peanut butter toast for dinner."

"That's not dinner." He glares at me, and I just shrug, turning around when my toast pops up and smearing peanut butter on it. "You can't just eat toast."

"Why not?" I ask, getting on the stool I always sit at, and it dawns on me that we have assigned seats.

"There is no meat," he says, chewing another bite. "It's toast."

"And it's my favorite," I say, taking a bite of the toast.

"It's gross," Dylan says while he chews. "I never want to eat it again."

I roll my eyes at him. There may have been a time or two that peanut butter and bread were the only things I could afford, and there may have been a time or two he hated it but ate it because there was nothing else to eat. "It's not gross."

"We ate it once for a whole month," he says, and I laugh.

"It was a week, and it was just for lunch," I say, and he shakes his head.

"You still need to eat something," Justin says, and I laugh.

"I'm still full from lunch," I say. "And this is what I want to eat." I point at the plate. "Now leave me alone or I'll eat your pizza," I say to Dylan who looks away.

For the rest of the meal, Dylan and Justin talk hockey, and when I'm done, I get up and start cleaning the kitchen. "Where is your vacuum?" I ask Justin, and he looks at me. "What?"

"You're not cleaning the house," he says almost as if I kicked him.

"I'm just going to pass the vacuum and maybe do the mopping," I say, and he shakes his head.

"The woman comes Monday and Friday," he says, and I look at him.

"What woman?" I ask him

"Cristine," he says. "Nice lady. She also does the laundry, and she buys the food."

"You have someone who does your laundry?" I ask him, although I don't know why I'm surprised.

"No," he says. "*We* have someone who does our laundry."

"Oh, no, buster," I say. "We do not. I do my own laundry, and I'll do yours, too."

"Sweetheart," he says, and whereas before, it made my stomach flutter, now I put my hands on my hips.

"Oh, no, don't you sweetheart me. If you want me to stay here, I will do the cleaning and the laundry." He glares at me. "And the cooking."

"Dylan, are you done?" Justin turns to him, and Dylan brushes his hands together. "Wash your hands."

"Okay, Justin," he says, getting off the stool and bringing his plate to the sink. "Can we watch a short movie?"

"Sure," I answer him, and he looks at Justin.

"You can choose." He smiles at him, and Justin smirks at first and then totally smiles. Dylan walks away, and Justin watches him, then turns to me.

"You are not cleaning my house nor are you doing my laundry," he says, and I cross my arms over my chest.

"Fine. I won't clean your house or do your laundry. But I will clean up after myself and my son in your house." I point at him. "And I'll do my laundry." I smirk now. "And if yours happen to fall in at the same time"—I raise my hands—"oh well." He glares at me. "I can't give you anything for having me and Dylan stay here. I can't even pay for the clothes you bought."

"I don't want you to give me anything," he says softly. "Just being here is all you need to give me."

"Can you just let me give you the only thing I can?" I ask. "You don't have to cancel your cleaning lady but let me just tidy things up if I can."

He put his hands on his hips and huffs out. "Fine, but no vacuuming or mopping."

I throw my hands up. "There is nothing left."

He just shrugs. "Well, then you can just relax and come and watch a show with us." He walks around the counter and kisses me. "Now let's go." He grabs my hand, and our fingers link together, and he kisses the tips of my fingers.

We walk to the back room, and I sit on the couch, curling my feet under me. Dylan comes to cuddle into my side. Justin gets on the other side of me, putting his arm around me and pulling us into him. We watch two episodes of a baking show, and when it's time for bed, Dylan is already half out of it. He kisses us both good night and slips into bed.

"Tomorrow," he says when he grabs my hand and we walk into his bedroom, "you can take the SUV to work, and I'll take the car." He walks over to what is now his side of the bed and pulls the covers back. "Get into bed, sweetheart." He smirks at me. "Gotta get back in the zone." I shake my head and go to the bed, and in fifteen minutes, my top is off, and we are lost in each other. We kiss until we are breathless, and I fall asleep again in his arms.

The morning routine feels like we've been doing this since the beginning, except when he slips out of bed at four to go work out and then comes back to shower and wakes me with kisses.

Nighttime comes with me usually getting there before them and starting to cook, which I love. Then sitting down and telling each other about our days. It may be just a little thing, but it's everything.

After I clean up, we end up in the pool where we stay

way later than we should. We create our own get to know you game, each one of us asking the other one what do you love more.

On Wednesday, I walk into work with a smile on my face that doesn't leave me the whole day, and when Cheryl comes in, she comments on how happy I look. "You've got that look," she says right before she walks out the door, and over her shoulder, she finishes her sentence. "The look of love. Have a great night." She waves her fingers in the air, and I sit here at my desk stunned. I just watch the door that she walked out of, and I'm not sure I heard her right. I can't have the look of love. I get up from my desk and go into the bathroom and look at myself in the mirror. The circles under my eyes are almost not there, my nose is a bit red from the sun because we've been in the pool since Sunday. Little tiny freckles are coming out on my cheeks. My hair is shiny, and it's also curled a little. I'm wearing a new blush pink T-shirt with white jeans and brown sandals. I touch my cheek, and I don't feel any different, but it's there, it's in my eyes. I put my hand to my stomach, and I suddenly feel sick.

"Am I in love?" I ask the mirror, and I don't know why I'm surprised when it doesn't answer me back. I knew I liked him; well, I knew I liked him a lot. I walk out of the bathroom and grab my purse to leave, and that night, he just looks at me, and when Dylan goes to bed, he stands in front of the bed.

"Sweetheart," he says my name, and I look up. I'm wearing another bedtime outfit. This one is shorts and a loose tank top. "Look at me."

"What?" I say, trying not to give him anything.

"What's going on with you?" he asks, and he stands there in his shorts that he always wears low on the hips, and I have the sudden urge to bite him. "You were quiet all night even in the pool."

"Nothing," I say, avoiding his eyes and slipping under the covers.

"Are you nervous that my parents are coming?" he asks, and I nod my head.

"Yes," I lie, hoping to throw him off.

"It's going to be fine," he says, coming to me. I also didn't tell him that I plan on going back to my house tomorrow. "By the way, I need your key."

"The key?" I ask him, confused.

"To your apartment," he says, and I look at him, blinking. "I have a crew going in this weekend to patch up all the holes."

"But," I start to say, "I was going to stay there."

"Yeah," he says, getting into bed. "And why did you think you would stay there?" He turns to me.

"Well, your family is coming, and ..." I start to say, and he pulls me to him, and my arms automatically go around him.

"And?" he says, leaning down and kissing my lips.

"And I was giving you some space with your family," I say.

"Well, it's a good thing that you won't be able to get into your place until the following week," he says with a smirk, and I have to wonder if he knew all along that I would try to make a run for it.

THIRTY ONE

JUSTIN

"*L*ET'S GO, BUDDY!" I yell down the hall toward the bedroom. Caroline comes out of the bedroom, and she looks like she's going to throw up. "You look beautiful." She is wearing a short-sleeved white dress with gray stripes and a matching belt around her tiny waist in a bow. She is wearing the brown sandals that she has been wearing for the past four days even though she now has twenty pairs of shoes. Because not only did Zara overdo it, but there has also been extra packages coming every single day.

"Yeah." She puts her hands to her stomach. "I really don't know what someone wears when they meet the family of the guy she's …"

"She's dating," I finish for her. "You're my woman." She glares at me. "Come here." I pull her to me, and she looks up at me. "Sweetheart."

"You guys with the kissing," Dylan says, walking past us.

"I'm getting a snack for the car."

"We leave in two!" I yell to him. "Now, tonight is going to be good." She doesn't even smile. "Great, amazing … they are going to love you."

"Yeah, yeah," she says softly, and we walk out together. She kisses Dylan on the top of the head and then leans up to kiss me. "Drive safely."

"You, too," I say, watching her get into the SUV and driving away. I get into the car and make my way to the arena, parking in my regular spot. "Let's go, buddy," I say, opening the back door for him, and we walk in together like we always do.

"See you on the ice," Dylan says, walking to his changing room, and I turn to see Ralph.

"Hey," I say to him, and he nods.

"You have some visitors." He motions over to the changing room, and when I enter, I see it overrun with the men in my family. Matthew and Max sit side by side, their hockey bags in front of them as they search through them. Evan and Viktor are sitting together on the other side, leaning with their backs to the wall and their eyes closed. Their hockey bags are not even open. Mini Cooper is sitting with Michael as he ties his skate. The kid has gotten so tall he might be past me now. My father sits on the bench by himself as he puts on his skates.

"You can't skate faster than me, Dad," mini Cooper tells Matthew. "You're old."

"I'm going to smoke you," Matthew says.

"He really is getting up there in age," Max says, and I laugh.

"What are you guys doing here?" I say, and my father looks up at me, and he smiles big. "Dylan!" I yell down the hall, and he sticks his head out of the room he's in. "Come here." I motion with my hand and wait for him to jog over.

"There he is," Evan says, finally opening his eyes.

"Buddy, I want you to meet my dad, Cooper." I point at my father, and he just smiles at him. "That's Matthew and Max. You know Evan and Viktor, and those two rats are my nephews, Michael and MC."

"Look at this kid," Matthew says, getting up and slapping my shoulder. "You look good," he says and then hits me in the stomach. "You look like you been eating doughnuts."

"You fuc-" I start to say, but then I catch myself. "You wish."

"That's Cooper Stone," Dylan whispers, and I smile, putting my hand on his shoulder. "Are you guys coming on the ice with us?" Dylan asks with his eyes big when everyone answers. "Cool," he says, then looks at me. "I'm going to go get ready."

"See you out there," I say, and I watch him walk out of the room.

My father now gets up and looks at MC and Michael. "Are you two ready to go?" He holds his helmet under his arm when they nod and get up, walking toward the ice. "You look good," he says, and I walk to him and give him a hug. "Looks good on you."

"Thanks, Dad," I say, and he walks toward the ice now. "You guys said you were coming in tonight."

"Yeah," Viktor says, opening his eyes now. "Then the chain texting started."

"Then plans started being made," Evan says. "And poof, we're packing up a day early. Now we are in a strange house, and baby Zoey is over it. She didn't get to sleep until five."

"Four thirty," Viktor says. "Then again at six."

"What are you talking about?" Evan says. "She's two months old, so that's her thing."

"How does a little thing have such deep lungs?" Viktor asks, and the guys laugh now. I sit on the bench and start getting ready.

"It's only starting," Evan says. "Wait until teething."

"Fucking horrible," Max says. "I swear I almost went bald on both sides of my head."

"So what's the story?" Matthew says, looking at me. "He yours?"

I just look at him. "Yeah, pretty much."

"Holy shit," Max says the same time Viktor holds out a hand for Evan to pay him money.

"I never thought I would see the day," Matthew says. "You with a kid."

"I used to babysit all the time," I tell them, putting on my skates.

"Yeah, to get the girls to come over and help you," Max says.

"Shut up," I tell them.

"How serious is this?" Viktor asks me.

"Very," I tell them even though we haven't had any conversations about it.

"She living with you?" Matthew asks me.

"Yeah," I say, and then I look up while he smirks and crosses his arms over his chest.

"You going to let her leave?" Max then asks.

"Nope," I say, and now Evan and Max moan.

"He's a fucking crazy like Matthew," Max says, shaking his head.

"No one is crazy like Matthew," Evan says.

"I bet you double or nothing," Viktor says. "He's a touch worse." He points at me.

I'm about to answer him when Michael comes into the room. "Dad, my leg hurts," he says to him, and I look at him. He's the same age as Dylan.

"Where?" he asks him.

"Where Alex hit me with the stick," he says, and Max shakes his head.

"You'll be fine," he says. "Go sit on the bench for a bit."

"What was that?" I ask Max.

"Alex was not happy when she was told it was boys only," Max says. "She took the hockey stick and slashed Michael with it."

"Oh my God," Evan says, putting his hand over his mouth to stop the laughing.

"Don't laugh," Max says. "Where do you think it comes from? Those Stone women."

"Okay, let's go," I say, getting up, and Viktor and Evan finally open their bag and get their things on. I walk out to the ice and see that Dylan is skating with MC. They both skate for the puck, and MC is a touch faster because he's taller.

"Bring the puck back!" my father yells and makes them, and Dylan lifts MC's stick, and just like that, he's skating down the ice toward my father.

"That yours?" Matthew asks from beside me, and I nod.

"That kid is going to make it."

"What?" I ask him.

"See the way he skates there?" He points at Dylan who skates as if he's gliding. "You can't teach that, and if you do, you get it when you're fourteen." He turns and looks back. "Max, check out the kid."

"Where?" Evan asks. "I have to go one-on-one with him."

"He's eight," I say, and Viktor just laughs. I look at them with their New York shirts.

"You couldn't just wear Stone Camp shirts?" I ask, and they all shake their heads.

"Assholes," I say and skate on the ice to my father.

"Hey, Dad," I say and then look in the corner where Dylan is fighting MC for the puck. He fakes right but then puts his stick between his own legs and knocks it away from MC, who just smirks at him as he shoots it in the net. I'm lucky that we had an empty ice this morning while all the other campers are on the other three rinks.

"That kid is ..." my father starts, and Matthew joins us.

"He's better than you guys were." He laughs and skates to Dylan, and he starts to tell him and point at him and then to the center of the ice.

"Come on, Dylan," Evan says, skating on the ice. "Let's see who's number one now."

Dylan smiles and spits out his mouth guard. "Justin is number one." He skates to me, and I put my hand on his head.

"Let's show them what we're made of, kid." I smile to him and skate to the middle of the ice. "Dylan and me against Evan and Michael."

"Let's go, Michael!" Evan yells.

"Uncle Evan, I don't want to," he moans, getting off the bench and coming over to us. "It's summer. Mom said I don't have to play hockey in the summer."

"You know Uncle Evan," MC starts to say. "Uncle Justin did score more points than you last year." He smirks and stands next to Matthew who just shakes his head. "Stats don't lie, right?"

"Could be but my numbers are still higher than M&M over there," he says and looks at me. "We doing this?"

"Yeah," Dylan says and gets into position. My father comes over and holds the puck in the middle of center ice, and Michael and Dylan both look at him.

He drops the puck, and Dylan is the first on it. He almost runs past Michael, who is skating behind him, and I look as Evan just smiles at him. "Let's see what you got, kid," Evan says, skating backward, and he looks at me and then I just nod at him. He tries to take the puck away from Dylan, but he turns his body and then goes around him, and all he can do is watch him skate to the goal and tip it in. The whole bench breaks out in laughter.

"I did it," Dylan says, skating to me. "I did it."

"You did, buddy," I say, holding up my gloved hand. "Okay now, let's go teach some kids," I say, and we get off ice one and walk over to ice two and three. We separate, and when it's lunchtime, we all gather upstairs for lunch. I look for Dylan, who is sitting with Michael, and they are laughing at something. "How great is this?" I say to the guys who look around.

"You are doing a good thing here," my father says. "All

301

these kids not having the chance to get on the ice, and you are paying for them to do all of this." I shrug.

"There are a couple that if they are given a free ride would just be out of this world," Matthew says.

"I have an idea for the Horton Foundation." Max says of the foundation that he started long ago. He works with the child's oncology department because his sister is a doctor there. Her stepson is a survivor, and she helped treat him.

"Yeah," Evan says. "I'd pitch in money to help kids."

"You guys are all copycats," I tell them, taking a bite of my chicken.

"But with all that said, it's a good thing."

"Your kid," Viktor says now, and I look over at him. He was quiet at first, and he took some time to come around. But after he went through his recovery and got with Zoe, he really blossomed and opened up. It was good to see. "He's got hands; he's got speed. If he had just a touch more height, he could even be three levels ahead. But it will come."

"His hands are insane," Evan says. "I was with him and the other kids his age. The kid didn't even look up when he is doing the drill, but he just stared straight and let the puck feel the stick."

I smile. "I taught him that," I say, and I look over at my father, who just smiles as he remembers teaching me the same thing. "He really is great," I say, my chest filling with this enormous pride that I didn't even know was there. I look over at him, and it just clicks into place. Everything was there. I knew that I liked what we had, and I knew that it was special. What I didn't know was that I would do whatever I needed to protect it. Now I just have to convince his mother.

THIRTY TWO

CAROLINE

$\mathcal{F}$OR THE WHOLE day, I am on pins and needles. I keep coming up with excuses on how to bail for tonight, but Dylan is with him. I pick up the phone no less than one hundred times an hour, phrasing a text, but in the end, I never send anything.

"You look like you are ready to crawl out of your skin," Cheryl says when she pokes her head into my office at two o'clock.

"Yeah," I mumble. "I'm meeting Justin's family tonight," I say, and she comes in smiling.

"How exciting." She sits down in one of the empty chairs. I look toward the window, seeing the sun outside shining.

"It's just ..." I start to say and she crosses her arms over her chest. She is wearing one of her long white flowy skirts with a bright pink top.

"It's just that you don't think that you fit in." She finishes the sentence for me. "You aren't worthy." She doesn't stop either. "That he deserves to have better."

"Pretty much." I lean back in the chair. My legs shake, and my fingers strum. "We are from two totally different worlds."

"See, that is where I think you're wrong," she says, and I look at her. "*You* are not that different. Do you smoke?" I shake my head. "Does he?" Again, I shake my head. "Do you do drugs?" I roll my eyes. "You see where I'm going with this."

"Okay, I'm not a drug addict," I start.

"You are in this place because you fell in love with a man," she says.

"I don't know if I ever really loved him," I tell her. "I was seventeen when I got pregnant, eighteen when I had Dylan. My parents kicked me out, and he took me in. How do you know what love is at that age?"

"Exactly." She raises her eyebrows. "You are a survivor. That is what you are. You are doing what you are doing for your child, which makes you just like everyone else in the world."

"Yeah," I say. "I'll remember that tonight when I look around and feel like I want the earth to swallow me up."

"You do that," she says, getting up. "See you Sunday."

"Have a great weekend, Cheryl," I say to her, and she walks out with her signature wiggling fingers in the air.

I close the computer and make my way back to the apartment. The phone rings right when I turn on the street, and I press accept on the Bluetooth. "Sweetheart."

"Hey," I say, the smile filling my face without me even knowing.

"Where are you?" he asks.

"Two minutes from your place," I say.

"Okay, I'll be there soon," he says. "See you soon, sweetheart."

I pull into the parking spot and then walk to the elevator. I'm about to press the button when I see his car coming into view. I stand here smiling, walking back to his parking space. He gets out, and his eyes fly to mine, the smirk going to a full smile. I look at the back, expecting Dylan to come out, but it's not Dylan. It's a man who looks exactly like Justin, and just like that, I feel like I'm going to vomit.

He looks at me and smiles, and then the door opens again from the front seat and another guy gets out, and he's just as tall as Justin with more muscle. Then I hear Dylan. "Mom, Mom!" He calls my name when he comes out of the car and runs over to me. "Guess what I did?"

I look down at my son radiating with happiness. His eyes are light and bright, his face with a light tan from spending so much time in the pool. "I beat Evan."

"Did you?" I ask, and he nods his head and looks over his shoulder at Justin. "Tell her."

"He did," he says as he comes to me, leaning down and kissing me on the lips. Then he stands next to me and puts his arm around my shoulder. "Sweetheart," he says. "I'd like you to meet my dad, Cooper, and my brother, Matthew."

I don't know how to greet them. Should I put my hand out to shake theirs or should I just nod and smile and wave? How does one greet the father of the man she's fallen in love with? "It's very nice to meet you," his father says, coming to me and giving me a hug. "You've got yourself an amazing young man," he says, and I have no words as he steps back and gives Matthew a chance to greet me.

"Great to finally meet you," Matthew says, coming in and giving me the same greeting as his father.

"Let's get upstairs," Justin says and grabs my hand, walking to the elevator.

"Can we go to the pool when everyone gets here?" Dylan asks. I look over at Justin, wondering who the fuck is everyone.

"Sure," Matthew says, looking down at his phone. "They just loaded up the cars and will be here in ten minutes," he says, looking up.

"I'll make sure I get food delivered," Justin says, taking out his phone. When the elevator doors open, we all get in.

Matthew and Justin are talking about what to order, and Cooper is talking to Dylan, and I'm trying to become as invisible as I can. When the elevator doors open, the boys walk out, and Justin slowly slides his fingers in mine. He leans over and whispers, "Relax." Dylan grabs the keys from Justin and opens the door for everyone.

"Are they almost here?" Dylan asks, and Matthew looks at his phone.

"Actually, they are parking right now," Matthew says, and I look over at Justin.

"Excuse me," I say to them and walk toward the bedrooms. I'm even shy to walk into Justin's room, knowing that his father knows where his room is. I'm in front of the bed when I feel him behind me. His arms going around my waist to stop me from walking.

"Sweetheart," he says soft and low. I close my eyes while

his front presses into my back, and my right hand comes up to hold the arm around my waist. "You have to relax."

"I don't know if I can do this," I say quietly and turn in his arms. "I don't think I've ever been this nervous in my whole life. It's just too much."

"It's going to be great," he says to me, leaning forward and giving me a soft kiss. "I promise you that it's going to be amazing, and if at any time you feel even a bit uncomfortable, all you have to do is tell me, and we can take a break."

"Justin, this is huge," I say finally. "Your family ... it's your whole world."

"Sweetheart," he says again softly and leans down to kiss me, and this time, I get lost in him. His tongue mixes with mine, and I swear my heart speeds up for a whole different reason. He pulls me even closer to him, and right when I turn my head to the other side to deepen the kiss, I hear Dylan.

"They are kissing again!" he yells over his shoulder, and Justin tries not to laugh as I hang my head forward. "Mom, come meet Justin's mom." He whispers, "She looks like a princess."

Justin smiles and kisses my forehead. "They are going to think we came into the room to make out." I close my eyes.

"You ready?" he asks, and I nod my head. "Let's do this."

I follow him out, and the whole place is overflowing with more people than I can count. "Well, well, well," a girl says. I look at her, and she has the most beautiful blue eyes. "Caught with your hand in the cookie jar," she jokes, and Justin shakes his head.

"This is Allison," Justin says, and a man comes up to her

and puts his arm around her shoulders. He's tall, and his black hair is folded over, and he is holding the hand of a little girl who looks exactly like her mother. "This is Max, her husband, and their daughter, Alex."

"It's so nice to finally meet you," Allison says, coming to me and taking me in her arms. Her husband smiles at me and nods, his arm never leaving her. "Why am I not surprised that you managed to snag the most beautiful woman I've ever seen?" she says to Justin and pushes his shoulder. "Michael!" she yells. "Come meet Dylan's mom." She turns to me. "I've heard nothing but Dylan, Dylan, Dylan since he came back."

"Hi," Michael says from beside Dylan, and he looks just like his father.

"Here." A woman comes over with strawberry blond hair and hands Justin a baby who just looks up at him. "Go see Uncle Justin."

"This," Justin says, cuddling the baby in his arms, "is Trouble number two or number one, depending on the day." The woman throws her head back and laughs, and I finally get that she is Zoe.

"It's so good to meet the one who has this one on his toes," she says, leaning forward and giving me a hug. "You are too pretty for him."

"Shut up," Justin says, and she gasps.

"Not in front of the baby," she says, and the little girl in Justin's arms just smiles at her. "Viktor," she says, looking over her shoulder, and a man comes forward, his brown eyes lighting up when he spots his daughter. "This is my husband, Viktor."

He reaches his hand out, and I shake his. "Nice to meet you," he says, smiling. "You did a good job with Dylan."

"Thank you," I say, and I swear my heart speeds up and my neck gets hot.

"Okay, where is Mom?" Justin asks, and Zoe looks around. "I think she's in the bathroom."

"There she is." The voice sounds familiar as I look over and see Zara. She takes me in her arms when she gets to me. "My favorite muse," she says. "I had the best time shopping."

I laugh now. "I really hope that you're done," I say. "I have more clothes than I know what to do with."

"Um, if I have a credit card," she says, "I put it to good use." I look over as the door opens, and Evan comes in with a little girl on his hip. She has the same hair as her mom, and it's up in little pigtails.

"Holy shit, that's his woman?" he says, looking at me and then looking at his wife who glares at him. "Sorry, sweet Zara."

"Barf," Justin says from beside me. I watch him rocking side to side, and the baby slowly falls asleep. He looks like he's done this before. He looks like he was born for this, and my heart suddenly clenches in my chest.

The door opens again, and in comes a woman who can only be described as a princess. Her hair is down and curled all down her back, and her green eyes are the perfect almond shape. Cooper walks over to her and leans down and kisses her lips. He says something to her, and she just smiles up at him, and you can feel the love they have for each other all around them. He puts his arm around her, and she looks around. When her eyes meet mine, she smiles, her whole face lighting up, and she walks over to us.

"There she is," Justin says with a huge smile on his face as he cuddles the sleeping baby in just one arm. "That's my mom," he says, and I look at the woman who made the man who has slowly made his way into my heart.

"You are so, so beautiful," she says. Taking me into her arms, she hugs me tight. "Look at her," she says, looking at Cooper. "She's stunning."

"Thank you," I say shyly and then look at Justin, who looks like a kid on Christmas morning.

"You did good, son," Cooper says with a smile. Justin puts his arm around me, pulling me to him, and kisses my head.

"Hit the jackpot," he says, and I know that this moment will also live with me forever along with the silent words I whispered to myself. *I love you.*

THIRTY THREE

JUSTIN

"*T*OMORROW NIGHT," MY mother says at the table, "we are going to have dinner at our place."

"The house is huge," Allison says. "The backyard has a pool and a treehouse."

The rest of the dinner is loud as expected with my family. I look over at Caroline, and she is deep in conversation with Allison and Karrie. "Don't fill her head with anything," I say, leaning over and kissing her neck.

Karrie shakes his head. "It's finally good to have another woman who has to deal with the crazy Stone men."

"Hey," Matthew says from beside her.

"Don't hey me," Karrie says and looks over at Caroline. "Has he used his soft voice to change your mind yet?"

Caroline opens her mouth. "He does call me sweetheart when he wants me to do things."

"That is not true," I say, laughing. "I call you sweetheart

because ..." Looking around the table, I wait for one of the other guys to chime in, but they all avoid eye contact. "I call her sweetheart because I want to."

Allison throws her head back and laughs. "You're one to talk, Angel." Matthew makes fun of her nickname.

"I call her angel because she is one," Max says, and I have to roll my eyes.

"You know he stole my sister," Matthew says to Caroline, and everyone just groans.

"I did," Max says. "Tossed her over my shoulder." He smiles and looks at Allison, who looks at him, pretending to be annoyed, but leans forward and kisses him. "Made her mine."

"That," Caroline says. "That is what you do." She points at me. "You get all annoying and then kiss me, and it's like a soft spot." I lean into her now, and her breath hitches.

"Your parents are watching," she whispers. "The whole table is looking."

"I don't care," I say, and kiss her once and then twice, and on the second one, she cups my cheek with her hand. "Still don't care."

"See," Karrie says. "It's the Stone charm or curse. You used to make fun of us all the time. Fake barfing in the corner. Now look at you, all smitten."

Everyone at the table laughs, and by the time everyone leaves, it's way past ten o'clock.

"Don't do anything I wouldn't do," Matthew says, looking at me.

"Yeah, like handcuff her to a bed." Max follows suit, and I push them out of the door with both of them laughing, and

Dylan is dragging himself.

"Do I have to take a shower tonight?" he moans, and I nod at him while Caroline loads the dishwasher.

"You were in the pool," I say. "Just go and rinse yourself off real fast, and then you can get into bed." He moans and turns around, walking to the bathroom.

"So ..." I put my hands on the counter on each side of her, and I move her hair to the side, exposing her neck for me to kiss. "That wasn't too bad." I spread kisses along her neck, softly moving all the way up to her ear.

"It was," she starts then turns her face to the side, and my lips kiss hers. "It was a lot."

"They can be a bit much." I give her more kisses.

"That is an understatement."

Dylan yells from his bedroom, "I'm going to bed!"

"Let's go to bed," I say, and she shakes her head.

"I'm going to load the dishwasher, then go shower," she says, and I kiss her neck one more time and go take a shower. I wait for her in bed, but my eyes give up. When my phone alarm goes off the next morning at four, I turn it off and turn to cuddle her in my arms until her alarm goes off.

"One more day," I say, and she looks at me with one eye open. "Our date. One more day."

I get out of bed while she stretches and go in search of coffee. I'm not even going to lie. My ass is dragging today, and it shows on the ice when the kids actually beat me. When I walk out of the arena that night and get in the car to get Caroline at home, I swear I could take a thirty-minute nap. When she gets into the car, she looks tired.

"I can't wait for tomorrow," she says, and I'm thinking that

317

she is talking about the date. "No alarm, no rush no work."

"You don't work at the hotel tomorrow?" I ask, and she shakes her head.

"No, it was a quiet week. They only have three rooms rented out," she says, and I nod.

When I walk into the backyard of my parents' rental holding Caroline's hand, it just feels good. Dylan runs over to the kids, and it's like he's been with them the whole time. He and Michael run over to the treehouse, and my mother comes over to us. "Hey, you two," she says, and I drop Caroline's hand to hug her. My mother hugs Caroline who just smiles and then looks at me, and I can see she still feels shy around Mom. We sit by the pool together talking, and at dinner, it gets louder when Vivienne, Karrie's best friend, walks in with her husband, Mark.

"Je suis arrive," *I have arrived*, she says, and the kids run over to her, especially Chase who she bends and takes in her arms blowing kisses in his neck.

"Ignore everything that she says," I whisper to Caroline right before Vivienne comes over.

"I have to say I always knew you would settle down with a model," she says, and Caroline looks around. "She is exquisite."

"Oh, I'm not a model," Caroline says, and Vivienne laughs.

"Well, you are doing the world a disservice then." She holds out her hand. "I'm Vivi." She smiles. "And that eye candy over there is my man." She winks at Caroline. "Cheri," she calls Mark, and he grabs the beer Matthew is handing to him and comes over. "Come meet Justin's girl." She looks over at Caroline. "I hope he's treating you well." Then she leans in and whispers, "In and out of the bedroom."

"Vivienne." I shake my head.

"Okay, fine, in the kitchen also. I mean, in the shower and the couch. Ooohhh," she says, "the car." Then she turns to call for Mark again.

He walks over, and she wraps her arms around his waist. She has been around since I can remember and never ever brought a man around. Then she finally caved, or he beat her down, we are not sure which. He smiles at Caroline as they share introductions, and then he walks away.

"Are all the guys in your family hot?" Caroline says, and I glare at her.

"I mean, you are the hottest." She's laughing, and I grab her and kiss her hard, sliding my tongue into her mouth, and she pushes me away. "Don't you dare in front of your family."

"But you're mine," I say, and she crosses her arms over her chest. "Sweetheart."

"Don't you sweetheart me," she says, and she walks away from me. I put my hand in my pocket, trying to make my cock go down, and my father comes over.

"What did you do?" he asks, laughing

"I stuck my tongue in her mouth," I say, and he shakes his head.

"She's a great girl." I look at him. "Raised a great son."

"She did," I say, and we watch Dylan.

"I just ..." he starts to say. "It's not just her you have to think about, son."

"I know," I say, holding my breath and trying not to imagine my life without her in it.

"Do you think that maybe you rushed things a bit?" I look

at him, and for the first time, I turn to look at my father with anger. Sure, I got mad at him as a teenager, but this is different.

"Were you sure about Mom three days in?" I ask him, and he looks over at me.

"I'm not the enemy," he says.

"She's the one," I say, shrugging. "I don't know why, and I can't explain it. But I know."

He nods his head. "As long as you know what you're doing."

"I wouldn't make her meet my family and move in with me if I wasn't a hundred percent in this."

"Cooper." My mother calls him, and he walks away. I stand here with my heart racing, and my stomach full of nerves. I try not to let it get to me, and I bury it for now, but I know that I'm going to have to sit down with my parents and squash whatever doubts they have.

After dinner, I'm looking for Dylan, and he runs over to me.

"Can Michael sleep over?" he asks, and I look at Caroline, who just watches me.

"Sure," I say.

"Can we sleep in the game room and do a fort?" he asks, and I shake my head.

"You can sleep in the game room but no fort." It scared him the last time, and I can't handle that again.

"Mom!" Michael yells, and Allison looks over. "I'm sleeping at Uncle Justin's with Dylan."

"Whatever," she says, and I have to say this, this right here is what my family is. We trust each other with everything we have. "I'll take them tomorrow."

That night, Caroline is on pins and needles, and she gets up every hour to check on them and make sure they are okay. "Sweetheart," I say after the tenth time, "if they need you, they will call."

"But," she starts to say, and I pull her tighter against me. "He's never had a friend sleep over."

"Sweetheart," I say. Rolling her to her back, she opens her legs for me, and I lean down and kiss her.

"We are not even dropping the puck, Stone," she says. "Can you imagine Michael catching us?"

"Chances are, he'll know exactly what we're doing. He caught his parents in the act two or three years ago."

"Oh my God," she says, and I bury my face in her neck and turn to the side. It takes her a while, but she finally falls asleep.

"Are you sure you have everything?" Caroline asks Dylan for the tenth time, and he looks at me for help.

"Mom, I have everything, and if I need anything, I'm going to ask Allison or Max," he says.

"You can call whenever you want," Max says by the door.

"We are going to pick him up at around ten," Caroline says and then looks at Dylan. "We have church."

"Kiss your mom," I say, and he comes over and hugs her around the waist, and she whispers to him. Then he walks to Michael, and they walk out with Max looking at us.

"I'll send you texts," he says and looks at Caroline. "It'll be okay." Then he leans in and pretends to whisper, "I'd feel bad, too, if I had to be alone with Justin."

I push his shoulder while Caroline laughs. "Get out." Shoving him out the door, I can still hear the sound of his laughter through the door after I slam it shut.

"What are the chances that we don't go out for a date?" Caroline asks, and I see her fidgeting with her fingers.

"Zero," I say. "Go get ready."

"But ..." she starts to say.

"But nothing. Go get dressed. I'll use Dylan's shower," I tell her. "Be ready in an hour."

"Now that Dylan is gone, we can shower together." She tries not to laugh, but she sees me glare, and the laughter escapes her mouth. She turns and walks to my bathroom and closes the door.

I feel so nervous when I grab my things and go to the other bedroom and get ready. I'm fastening the button on my right wrist when she comes in the room, and I stop what I'm doing. She's wearing the white lace dress, and it's long sleeves. Her hair is tied up on top of her head in a ponytail. The dress goes until her mid-thigh and then flares out just a touch with a ruffle. "Can you zip me?" she asks, and I look at the rest of the dress. It goes high to her neck, the lace playing peekaboo with her skin. She turns, and I see that she isn't wearing a bra, her skin a soft tan. I lean forward and kiss the back of her neck and slowly zip her up and then put my hands on her hips. She turns around in my arms. "You look so hot."

She smirks, and I look at her, seeing that the dress goes tight at her waist a bit, showing off her hips.

"You're stunning," I say and lean to kiss her again.

"I'll be ready as soon as I put my heels on." She smiles. "You might have to hold me up." Laughing, she walks out of the room.

"Forever," I say quietly to the empty room. I adjust my hard-on now and run my hands through my hair. Going into my bedroom to get my belt, I find her sitting on the bed, leaning forward to tie the strap around her ankle. I grab my brown belt and shoes, putting on the matching blue jacket and pulling out the cuffs.

"I'm ready," she says, and I turn to see that the heels are white. A strap around her toes and another around her ankle. Her legs look longer than ever. "So where are we going?"

"It's a surprise," I say, and I'm suddenly afraid she is going to hate this surprise. I grab her hand, and we walk out of the apartment with her holding my one hand with both of hers. When we get into the garage, I walk over to the red sports car. She stops walking. "What's the matter?"

"Can we not take the flashy car?"

"What, why?" I look from her to the car.

"Don't take this the wrong way," she says, "but this is a big deal to me. I've never gone on a date, and my first date is with Justin Stone."

I try not to laugh. "And I know people are going to look at us tonight, which I'm still not okay with, but it is what it is." She looks down. "Just, can we not draw more attention to ourselves?"

"We can take the BMW," I say, walking over to the car and opening the door for her. She turns around before getting in.

"I know that we haven't even left yet …" She looks down and then up again. I can see her hands shaking. "But this is the best date I've ever had."

I put one hand on her hip and pull her to me while the other hand goes to cup her cheek. "It's just the beginning."

THIRTYFOUR

CAROLINE

"IT'S JUST THE beginning." His words hit me straight in the heart. My stomach flutters, and my knees almost get weak as his voice goes lower. He leans forward, and I finally kiss him. I've been dying to kiss him since I walked into the bathroom and asked him to zip me up.

He stood there in his blue pants and white dress shirt, and everything fit him like a glove, and all I wanted to do was unbutton his shirt one button at a time and just stay in. I wanted to just be with him, but here I am, getting ready to go out, wearing a dress that is so soft on my body and probably cost as much as my rent for six months. I'm not even going to think about how much the shoes cost.

"If we don't get in the car now, this date is going to go from us going out to me carrying you back upstairs," he says, kissing me again, and my mouth opens for him. My hand goes to his waist as I hold his jacket that feels like silk in my hand.

"I, for one, will not say no," I say, and he looks at me. "I know that you want to take me out. I know that you want to give me this." I lean in now and kiss his neck right inside the open collar of his shirt. "But this, just being with you, is"—I shrug—"well, it's everything."

"If you could plan this date, what would you want?" he asks, and I get even closer to him. His hand falls from my face and wraps around my waist.

"You won't be mad?" I ask him, and he shakes his head. "Well, it would be me and you." I look up, and our eyes meet. "Your bed." I look down. "And lots of penalty shots." The hockey lingo comes out as I try not to sound like a horny girl who just wants him for sex.

"So if I understand this …" he says, "you want to spend the night in bed with me?"

"Yes," I finally whisper while my heart beats so hard in my chest that I'm sure he could probably hear it. My mouth is dry, and it feels like I have sand in the back of my throat.

"You won't feel like I'm treating you like a—" I put a finger to his mouth to stop him from talking.

"I'll feel like you want to spend time with me. I'll feel like you want me all to yourself, and I'll feel more special than if you take me out to show me off." I swallow now, and it's almost as if I have a lump in my throat.

His hand falls away from me, and I suddenly want to kick myself for being so open. I should have just gone with him and had the romantic dinner that he probably spent a lot of time planning. He takes my hand, and I'm waiting for him to open the door, but instead, he walks back to the elevator.

But he's not walking slowly; he's almost speed walking, and it's taking all my concentration to keep up with him and not fall on my face. The elevator somehow opens as soon as he presses the button. He walks in and presses the button for his floor, and then he turns and presses me into the wall. "I promise you that we'll do all the hearts and flowers date soon."

I take a deep breath, and the ping of the elevator makes us both look at the door as it opens on his floor. He moves away from me and lets me walk out, and when I get to his door, he takes the lead. He grabs me by the hips and turns me around, scooting down so we are at eye level.

"Everything," he says right before he takes my mouth in a hungry kiss. One hand grabs the handle of the door, and when it opens, we stumble inside, our mouths never leaving each other. My hands peel his jacket from his shoulders, and he presses me into the wall by the front door. He lets go of my lips the same time his hands go to my hips, and he slowly raises the skirt while he kisses me right behind my ear where he knows it makes me shiver. I moan, closing my eyes, and just take in his hands on my bare legs and his tongue sucking in while he takes little nips of my earlobe. My hand pulls his shirt out of his pants, and I think I'm panting, or maybe it's just echoing in my ears. His hand goes around my waist, and he carries me to the wall next to his bedroom, and his cock is right where I want it. Except too many layers of clothes are between us.

"Too much," I say, and he stops and looks at me. His eyes almost looking black. "Too much clothes," I say. He puts one hand on the back of my head and pulls me to him, nipping my bottom lip, and when I gasp, his tongue enters my mouth. My hands slowly work on the buttons, and the kiss gets rougher. It's all tongue, teeth, and hands.

He unzips my dress, the sound lost in the heavy pants of our breath. He peels the dress from my shoulders at the same time I push his shirt off him. His mouth goes to one of my nipples while the dress hangs on my hips. My back arches off the wall, and he picks me up. While he bites my nipple, he walks to his room. I swear I'm about to have an orgasm, and the only thing he's touched are my breasts.

He walks into his room, kicking off his shoes, and then he places me down on my feet, and I wobble on the heels. I wish I could kick them off. I want to kick them off, but he looks at me.

"I had this whole thing planned," he says, his hand coming up, and his thumb rubs over my lips. "Wine and dine and then take you to bed." I want to roll my eyes and groan. "I want to take my time with you." His voice is low, and just the way he says it fills my body with goose bumps. His hand moves down to my pebbled nipple, rubbing it. He puts his thumb into his mouth and then rubs my nipple again, and I swear my eyes want to roll in the back of my head. "I'm going to take my time with you," he says, "but not this time."

"Justin," I whisper or pant out his name.

"It's going to be fast," he says as his hands push the dress down over my hips, leaving me in the white lace thong that I slipped into after the shower. "It's going to be hard," he says, looking down at me. "And it's probably going to be faster than we both want." I take a deep inhale as I watch him unbuckle his belt. "But that is only going to be round one." His pants fall from his waist, and he's standing there in black Calvin Klein boxers. His cock is hard and ready, and I hold my breath as he peels them down, and I finally see him naked. His cock is huge and perfect, and I want to touch it. My hand comes out, and I fist it in my palm, and now it's his turn to hiss. I move my hand up and down once and then another time before he is suddenly not in my hand anymore. Instead, he is on his knees in front of me, pulling my panties to the side while his mouth devours me. He pulls my clit into this mouth, and I have to hold on to his shoulder or I'll fall over. "Fucking perfect," he says right before his tongue fucks me.

"I can't," I say, and I don't know what I'm saying or asking for. His fingers are now inside me, and my hips move on their own. "Justin," I say right before he moans into my pussy, and I come on his fingers and tongue. I shiver the whole time, my nails for sure ripping the skin on his shoulder. He waits until I'm stable and then comes up and kisses me, and I taste myself on him.

He unties one ankle strap and then the other. "Lie back and open up for me," he says, going to the side table where I know he has his condoms. He grabs one and comes back to me, my eyes never leaving him. His perfect body, his arms that are defined all the way to the side muscles on his hips. I sit up now when he gets closer, and I'm finally able to bite that side hip that I've been dreaming of doing. He hisses, and I move my head just a touch and cover his cock with my mouth. I devour his cock as much as I can. My hand comes up to hold him and he lets me for less than a minute. "I'm not coming in your mouth," he says. "First time, I come in you." He opens the condom wrapper. "Now lie back and spread your legs for me." I lie back, my eyes on his as he slides the condom down his cock, and he puts one knee on the bed. "I'll buy you another pair," he says, and I am so mesmerized with him that I don't know what he's saying before he tears my panties off in one move.

"Spread your legs for me." I open my legs wider for him, and when he crawls to me with his cock in his hand, I don't move, I don't breathe, I don't even think I blink. "I've been waiting for you," he says, rubbing his cock up and down my slit, "for what seems like forever." He places his cock at my entrance, trying to control himself. "Everything has led to this one moment with you." He looks down at his cock, and I look with him as his cock slowly enters me.

"I love you," I say without even realizing the words have left my mouth, and his head snaps up to look at me.

"I've loved you for what seems my whole life," he says, and with one firm thrust, he buries himself in me. His arms come to the side of my head. "I love you," he says again, and a lone tear escapes the side of my eye and rolls to the covers. "Love you forever," he says, and he makes love to me.

"I'm yours." I arch my back and lock my ankles around his back. "Don't hold back. Show me," I egg him on.

His arms hold him up beside my shoulders, and he spreads his knees, pulling out of me only to pound back in hard. So hard my legs unhook and fall to his hips. He does it again, over and over, and my hands now hold his arms as I groan.

"I'm almost there," I say, trying to swallow. He leans down and buries his face in my neck. He fucks me so hard, the only noise in the room is the sound of our skin slapping together, and I want more. "Harder," I say, and he gets up on one arm and moves one of my legs over his shoulder. With this angle, I swear he's going to tear me open. "Right there," I say, and he gets up on his knees, his cock never stopping. Putting his thumb into his mouth, he licks it, and I take turns watching his cock disappear into me and him sucking on his thumb. Then his thumb is moving to my clit, and he rubs it in little circles. "Oh, God," I say, and I want to grab him by the hips and dig my nails into him and just make him not move.

"Fuck," he says, "you got to get there." His thumb moves faster. "Your pussy is choking my cock," he says. "Fuck, get there," he says, hissing and I do. I get there at the same time as he pounds into me two more times before he roars out his release.

THIRTYFIVE

JUSTIN

"*T*HE WATER IS cold," Caroline says as she sits on me in the bath, my cock still in her. "But I'm too tired to move," she says, putting her head on my shoulder. When I get up, she tightens her legs around my waist, and I laugh.

"Sweetheart," I say, getting out of the tub, and the water is slashing everywhere. I grab a white towel and throw it over her and rub my feet on the mat before walking to the bed and seeing her shoes tossed beside the bed next to her torn panties and her dress right in the middle next to the bed. My pants, shoes, and socks are right next to it. I pull her off me and put her on the bed. Little red marks are all over her from the bites I've given her along with little dots from my beard between her legs.

"I just need a minute," she says and rolls to her side. I laugh, walking back into the bathroom and taking off the sixth condom we've used in four hours. I grab a pair of boxers and walk back into the room, hearing her soft snores. I check to see it's only eight thirty, so I grab my phone and call Max.

"If you are calling me at eight thirty, I'm assuming you struck out," he says, laughing.

"I'm calling to check on Dylan," I say. "Is he okay?"

"Yeah, he and Michael are like two peas in a pod. We haven't heard from them since they came in except when they were starving." He laughs. "Wait, your sister is pulling my …"

"Why are you calling us?" she hisses. "You don't take a girl out on a date and then use the phone. That's rude."

"We're home," I say, and she moans.

"Oh my God, Justin. Do I need to have the whole you need to wine and dine conversation with you?"

"You can please spare me the dating dos and don'ts. You got married at twenty-one." I laugh and grab a bottle of water. "Can I please talk to Dylan?"

"We're coming to church," she says. "Everyone is going to meet at your house at ten, and we can go together."

"Um …" I say. I'm not sure what to say or how Caroline is going to react. "Okay."

"Dylan!" I hear Allison yell. "Phone."

"Hey." He comes to the phone.

"Hey, buddy," I say, smiling and suddenly missing him. "Everything okay?" I ask, and he goes on and on about all the games he's played, and how they did stick handling and scoring on Evan twice. "Okay, if you want to come home tonight, all you have to do is call."

"See you tomorrow," he says and hangs up. I pick up my jacket and walk back to the bedroom, and she turns her head when I walk in and then stretches.

"I'm hungry," she says, and I laugh. "Are you going to feed me?" She looks at me up and down. "Why are you dressed?"

"What do you want to eat?" I ask and walk to the bed and sit beside her. "I can get naked if you like."

"Yes." She cranes her head to me, and I kiss her. "But first food." I laugh and get out of bed, warming up some of the leftovers from yesterday, and she walks into the kitchen wearing my dress shirt. Only one button fastened. We eat side by side on the stool, and when we finish, she gets up to clean.

One thing leads to another, and by the time we are done, I'm fucking her on my counter. Every single time I think it won't get better, it does. She blows my mind. She asks for what she wants and takes it also. When we finally fall asleep, it's with her draped all over me, and in the morning, I wake with my cock buried in her mouth.

"What time is everyone coming over?" she asks, sitting on the stool wearing a robe.

I look over at the clock. "In about ten minutes," I say, and she freaks out.

"We had sex ten minutes ago," she reminds me, and she really doesn't have to since I'm still half hard. "They are going to know."

"How?" I laugh, and she shakes her head and goes into the bedroom.

"It's a glow," she says over her shoulder, grabbing a pair of panties and getting dressed in front of me. I grab a pair of blue shorts and a white polo shirt.

She pulls the long dress over her head, and I look at her.

How can one girl make a cotton dress look so sexy? It has short sleeves with white and black lines across her chest. Going tight until her waist and then flowing down with the black lines going downward. She slips on the brown sandals. I walk to her and take her in my arms. "No." She pushes me away. "I already have the glow."

I laugh when I hear Dylan. "Mom, Justin, I'm home."

He comes in and hugs first Caroline and then me. "Go get changed," I say, and I walk out of the room and see that my whole family is coming into the apartment. "Hey."

"Hi," my mother says, coming to me. "I hope it's okay that we come to church with you guys."

"Yeah," I say and feel Caroline beside me. "Did you guys make plans for after church?"

"Yes," my father says, coming and smiling at us. "We have a caterer already setting up at our rental."

"Perfect," I say, and it takes a full twenty minutes to get everyone in the car, and when we arrive, I look over at Caroline. "Do you think the church is ready for us?"

"There is no one ready for you guys," she says, smiling and getting out of the car. Opening the back door, she waits for Dylan to get out. I stand by my car with my hand around Caroline and one on Dylan's shoulder. The trucks come and I swear if you count it might even get to fifty.

Caroline looks down, and I feel her stiffen beside me. "What's the matter?"

She looks around. "This isn't the best area." She blinks now, and what started as a great morning is quickly turning downhill.

"My family doesn't care about that," I say and lean down

to kiss her.

"Let's go," Matthew says to Karrie, holding her hand and then the kids walk in front of them. Max and Allison are right behind them with Alex holding her father's hand. Zara and Zoe walk together with Viktor, and Evan's right behind them holding the kids. Vivienne is chatting with Mark and laughing.

My parents walk with us toward the church. The minute I take a step on the sidewalk, I hear Dylan's name being called, and my neck suddenly burns.

"Dylan!" Andrew yells his name from the side of the church and waves his hand in the air, and I stop in my tracks because Caroline starts to shake beside me.

"Oh my God," Caroline whispers. Andrew walks over to us, and you can tell he's high as fuck. His jeans are hanging on his hips and have brown stains down the front of them. His once white shirt is two sizes too big, and looks yellow. His hair is stringy and so dirty it's matted to his head. His eyes are so dilated they look almost black. His nails have dirt in them, and the sores on his arms are very apparent.

"Dylan," he calls him, but Dylan doesn't move from beside me. Everyone around us stops walking, and you can hear a pin drop. "What the fuck, Caroline?" he shouts when he gets close enough. "Are you trying to keep my son from me?" he hisses when he stands in front of her, and I notice that he's wearing two different shoes, and one is three sizes bigger than the other.

I move myself in front of Caroline when I feel that he's getting too close to her for my liking, and I suddenly feel Matthew at my side. "What the fuck do you think you're doing?" he spews to me. "Trying to keep me from my kid?"

"Caroline," I say, my eyes never leaving his. "Go inside."

I look to the side at her and see she has tears streaming down her cheeks, and my mother is now by her side along with Karrie. Allison, Zoe, Zara, and Vivienne are trying to usher the kids away from this scene.

"Andrew," Caroline finally says, shaking her head. "Not here."

"Fuck you!" he shouts at her. "Fuck you and your perfect little attitude!" My blood is boiling, my hands shaking with anger.

"Dylan," Caroline says, "let's get into church." She turns and leads Dylan away, who has his own tears rolling down his chin. He walks with his mother toward the church when Andrew jumps and shouts at them.

"Don't you take him away from me." Andrew tries to get to them, but I step in front of him, and he pushes my shoulder. "Fuck you, man." His body odor is almost unbearable.

"She doesn't want to see you," I say, and he just leers at me as he watches Caroline walk up the steps to the church. Allison stands beside her, and my mother has her arm around Dylan's shoulders as she looks back at the scene.

"Fuck you!" he yells at the top of his lungs, jumping up and down and punching the air. "You ruined my fucking life!" he yells louder, not caring that he's making a scene and everyone is watching him. "Get your fucking ass back here, you fucking bitch." He jumps up and down again, trying to get to them, but we aren't letting him anywhere near them.

"Enough!" I yell, and my father grabs one of my arms to pull me back as I advance on him.

"Fuck you, man!" He looks at me and stands straight. "I'll fucking kill you, man, and you won't even know what is happening." He smirks at me and pretends to come at me, then turns back and yells right before Caroline steps foot in the church. "Get back here, you fucking bitch! You ruined my life!" he spews, this time spitting everywhere. Caroline and Dylan just look at him. "You and that fucking piece of shit kid you forced me to have."

Everything happens so fast that I don't even realize it's happening. But my hand just flies up out of reflex, gripping him by his neck and stopping him from speaking or breathing. He sputters, and his hands go to his throat on top of mine as I squeeze without even thinking twice.

Matthew pounces, yelling my name. "Justin!"

"Justin!" Caroline yells from the top of the stairs. Allison holds her hand to stop her from running to me.

At the same time, my father grabs me. "Justin, let him go," he says in my ear, and Max and Viktor are beside us.

"You stay away from them," I say, and he just tries to get my hand to loosen from around his neck. "Fucking far away from them." I finally let go, and he coughs as he tries to catch his breath. His scrawny hands go to his throat.

"You are going to be sorry about this," he says, turning away. "More than you know."

"Get away from here," Viktor says. "Do yourself a favor, man, and don't make your son see you like this."

"Fuck you!" Andrew says. "Fuck all y'all!" He laughs and then turns to look at Caroline, who is holding Dylan while he sobs. "And fuck you two!" He puts up his middle fingers and then smiles, showing off rotten teeth. "I'll see you soon," he says and motions with his hand a gun shooting me. "Sooner than you think." He turns to walk away, and I push through everyone to run to Caroline and Dylan.

She finally lets go when she's in my arms and sobs out. Father Rolly steps outside with us. "You should take her home," he says and then looks at her. "You go home and take care of yourself." Then he looks at me. "It's about time she found someone who is going to carry her instead of bury her."

My eyes follow Andrew as he walks away from us, and I look to my side as my father holds my mother in his arms. "Let's get out of here."

ThirtySix

Caroline

*W*HAT STARTED AS one of the best days of my life turned so violently to the worst. All I can hear is Andrew yelling for Dylan. At first, I thought I was having a nightmare, but then I saw him walking toward us, his hands going everywhere, and I knew he was high. I've been around him long enough to know when he's at the top of his high. And it was now, and there was no way I could shield Dylan from this. He stands beside me, and I swear I can feel him shaking.

My heart stops as he starts swearing, and I'm ready to just bolt into the church and shield Dylan from this. But it's almost as if it happens in slow motion or maybe it's just me having an out of body type of experience. Then his words hit me straight in the heart, not because I care, I've heard him say this every single time, but because Dylan is here and he's watching and listening to every single word. "You ruined my life." I hold Dylan in my arms, and I'm about to tell him to ignore him. "You and that fucking piece of shit kid you forced me to have."

He sobs out this time, and everything after that just happens so fast. Justin's arm shoots out to grab Andrew by the throat, and I'm screaming for him. He finally comes to me and takes me in his arms. My knees give out, and I don't know if I'm walking or being carried to the car.

"You aren't driving anywhere," Matthew says to Justin. "You need to take care of your woman and kid, man," he says, and we are all put in the back seat of a truck, and Matthew gets into the front seat with Cooper beside him.

"I'm so sorry he said that," Justin says from beside me, and then he leans over and puts his hand on Dylan. "It's going to be okay, buddy."

He pulls me into his arms, and I try to be strong, try not to have Dylan see me cry, but I can't help it. My heart hurts that he had to hear all that. That he has even one doubt that he is loved. I quietly sob in my hand, trying not to make too much noise, and the only thing I can hear is Justin's soothing words. "It's going to be okay."

We get back to Justin's place, and when Cooper gets out of the truck, he opens the back door and grabs Dylan, holding his hand until Justin is there beside him and he reaches his hand up so Justin picks him up. "It's going to be okay."

Cooper's phone rings, and then he looks at Matthew. "Do they bring the food over?"

"I don't think it's a good idea," he says, and he has this conversation as if we aren't here. "Maybe have Michael come over so he doesn't have to think about anything."

Cooper gets back on the phone, and I suddenly just need to lie down. My head is almost spinning. "I need to lie down," I tell Justin, who just nods his head. When we get into the house, I walk straight to the bedroom, and Dylan follows us. "I think I'm going to be sick." I put my hand to my stomach, and I make it to the bathroom just in time before everything comes out, and I hear Dylan start to cry again.

"She's going to be okay, buddy." I hear Matthew say. "Justin would never let anything happen to her," he says, and then the door closes, and Justin is there behind me, holding out a cold rag.

"Sweetheart," he says softly, squatting in front of me.

"I'm so sorry," I say, the tears flowing now as I look at him. "I'm so sorry I brought this to you, and that your family had to see that."

"You have nothing," he says quietly, "nothing to be sorry about."

"Dylan," I say right before the sob rips through me, and I put my hand in front of my mouth so he doesn't hear. "I never wanted him to hear that. Ever."

"Sweetheart," he says, taking me in his arms and sitting on the floor. "Please stop." We sit here until my sobbing stops, and my eyes feel so heavy it hurts to have them open.

"I don't think he means it," I say. "I mean, the bitch part he means, but the part about Dylan."

"Shh," Justin says. "The last thing you need to do is make excuses for him."

I get up now. "Dylan," I say his name, and Justin gets up, and we walk out of the room and see that Matthew and Cooper are in the living room talking in whispers. "I'm going

347

to check on him."

"Okay," Justin says. "I'll be right in." He kisses my lips, and I walk to the game room. Dylan is lying on the couch with the television off, just looking at the wall.

"Baby," I say, sitting beside him and rubbing his head. "Are you okay?"

"He hates me," he says the words I never wanted him to say. "He called me a piece of shit."

"He …" I start to make excuses for him, and then I stop. "He's sick."

"No, he's mean, and a bad person, Mom," he says to me. "You don't treat the people you love like that."

"You're right," I say. "I don't want you to ever have to doubt how much I love you."

He looks at me, my little boy who is turning into a man before my eyes. "I know, Mom."

I sit on the couch next to him with my feet under me, and we fall asleep. I don't even know how long I'm sleeping, but the doorbell rings, and we both jump up, running to see who it is. Both of us hoping that Andrew didn't follow us here.

I walk into the living room and see that Justin's mom, Parker, is now here, but it's the two police officers that draw my eyes. "Justin," Matthew says, coming into the room behind them.

"How can I help you?" Justin says, and his eyes fly to mine. My heart starts to beat faster than normal, and I think I'm going to have a heart attack. Dylan runs from beside me to stand next to Justin.

"We are sorry to be doing this," one of the cops says, "but

348

we have no choice."

"Do what?" Cooper asks, and if I thought I was going to die before, nothing prepares me for what is about to happen.

"Justin Stone, there is a warrant for your arrest for the assault on Andrew Woods," the officer says, and I feel like the floor is moving. My head is spinning, and I can't control it. "We are going to have to cuff you," the officer says.

"Seriously?" Matthew says. "In front of his kid." Dylan stands in front of him crying, and there is suddenly screaming. Someone is screaming, and the floor is coming closer and closer to me as my knees suddenly buckle, and I hear Justin yell.

"Matthew, Caroline," he says, and Matthew catches me right before I hit the floor, and the screaming stops. I suddenly realize that the screaming was coming from me.

"You can't take him!" I say to the officers, trying to get out of Matthew's hold. "Get off me!" I scream at him. "You can't take him!"

"Don't say a fucking word," Cooper says to Justin. "Not a peep."

"I want my lawyer," Justin says right before the clicking of the handcuffs fills the room. "Sweetheart, I'll be back."

"You can't take him!" I yell at them and fight to get free. "You can't take him! He didn't do anything!" I sob and fight to get to him, to hold him, to kiss him one last time. "Please," I plead with everyone around me. "Please don't take him." I finally collapse in Matthew's arms while Parker holds Dylan, whose sobs now echo mine.

"Justin!" Dylan yells his name.

"It's going to be okay, buddy." He looks at Dylan. "I need you to be strong for your mom," he says, and Dylan breaks free from Parker and throws himself at Justin, hugging him around the waist. "It's going to be okay."

"Don't let them take you," Dylan pleads while he sobs and shakes. "Don't take him." He pleads with the officer who just looks down.

Cooper makes his way over to Dylan and has to peel him off Justin, who just yells for Justin as he's pulled away and led out of the apartment. Cooper hands Dylan to Parker.

"Get over here now." I hear Matthew say to someone as he holds the phone to his ear, and Cooper runs out of the apartment, following Justin as he is led off.

"I ruined him," I say to Matthew. "Everything is my fault."

"No, it's not," he says. "You have to be strong for Dylan." I look over at my son as Parker whispers to him, and he sobs out, calling for Justin.

"Baby," I say to Dylan, and he comes over to me. Matthew finally lets go of me, and Dylan crashes into me and the both of us sob in each other's arms. Matthew is on the phone nonstop. The front door opens, and both of us look, hoping it's Justin, but it's just Max and Allison, who has her own tears running down her face.

"Go," she tells Matthew. "Take Mom." Parker gets up and looks over at me, her eyes with her own tears, and I swear I can almost hear her say she's sorry. She rushes out of the apartment with Matthew at her side.

"Where is he?" I ask them, and Max comes to sit beside us, and the door opens again, and this time, Viktor walks in.

"They are taking him in," Max says. "We just heard it on

SportsCenter."

"Oh my God," I say, putting my hand to my stomach. "I'm going to be sick," I say, turning and running into the bathroom. Whatever is left inside me comes out, and I close my eyes and vow to make it better for him. It's my turn to protect him, even if it means breaking my heart in the process.

ThirtySeven

JUSTIN

$\mathcal{I}$ SIT IN the lock-up cell the whole night, not once closing my eyes because when I close them, all I see is Dylan rushing to me and calling out my name.

When they placed me in the car and pulled away, I looked out the window. "We just want you to know that we had no choice," one of the officers said.

I didn't say a word the whole time, and my lawyer arrived five minutes after me, and I got my hands out of the cuffs. "You know this is a bullshit case. I have seven eyewitnesses who say Mr. Woods threatened my client."

He pushed and pushed, but the law was the law, and they couldn't do anything until I saw a judge, and that was only happening at eight this morning.

They did give me five minutes with my father and Matthew, but the only thing I cared about was Caroline and Dylan. "Stay with them." I looked at Matthew, and all he did was nod.

"Mr. Stone." My name is called, and I stand up. "You're up next."

"Thank you," I say and walk with him down the concrete hallway, and he stops at the big brown door.

"I'm sorry I have to do this," he says, and I just nod at him and turn around to have him cuff me. I would do whatever they tell me to do if it gets me one step closer to Caroline and Dylan. I walk into the courthouse, and my eyes fly to the people in the room. All the men in my family fill the first row with my parents at the end. I make eye contact with Matthew, who just nods. I also notice a couple of reporters in there, and I roll my eyes.

"All you have to say when they ask you is not guilty. Your bail is set to be posted, so it'll be right after he calls out the number. We have a car waiting for you," my lawyer says. "I'm not going to lie, though. The press got a hold of the story."

"I don't give a shit. I need to get home," I say, and we stand in front of the judge. When the district attorney starts reading the charges, I almost want to snort when they call Andrew the victim.

The judge asks me how I plead, and I finally speak. "Not guilty, Your Honor." He sets the bail, and I don't even hear how much nor do I care. When he hits the gavel, I look at my lawyer, and he looks at the DA, who nods his head. "Go."

I walk to my family, and my mother gets up and walks next to me with my father on her side, and Matthew on my other side. Max, Viktor, and Evan walk in front of us. "Caroline?" I ask Matthew. He avoids eye contact, and my stomach sinks. My mother grabs my hand, and I look at her. She tries to pretend she is okay, but she just shakes her head.

The car is waiting, and I get in the back with my mother and father, and Matthew gets in the front behind the wheel. The reporters try to take our picture, but I turn my head, and when we are away, I ask the question again. "Where is she?"

"At your place," Matthew says. I look at his eyes in the rearview mirror, and I know he isn't telling me something. The drive home takes more time than I care for, and when I get out of the car, my father calls my name before I take a step toward the elevator. I look back at him, and he stands there with my mother beside him.

My mother has tears running down her face. "Justin, we need to talk," my father says.

"Dad, it's really not a good time," I say and try to turn around.

"I think this is the best time," he says. "Justin, you have to take a second." I turn and look at my parents. "I get that you have a connection with this woman, but, Justin …"

"What are you saying?" I look at my parents who have been by my side my whole life. By all of our sides without thinking twice. No matter how many times we fucked up, the only thing that was the same was their support for us.

"I'm saying you need to walk away," my father says, and now my mother talks.

"You want to save her," she says, and I shake my head. "I know how much you care for her and Dylan, but, Justin, this situation …" She swallows. "Justin, it's not safe."

"What the fuck?" Matthew says under his breath.

"Listen to us for a second," my father says. "We always have your best interests at heart. Always."

355

"Obviously not always," I say, putting my hands on my hips.

"Justin, the guy threatened to kill you," my mother says, almost shouting.

"Oh, for Christ's sake!" I yell. "He's crazy."

"Exactly," my father says. "What if the next time he comes with a gun? Justin, seriously, you are putting yourself in harm's way, and I think you need to think about it."

"I'm going upstairs now to the woman I love," I say, and my mother gasps. "That's right. I love her. I love Dylan. I love them both, and I know that if push comes to shove, I will pick them." I look down. "Even if I have to walk away from my family."

"Justin," my father says, and I shake my head. "Maybe you think you love her, but you just want to save her."

"What are you saying?" I look at them. "I love her. With everything that I have. Until my last dying breath, it will always be her. I will walk with her through fire if I have to, and if push comes to shove, I will."

"You could be throwing away everything you have," my mother says.

"Everything you've worked for since you were little could be taken away," my father says, and I hold up my hand.

"You can either be with me or not, Dad," I say, "but if you aren't on Caroline's side, then you aren't on my side. Now, I'm going to go up there and try to get her head out of her ass because if I know her like I think I do, she is probably already thinking of leaving. I have to tell you, if she leaves me, I'm not going to rest until she is with me. I will turn over every fucking rock on earth."

"I just want you to recognize the danger you are putting yourself in," my father says, and it's Matthew now who walks over to him.

"Dad," he says. "If you met Mom, and she had Allison and me, and my father was Andrew, would you walk away from her?" he asks quietly. "As a dad, I know what you're doing. I would do the same thing, but we both know you didn't raise your kids not to follow their heart."

"I blame you," my mom says to my father. "It's all your fault our children are like this." He grabs her around her shoulders and pulls her close and they look at me. "You're right about Caroline. She's already planning on leaving."

"What?" Matthew hisses, and I look at her.

"She came to me yesterday after everyone left, and she got Dylan settled down." She looks at my father. "She would have been gone if Allison hadn't walked into the room and grabbed her bag. She pleaded with us to just let her go."

Without waiting for anything else, I run to the elevator and press it five times. When the doors open, my parents and Matthew squeeze in with me before the doors close. "I need to talk to Dylan," I tell Matthew.

"I have it covered," Matthew says, and when I finally open the door to my house and see both of them sitting on the couch, it's now my knees that almost give out. Dylan jumps off and runs to me, tears running down his face, and I crouch down to grab him in my arms as he hugs me with everything he has.

"I'm here," I say to him as he cries in my neck. "I'm here, buddy."

"I love you," he whispers, and I hug him to me.

"Love you, too, buddy."

"I'm sorry it's all my fault," he says to me.

"It's no one's fault," I say and put him down. I see Caroline on the couch, trying not to cry, and I'm waiting for her to fight it. Waiting to see how high the wall she built is.

I walk to her, and I'm expecting her to fight it, expecting her to ignore what we have, but what she does is even better. She gets up and jumps into my arms much like her son just did. Her tears soak into my skin.

"I love you," I say. "Love you so much," I say into her neck.

"I love you more," she finally says, and I feel someone hug my waist and look and see it's Dylan.

"I'm here," I tell them both, "but I need a shower."

My mother goes to the kitchen. "I'll make something to eat. Dylan, come and help me."

"Go on. I'm not going anywhere," I say. Caroline releases me, and I see she is still wearing what she wore yesterday. He walks to my mother who takes him in her arms, and I walk to my bedroom with Caroline's hand in mine.

I close the door behind us, and she turns and hugs me. "I love you," she says.

"So much you were going to leave me?" I say, and she looks at me.

"You don't understand," she says.

"No, you don't understand," I say. "It wouldn't have changed anything if you left." She looks at me. "I would have searched my whole life to find you again."

She walks away from me. "You don't need this in your life."

"I need you in my life," I say. "I need you, and I need Dylan."

"Justin."

"Sweetheart," I say. "I just spent the whole night worried whether you would be here when I came home this morning. I need a shower, and then I want to sit on the couch and have a movie night with my family."

I walk to the bathroom, and she calls my name.

"Justin." I turn. "I was going to leave," she says, which I already knew. "I was going to escape and disappear. You protect the people you love."

I smile at her. "I would have found you. Without you, there is nothing."

I pull off my shirt and throw it straight to the trash. "Now do you want to join me in the shower?"

"Your family is here!" she gasps, and I turn and walk into the bathroom, and when I turn around, she's already naked and getting into the shower before me.

I step in with her, and my mouth finds hers. I kiss her like it's the last time I'm going to kiss her. Her arms go around my neck, and she gets on her tippy toes, tilting her head to the side to deepen the kiss. As I was sitting in that jail cell all night, not being able to hold her in my arms, the only thing I thought about was holding her and making sure she and Dylan were okay. I didn't care what they did to me. I just wanted them to be safe. "I love you," I say, kissing her neck and the water pouring over her.

"I love you," she says, breathless, and I pick her up, pressing her back against the tiled wall as the water washes over us and I slowly lower her on my cock. My mouth swallows her moans. I make love to her in the shower, and she gives me what I need.

When we walk back out, my whole family is now there, and no one says anything about us taking too long or that her hair is wet. For the rest of the night, Dylan and Caroline never leave my side.

THIRTY EIGHT

CAROLINE

"IT'S TIME FOR bed," I whisper to Dylan who has been by Justin's side since he came home. We both have. After he left, I told Dylan to go get his things, and that we were leaving.

He looked at me, and he knew it was the right thing to do. I was almost out the door when Allison caught me and sat me down. She never once told me that I shouldn't go. Instead, she listened to me and told me to wait for Justin, but I knew that if I waited for him, there would be no turning back.

The minute the door opened and I saw him, I knew I couldn't walk away from him. I tried. but no matter how much I spun it in my head, I just couldn't do it.

"Will you tuck me in?" Dylan asks Justin who just gets up. His family just left, and everything is going to go back to normal tomorrow.

"Give your mother a kiss," Justin says. Dylan comes over, and I kiss his head.

"I'll meet you in bed." He leans down and kisses me.

I get up and make sure all the lights are turned off and go wait in bed. I lie down, looking toward the door as I wait for him to walk in. After thirty minutes, I get up and walk into Dylan's room, and they are both sleeping. Justin has Dylan tucked in beside him. I walk out and go to our bed and try to sleep, and after tossing and turning, he finally walks into the room.

"I fell asleep," he says, crawling into bed and taking me into his arms. He falls asleep as soon as his head hits the pillow, and soon after, I'm falling asleep myself.

When his alarm goes off at four, he turns it off, and instead of going to work out, we get lost in each other. Our hands are hungry for each other, and for two hours, all we do is live in the moment. "I need a nap."

"So sleep," he says, getting out of bed, and I look at him.

"I have to go to work today," I say, and he shakes his head.

"You're not going back there," he says, and I sit up, holding the sheet to my chest.

"Excuse me?" I say, and he looks over at me as he puts his boxers on. I hate that he's so good looking and that I love him when he starts to get bossy.

"I don't want you going back there," he says, and I get out of bed, walking to put something on.

"I have a job," I say. "A job that I need."

"Yeah, and your ex who is slightly unstable is out to get you, so I don't think you going back there is a smart thing to do." It bothers me even more when he makes sense.

"I need to work, Justin," I say, and he shocks me.

"Come work for me," he says, and I glare at him.

"I need someone to take Amy's place." He slips on his shorts. "Do you want coffee?"

"Justin, I already live with you," I say, and he kisses my neck while he walks out and I slip on the shirt he was wearing last night. "I can't work for you." I follow him out of the bedroom and to the kitchen.

"If it makes you feel better, you wouldn't be working for me," he says, starting the coffee. "You would be working for my foundation."

"You know it's the same thing," I say. "Plus, now I have to pay for your lawyer." He slams the cupboard so hard I think it's going to come off its hinges.

"Don't say that shit again." He points at me. "Andrew is not your fucking problem."

"Well, if it wasn't for me," I say, and he just glares at me.

"Don't piss me off, sweetheart," he says.

"Don't piss me off, Justin," I say to him, and then Dylan comes out and rubs his eyes.

"Are we going to camp?" he asks, and Justin shakes his head.

"I'm hungry," he says, going to the pantry and grabbing a doughnut out of there. He takes a bite and is chewing it on the way back to his room.

"I don't want you going back there," he whispers. "What would I tell Dylan if something happened to you?"

"That's not fair," I say, refusing to think about it.

"Just think about it," he says. "Sit down and think about it."

"Even if I don't want to, Justin, I have no choice," I say, and when he starts to say something, I cut him off. "I am not taking money from you."

"Sweetheart," he says, and I glare. "Stop being so stubborn."

"I have to go get ready," I say to him and walk to the bedroom. With a heavy heart, I get dressed in jeans and a shirt. I kiss Justin and Dylan goodbye and make my way to the church.

When I walk in, Father Rolly is there waiting for me. "Caroline," he says and comes over to me. "I've been thinking about you since Sunday."

"I'm sorry I didn't come into work yesterday," I say, and he waves his hand in the air.

"I read about Justin in the paper." He starts to say. "You'll know that I went down to the police station yesterday to give my side of the story. I saw everything and so did a couple of the parishioners."

"Thank you so much, Father," I say.

"It's a shame that his team is suspending him," he says, and I look at him.

"Sorry, what?" I ask, confused.

"The team put out a statement last night saying that until they get to the bottom of it, he is suspended," Father Rolly says. My heart sinks, and I sit down in the chair.

I'm about to lose it when the door opens, and I'm suddenly terrified it's Andrew. My hands start to shake, and I hate to admit that Justin is right. I think I hold my breath until I see it's Parker with Viktor following her. "What in the world are you guys doing here?" I ask, my heart beating normal now.

"I was going to hit up a meeting," Viktor says, and I look at him. "I'm three years clean."

"I'm sorry. I didn't know that," I say, and I have so many questions. "Father Rolly, this is Justin's mom, Parker, and his brother-in-law, Viktor."

"Father," Viktor says, nodding at him.

"I just found out that Justin is suspended," I say low and try not to let the tears come, but they do anyway.

"It's going to be fine," Parker says, and I nod and look at Father Rolly.

"I'm sorry to do this to you, but," I say, taking a deep breath, "I can't work here anymore." I'm expecting him to be a bit mad, but instead, he smiles. "I know I need the job, but just now, I was shaking thinking that Andrew was walking in here."

"The job is going to be here no matter how long you decide," he says, and then I look over at Parker.

"Will you come with me?" I ask and she just smiles. Then I look at Viktor. "Cheryl is going to be here in five minutes. She runs the meeting, and she is amazing."

"I'll wait here," he says and looks at Parker. "You better tell Zoe that you decided to leave me and not that I just dropped you off."

Parker laughs and goes over to him. "You're my favorite," she says. "Don't tell the others."

"You know that we talk, right?" Viktor tells her. "Last week, you told Evan he was your favorite." Parker gasps.

"He was not supposed to tell you that," she says. "I really mean it with you."

"That's what you told Max," Viktor says, and Parker throws up her hands.

"I'm ready to go." She turns to me. "We're leaving." I walk out, and she gets in the car and puts her seat belt on. "So where are we going?"

"I have a couple of things I have to do, and I would like for you to be there," I say, and she just smiles. When we pull up to my old apartment I turn off the truck. "This is my place," I say, and she looks around.

I walk out, and she follows me, and I wonder if she is scared. When we get to my place, we walk up the five flights of stairs. I turn the key and when I walk in, the smell of fresh paint hits us right away. The windows are closed, and the air is thick. I see that the futon is gone, and the mattress is not there either. "This is my home," I say, turning in a circle. "Not much to see," I say, laughing with all the nerves. She smiles at me and has tears in her eyes. "Wow, this is harder than I thought," I say and now it's me who's scared. "I love your son."

"I know," she says, and she holds her hands together.

"I met Andrew when I was sixteen, and I thought he hung the moon and stars." I try to swallow, and I'm suddenly sweating. "And at seventeen, I got pregnant. I'm not going to lie. You think that at that age nothing can touch you. It's never going to happen to you."

"It takes one time." She laughs.

"My family kicked me out. I basically had to choose between my child, who I loved with everything that I had even though he was just a little pea"—I brush a tear away—"or my parents."

368

"Oh, Caroline," she says.

"Andrew was supposed to be the it thing. He played football and he was the best quarterback out there, and he got picked up by the biggest university. With that came housing if we were married, so in a small ceremony, we got married. Then he got hurt junior year. Sacked in the stomach, and when the guy landed on him, he crushed his ACL." My hands start to shake. "I didn't know he was on drugs. I was a new mom with no help, and Dylan had colic. If he was around, he was moody and angry, and I just thought that it was because he was frustrated."

"Caroline," she whispers, "you don't have to do this."

"But I want to," I say. "I have to. You were the first woman Justin ever loved." She smiles, and the tears roll down her cheeks. "When I finally realized what was going on, he was too far gone, and I was already going down that black hole with him. I have never done one drug in my whole life, but then, I owed over fifty thousand dollars in credit card debt, six months of rent, and let's not forget about the dealers that he kept taking shit from and never repaying." I close my eyes.

"I came home one day, and he was on the couch fucking our landlady because he didn't have rent." Parker gasps. "Three months later when he came home and was coming down from his high, I told him he had to sign a paper so I could get extra diapers from the church. I lied. They were divorce papers that I got online, and the next day, I filed them at the court, and just like that, without him knowing, I cut the tie I had to him. But I still had Dylan, and I tried to shield him and, well, protect him from what his father was. I think I did a pretty good job."

"No!" Parker almost screams. "You did an amazing job. He's wonderful and kind and smart. But the best thing he has is his heart of gold. You can't teach that."

"I tried to pay off the bills, but whenever I got ahead, Andrew would come around, and well, he would take and steal, and he just kept pushing me down. I moved six times and tried not to let him find me, but when you have a low income, there are only certain places you can rent, and he knew them all. I know that I'm not what you wanted for your son. I know that you want someone who doesn't have all this baggage and problems. You guys have a family that people dream about. You love and support each other, and when push comes to shove, you guys go to war for each other, and well, then you have me. It's just me and Dylan, just the two of us." I cry now. "But I love him so, so much. I didn't think I could love someone this much. I wanted to run and give him a chance to find someone better." I look down. "You protect the ones you love. And I love him with every-thing I have to give, which isn't much."

"But to him, it's everything," Parker says. "I'm not going to lie to you. We were scared for him. Andrew is not stable, and that has nothing to do with you. But as a mom …"

"You want your kids safe no matter how old they are," I fill in for her. "I can't walk away from him." I shake my head. "But I don't want him to have to choose between me and his family."

"He won't have to choose." Parker now comes to me and takes me in her arms. I sob when she hugs me. "He'll never have to choose. You and Dylan are a part of him, and my boys know what they want."

"He's stubborn," I say, laughing. "And annoying."

"Oh, honey, it's going to get so much worse." She laughs. I step away from her and go to the bathroom, grabbing some toilet paper for us.

"He almost forbade me from going to work today," I say, and she laughs when she dabs her eyes. "Which is even more annoying, since he was right."

"If you tell them I said this next part, I will deny it," she says and leans in. "They usually are."

"Then he offered me a job with his foundation." I shake my head. "Which I'm going to have to take now since I need a job."

"He's going to be so happy," she says, and I nod.

"I have one more stop before I go to him and one, accept the job, and then two, yell at him for not telling me about getting suspended."

She laughs. "Let's go." She looks around. "I would take whatever you want to keep. You are never coming back here again, and that's coming from me, and if I have to, I'll tell Cooper."

"So it's the whole family that is like that."

"It's a Stone thing," she says, laughing, and for the first time in this apartment, I laugh with a full heart.

THIRTYNINE

JUSTIN

"*P*USH, PUSH, PUSH!" I yell and then skate back to the bench where the other kids sit. Walking into the rink today, I didn't know what to expect. Ever since the news hit that I was arrested, things have just gotten thrown at me. I was surprised when my agent called and told me that the general manager of the team and the team owners were not pleased with me, and they suspended me until further notice. I thought it would bother me more, but it didn't. I put my phone down and just walked to Dylan and Caroline.

I was also not sure how the parents of the camp would feel, and when I walked in, a couple of the dads came up to me and hugged me, thanking me for doing what needed to be done.

"Look who decided to show up." I hear and look toward the bench at Ralph who is wearing a track suit and his skates. "You just had to be Superman."

I laugh. "You know me. I want all eyes on me."

He throws his head back and laughs. "Of course, you do. You scored the hottest mom there was." I put up my hand and glare at him, and he laughs. "Point taken. Anyway, I wanted to be the one to tell you I just signed a new contract."

"No way," I say, happy for him. He became a free agent July first, and he turned down the shitty contract Edmonton offered him. "Where to?"

He smiles at me. "Actually, Matthew saw me skating and liked my work, and we got to talking, and he hooked me up with Nico. I'm going to Dallas."

"Does that mean I get ten percent for introducing you guys?" I laugh, and he shakes his head. "I'm happy for you. It's a great organization."

"Yeah, I'm excited about it. My wife, not so much, since all of her family is here," he says and then looks down and then up again. "She's expecting."

"Holy shit," I say, holding up my hand and waiting for him to high-five me, and he beams with pride. "That's crazy. Nico is the new owner, right? I heard about him taking over for his father. He has big plans for that club."

"Yeah, it's really early, and she doesn't want to say anything." He looks at the kids. "But fuck, I'm just so happy."

"I'm happy for you," I say, and then Matthew comes out of the back. "Stop stealing my people," I say, and he laughs now.

"I have to go. I just wanted to tell you," Ralph says. "See you later."

He shakes Matthew's hand and walks away.

"That was a good pick," I say to Matthew who stands there in his track pants. He's been at my side since this whole thing started. Actually, everyone has. All the men are hanging at the rink today. My father is teaching on the other ice with Max, and Evan is in the gym with mini Cooper.

"Where is Viktor?" I ask Matthew, and he looks down.

"He wanted to hit up a meeting," he says, and I look at him. "At the church where Caroline works." And just like that, I see that he went to make sure she is okay. "With Mom."

My eyes open huge. "What?" I almost scream. "Why would he take her there?"

"Would you say no to her?" Matthew laughs. "The best part is that she didn't tell Dad."

"Oh my God," I say, and then blow the whistle for the kids to get off the ice. "He's going to lose his shit."

"Yeah," Matthew says, and we both know how protective my father is about my mother. He doesn't let anything touch her that is bad. He shields her with everything he has. "Dinner will be interesting."

I look toward the clock and see it's lunchtime. "I'm dragging my ass today," I say, getting off the ice. I walk through the hallway and peek into some of the rooms to make sure no kids are lingering.

"Oh, shit," Matthew says, and I look at what he's looking at, and I see that Caroline is charging into the arena with my mother following her. "This doesn't look good," he says. "I know that walk," he continues. "It's not a good walk."

"I think she's charging," I say under my breath, and I see Caroline look around. When she finally spots me, I smile at her, but all she does is glare.

"Oh, I definitely know that look," Matthew says. "Just say you're sorry."

He tries to talk fast. "Doesn't matter if you don't know what it's about, just say sorry."

I look back, and she is in front of me now, and I see that she is even more beautiful. "Hey there, sweetheart," I start softly, and she just crosses her arms over her chest.

"Don't 'hey there, sweetheart' me."

Matthew mumbles under his breath, "Say sorry."

"Don't you start." My mother looks at Matthew, and he just holds up his hands.

"Why didn't you tell me you got suspended?" she asks. "I can't be in this if you aren't going to be honest with me."

"Okay, for one, being suspended isn't that big of a deal," I say. Sure, it pissed me off that my team didn't have my back, and I have a call with the general manager set for next week where I plan to tell him exactly how I feel about this. "I honestly didn't even think of it."

"If you want me to work for you, there has to be a contract of sorts," she starts saying, and I look at her. "When we are at work, I'm your employee and not your girlfriend."

I am about to say something, and Matthew is the one who puffs out. "You're his woman," he says. "He's not hiding that fact." Caroline looks at him, and he puts his hands up. "Just stating the facts."

"I'm not hiding that we are together, and if I want to come and say hello and give you a kiss, I'm going to come and give you a kiss."

"You come and say hello during lunch, and if I'm on break, you can kiss me," she negotiates.

"Fine," I say, accepting it. I'm not about to tell her that I'm going to do what I want. I'll ease her into it.

"Next, I gave up my apartment today," she says, and I look at my mother, who just smiles. "So I'm basically home-less."

"You aren't homeless; you live with me," I say.

"I told her that," my mother chimes in. "It was silly for her to pay rent if she is never going back there."

"Wait, you went to her place?" Matthew asks, and my mother nods her head. "Viktor is fired."

"Oh, you stop that," my mother says.

"I'm telling Dad," Matthew says, and my mother laughs. "Not kidding."

"Can we for a second get back to me?" Caroline says. "I want to pay rent."

"Fuck no," Matthew and I both say at the same time.

"Then I'll buy food," she counters.

"Sweetheart," I start to say, and she glares at me.

"Then you cancel the cleaning lady." She raises her eye-brows.

"Only if you quit your job at the motel." It's now my time to counter.

"Wait, you work two jobs?" Matthew says to her and shakes his head. "He lets you work two jobs."

"I do," she says, and Matthew just looks at me like *how could you?*

"Fine, I'll quit the job at the motel, and in return, I'll clean the apartment," she says, and I nod.

"Sure," I say, knowing full well that's never going to hap-pen. "What else?"

377

"Well," she says and looks at my mother. "I bought you a gift."

"Wait, what?" I say, and she hands me a white square box.

"Oh my God," Matthew says. "If she proposes to you, I'm going to die, and you'll never live it down."

"Caroline," I say, using her name.

"It's not a ring," she says. "And if it was, would you say no?"

"Say no," Matthew says.

"Matthew Grant," my mother says in warning.

"Mom," he says, "don't even."

"It's not a ring," Caroline says. "God, it's not a ring."

"Then I'll take it," I say, taking the box from her and opening it. It's a silver chain with a medallion on it.

"It's Saint Christopher," she says softly and steps closer to me, and I pick up the silver medallion with the saint on it and the words *protect us* on the bottom. "It's not new," she says, and she turns it over, and I read it.

Caroline & Dylan

"I love it," I say. Taking it from me, she pulls it out of the box, and I bend for her to put it on me. I stand, and she puts her hand on it.

"Does this mean you are officially living with me?" I ask, taking her in my arms. "And you are going to work with me?"

"For you." She raises her eyebrows.

"Same thing," I say and kiss her, and Matthew just laughs.

"It's not the same thing," she says against my lips but

378

wraps her arms around my neck while I pick her up.

That night, everything is back to normal, and the next day when we walk in together, it's done with me not worrying about Andrew just popping up.

I don't think I'll see him until we are in court, and then one day when I run back to the SUV to get something, he is waiting beside it for me. I stop in my tracks, and Matthew pulls up at the same time, getting out of his car without turning it off.

"Relax," Andrew says, holding his hands up. "I'm not here for anything."

"Then you better get the fuck away from my brother," Matthew says to him, and he smirks.

"What do you want, Andrew?" I ask him, standing here with my arms across my chest.

"I'm here with a proposition," he says, and I see he's wearing the same clothes as on Sunday.

"You have nothing that I want," I say, and he just laughs.

"Oh, that's where you're wrong," he says, waving his finger. "I have Dylan."

"The fuck?" Matthew says from beside me, and my heart starts to speed faster.

"Ten thousand." He says the number as if he's selling a fucking car. "You give me ten k in cash, and I'll sign over my rights to him."

Oh my God. "Bullshit," I say, trying not to smash his head into the truck.

"Get the papers ready and the cash, and I'll sign it," he says, shrugging.

"Tomorrow," I say, and his eyes light up. "You show up at

379

my attorney's office tomorrow morning, and I'll have your cash ready for you."

"Twenty k," he says fast.

"Ten," I say it again. "Not a penny more."

"Give me the address," he says, and I grab the card from my SUV and hand it to him.

"I'll be there at eight. If you aren't there by eight thirty, the offer will never happen again."

"Fine by me," he says, smiling and snickering. "Kid's been a dark cloud following me ever since he came into my life." His hand comes up. "I'll be there at eight."

He turns around and walks away, and I finally let out the breath I was holding and put my hands on my knees. "Did he just sell his fucking kid for ten thousand dollars?"

"I would have given him everything I have," I say, watching him disappear.

"You going to tell her about this?" he asks, and I shake my head.

"Not until he signs the papers," I say, and he just looks at me. "Nothing until he signs."

I don't mention it again, and that night when I get to tuck Dylan in and tell him I love him and he hugs me back, I put my hand on the medallion hanging around my neck.

The next morning, I make a stupid excuse about hitting the gym with Matthew, and I can see right away that Caroline doesn't believe me. But I kiss her and walk out to Matthew, who picks me up, except he's picking me up in an SUV instead of his car, and when I get in, I look in the back seat and see that all the men are there. "You didn't think you'd do this alone?" my father asks, and I don't say anything.

We get to my lawyer's office at ten minutes to eight, and every single minute that passes feels like an eternity. My father and Matthew sit beside the lawyer at the head of the table in the conference room. Evan, Viktor, Max, and Markos are sitting two by two in front of each other.

When it finally gets to eight, I start pacing back and forth, and at eight ten, he saunters into the office. "I fucking hate that fuck," Max says.

"You got the money?" he asks, and Matthew just shakes his head.

"Not until you sign this." I put the paper forward, and my lawyer speaks up.

"This is you signing away your parental rights," he says. "You at no time can contact Dylan Woods."

"Don't want to see his face either," he says as he signs on the dotted line, and I think my father is going to jump over the table.

"Are you sure you understand what I just said?" my lawyer asks, making sure that he gets all this on camera.

"Yeah," Andrew says. "The fucking kid isn't mine; he's his problem now." He motions to me with his head. "Now where is my cash?"

My lawyer hands him the envelope that I gave him when I came in, and Andrew opens it to see the bills. "Should have held out," he says, turning around.

When he is finally out of the room, Evan stands up. "I think I'm literally going to be sick." He puts his hand on his stomach.

"The guy just signed away a kid," Markos says.

"He's sick," Viktor says, and we all look at him. "Relax, I don't like him. I'm just saying that he's a sick man."

"I don't give a fuck what you say." Matthew looks at Viktor. "You're in recovery. Would you sell baby Zara?"

"I would die before I gave her up," he says without skipping a beat.

"The question now is when are you going to tell Caroline?" my father asks me.

"Tonight," I say, and when the lawyer gives me a copy of the papers and I walk out of his office, I get sick right next to the car.

FORTY

CAROLINE

"CAROLINE, CAN YOU please make sure that all emails have been verified?" Malika smiles at me.

I smile back at her. "I just did." I give her the ones that have to be changed.

"It's so good to finally have some real help here," she says, turning and walking back to her own office. When I first started here, I thought I would just be answering the phone, but Justin stuck me in a office, and Malika came in with a coffee in one hand for her and another one for me, and she went through everything that we did. I was in awe with everything that Justin's foundation does. I was also in shock when they told me that my salary was close to seventy-five thousand dollars.

"I'm just happy I haven't messed things up too badly." I smile when I hear voices, and look out of my office window, wondering if Justin is in. He was acting really weird the whole day yesterday, and this morning, he nearly ran out of the door.

When he went to bed last night, it was as if he wasn't there. Even when we got lost in each other, something was missing. I tried to tell myself that he was tired. I tried to tell myself that it was nothing and all in my head, but this morning, he barely made eye contact with me, and my stomach dropped when he left without so much as a backward glance. In fact, he couldn't run out fast enough.

"Hey," I hear, and I am taken out of my daydream, and I smile when I see it's him. "You almost done?"

"Yes," I say. "I'm done."

"Okay, I'll be done in about fifteen," he says, and then he looks at me and just fake smiles and my heart sinks.

I wait for him and Dylan to come and get me, and when he drives home, all I can do is look out the window. Dinner is quiet also, and he passes on going to the pool. I know it's the end. When Dylan and I come back from the pool, he's sitting outside, looking at the view. "We're back."

"Oh, yeah," he says, and Dylan comes out, and he grabs him and brings him close to him and buries his face in his neck. "I love you," he tells him, and then he puts him on his lap, facing out, and holds him as they watch the sun go down. I try not to sob. I try not to show my pain; after all, I'm good at hiding things. It's only when I step under the shower do I allow the tears to fall.

Same story, just a prettier bathroom. I get out and get dressed, and when I walk out of the bathroom, he's there sitting on the bed waiting for me. His eyes are down and papers are beside him, and I have to hold the doorframe to be able to stand. I love him so much that if me leaving is going to make him happy, I'll do it. "Is everything okay?" I try to talk without my voice cracking.

"No," he says and looks down at the floor, and my heart is shattered.

"I get it," I say, and he looks up. "It was a whirlwind, and everything happened so fast." He looks at me. "I'm just going to sleep with Dylan, and we can be out of here tomorrow."

"What?" he says.

"I get it, Justin," I say, the tears falling now. "It's fine." I smile, not wanting him to feel sorry for me or want to be with me because I'm crying. "We'll be okay."

"I'm so confused right now," he says.

"It's over." I say it for him, although I shouldn't. I should make him do the dirty work.

"What's over?" he asks, confused, and I want to yell at him to stop pretending.

"Us." I point at him and then myself. "This thing."

"We aren't over," he says, scoffing at me even saying that. "Far from it."

Now I'm the one who is confused. "Andrew came to see me."

"What?" I look at him and take a step forward.

He holds up the paper for me. "I did it for you," he says. "For Dylan."

My head spins as I try to think about what he did for us, what more can this man could do for us. I grab the paper in my shaking hands, and I unfold it and it looks like a case file and my eyes go line from line until I see the words.

Termination of Parental Rights.

My tears blur my sight, and I can't continue reading it when I see Dylan's name. My hands are shaking uncontrollably when I put one of them in front of my mouth. My body shakes now, and I can hear my teeth chattering. "What?"

"He came to me." Tears roll down his own cheeks and he looks me in the eye. The anguish is written all over his face, the hurt, the pain everything is written on his face. "I'm so sorry."

"For what?" I'm so confused. "Did you agree to let us go for this?" I shake the paper in my hand. "To have him out of Dylan's life, you gave us up?"

"Sweetheart," he says, his voice broken. "Never." He looks down "He signed it for ten thousand dollars."

The gasp comes out along with the sob, and I fall, shattered to the floor, and he comes to me. "I'm so sorry, I'm so, so sorry."

The wail rips through me. "Why?" I can't even think; I can't see the paper in my hand crushed between us as he rocks me. "How could he? That's his child. His blood," I sob. "His son. Why?" I shake in his arms. "Me, I get, but Dylan, that sweet boy who doesn't hurt anyone. Who accepts when all I can do is feed him peanut butter. The little boy who doesn't care that he only got one Christmas gift or that his birthday gift this year was just a meal at McDonald's and a visit to Dollar Tree. The boy who wore his shoes for two months more than he should have with a hole in the sole without saying anything because his dad's fucking drug dealer came and took our rent. Or that we had to wear our shoes and gloves to bed one night because the heating got cut off in the spring, but it was still fucking snowing." I close my eyes, thinking of Dylan. "My son, who doesn't deserve any of this. Why?"

"I don't know," he says softly. "I have no idea, but I had to," he says, broken. "Don't hate me. Please don't hate me."

"Hate you?" I ask. "Why would I hate you?"

"I gave him money for him to go away," he says, his heart broken. "He sat in front of me and signed the paper like he was taking out a library book, not signing away his son."

"After everything that he's done to you, you still gave him money?" I ask.

"I would have given him everything that I have," he says, and he dries my tears with kisses. "Right down to my last cent if it got him away from Dylan."

"I don't know what I did," I start to say, and I kiss him, "to deserve you." I peel his shirt from him. His hand slides under my shirt, and he cups my breast and kisses me again. He pulls my shirt over my head. "I love you," I say and then kiss him again.

He flips us around, and I'm on my back now in the middle of his room, and he moves my pants down and slowly kisses my leg all the way up my leg and he gets up. "I have to get a condom." I stop him from walking.

"I have an IUD," I say. "And in the shower, you didn't use one."

He covers me now with his body, and I push his shorts down. "Put me in you," he says. I grab his cock with my hand and place him at my entrance, and he slides into me. Our mouths find each other, and we swallow our moans as he makes love to me. Slow, ever so fucking slow. Until we both let go, and his name is on my lips. He falls down on me, and I hold him close. My arms and legs hold on to him. He rolls off me, and I get up off the floor. Going to the bathroom, I clean up, and when I get into bed, I look over at him.

"Is that where you went this morning?" I ask, and he turns to me.

"Yes," he says, and I look up at him. "He came to me yesterday when I went to get my wallet."

"That's why you acted weird all last night?" I ask, and he nods.

"I thought …" I start to say.

"You thought I was breaking up with you?" he says, and I roll my eyes.

"What was I supposed to think? You were distant yesterday, and then today, you didn't even kiss me goodbye." I pretend that it doesn't bother me, but all day long, I was on pins and needles.

"I was afraid that if I said anything, I would tell you, and then you would stop me."

"Did you go by yourself?" I ask. I want to know it all. "Please tell me everything."

"No. Matthew got there yesterday when Andrew was there, and if he tried anything, Matthew would have been another one arrested."

"Oh my God," I say. "Did he come with you today?"

"Everyone was there," he says. "The men, at least."

"Oh my God," I say, putting my hand in my face feeling embarrassed.

"We got there, and I was a nervous wreck. I thought he wasn't going to show. I think deep down I hoped he'd wake up and realize what he was doing, but he walked in there and had no care in the world."

"He's a horrible person."

"He's a son of a fucking bitch, and I fucking hate him," Justin says. "I made sure he knew that he wasn't allowed to contact him, and the only way he would have communication with Dylan was if Dylan wanted to talk to him."

"What do we tell him?" I ask, and he takes a deep breath.

"I have no idea. I was going to say nothing and hope that when he gets older, he has no memory of him," Justin says. "I hate Andrew, but he did do one thing. He made Dylan."

"I had more of a hand in it than he did," I say, and he laughs. "He's mine. I want to change his last name."

"Okay," Justin says. "We can go to the lawyer, and he can take care of it." He kisses me. "There is one more thing I did today, and I want you to know that I love you."

"Why does this sound like you did something that I am not going to be happy about?" I ask.

"Well, you might be pissed," he says. "Matthew said ..."

"Oh, Jesus, nothing good comes when you start a sentence with Matthew said."

Justin laughs and sits up, and I sit up with him. He reaches to the bed and grabs another sheet of paper, except this one is thicker than the one he just gave me. "I also did this."

I open the papers and see my name now on a credit card statement and see the balance is zero. I flip to the next one, and it's zero also. All the debts I had are paid. "What?" I ask, not sure I'm seeing right.

"How?"

"I might have stolen your social security number from

your file at work and given it to my lawyer," he says, and I just flip through the pages. "And I know you're going to be pissed, so you can pay me back, just with no interest."

I look up at him. "You're going to let me pay you back?" I ask, and he looks away from me.

"I was going to put it in Dylan's account," he says. "Or not."

"I can't believe this," I say in shock. "This whole thing."

"It's about time," he says, and I look at him. "It's about time that someone finally took care of you and not the other way around."

A tear escapes my eye. "You just have to protect and take care of us." My hand goes to his chest, and my finger plays with the necklace that he hasn't taken off. "I love you." There are no other words that I can say right now.

"I love you, too," he says to me. "Forever."

FortyOne

JUSTIN

"*I* DON'T KNOW about this," my agent, Carey, says to me. I smile at him and adjust my tie when I get out of my car and walk into the building. I fasten the button on my blue suit jacket, and we walk to the elevator. "I have a bad feeling about this."

"Relax," I say, getting in the elevator and looking forward. I see from the reflection that he's rubbing his forehead. I look at myself in my blue suit and white shirt. This morning when I put it on, Dylan laughed at me and said I looked like a banker.

"You know that, as your agent, I have to be on your side," he says. "But this … it's just …" He puts his hand on his chest, and I have to laugh again. He's been with me since the beginning. "I thought your brother was nuts, but this …" Now I laugh. "It might kill your career." He doesn't just represent me; he has my whole family under him.

"That's okay," I say. "I made enough money to last a long time."

We walk out, and the receptionist greets us and asks us to follow her. "Here we go," he says when we get to the conference room. She opens the door, and we walk in.

I spot all the key players sitting around the table. The general manager for the team, Hartley. The owners of the team, Albert and Charles, and finally, the coach of the team, Claude. "Gentlemen," I say, and they each stand and shake my hand. "Thank you so much for coming."

"No problem," Albert says.

"Anything for you," Charles chimes in after him.

"Well, not really anything," I say to them, and they don't say a word as I unbutton my jacket and sit down in front of them with Carey beside me.

"Well, gentlemen," Carey says. "I bet we are all wondering why we are here."

"I mean, I don't think it's actually that much of a surprise," I say. Putting my hands on the table in front of me, I fold them together.

"We were going to reach out to you," Hartley says.

"But you figured that before you reached out to me to get my side of the story, you would suspend me." I look at them and see Claude lean back in the chair and side-eye the rest of the guys. "And tell the press before picking up the phone and telling me?"

"Justin." Charles starts to talk. "You have to understand that our hands were tied."

"You were charged with assault," Hartley says, "in front of a church."

"Charged doesn't mean convicted," Carey says from beside me, and I know that he is nervous, but I also know by the way he just leaned in his chair that shit is going to go down. "Especially now that the DA has thrown the case out, and all charges were dropped."

"We stand by what we did," Charles says. "It's a family-run company, and we can't let it slide, even if we didn't want to."

"Funny you should say family," I say, looking at them, "because a family-run company would have called me to ask if I was okay. Would have been at the police station making sure I was all right. A family would have had my back no matter what." Claude just nods. "A family doesn't just turn their backs on each other because it's going to get messy."

"I agree," Claude says.

"See, me assaulting that man was me protecting my family," I tell them. "Not that any of you asked. I have been a part of this 'family'"—I raise my hands and use air quotes—"since I was eighteen years old. I've gotten on that ice every single day, having the backs of my teammates. I've never once questioned any of the decisions that you guys have made over the years." I smirk now. "And there have been some shitty ones, and some not so smart ones, but I've stayed true to my commitment to this organization and to who I thought were my brothers."

"Your commitment to the team is not in question," Hartley says.

"You're right, it's not. What's in question right now is how I can skate for an organization that doesn't stand with me," I say and then look over at Claude. "I'm sorry that I am doing this, especially to you." I then look over at Carey, who just

397

nods. "I refuse to get on the ice with this organization going forward. I will not be attending camp. I will not be on that bench, and I will never wear that jersey."

"Surely, you don't mean that," Hartley says. "You can't just do that. We can ..."

"You can, what, suspend me?" I shrug. "Whatever."

"You'll be in breach of contract," Charles says.

"Oh, well, I guess you can either sue me or pay me out," I say. "Or here is something, you can trade me."

"That's crazy. You are the franchise name," Harley says.

"And not even that was good enough to stand by me," I say, pushing my chair back. "I'll let you guys think about it, and Carey will call you this afternoon to know which option you pick."

"You would ruin your career," Albert says. "All because—"

"All because in my time of need no one was there," I say and then look at Carey. "You ready?"

"This is fucking bullshit," Hartley snaps.

"No, what's bullshit is getting a fucking phone call from *SportsCenter* asking me to comment on my suspension." I push the chair back in. "That's fucking bullshit."

"I'll trade you to the bottom of the fucking barrel," Hartley says, foaming from the mouth.

"You can try, but obviously, my agent has my back, and there is only one team I'll go to."

"Fuck you," Hartley says.

I nod at them, smiling. "Have a great day, gentlemen, and good luck in the future." Then I turn to my coach. "Claude."

"We'll talk soon," he says, and I turn and walk out of the conference room. Pressing the button on the elevator, I wait. I don't know why I thought they would come chasing after me or even apologize for what they did, but I don't get any of that, and it just makes my decision easier.

When we walk out into the hot sun, I turn to Carey. "I say give them five and call them with my offer."

"I'll let you know," he says and walks to his car. "Never a dull moment with you."

"Hey." I smile. "Could be worse."

I get into the BMW and make my way back to the rink when the phone rings, and I see it's Carey. "Don't tell me they called you already?"

"I was shocked also," he says. "You can thank Claude. He said he didn't want you sitting on his bench." I laugh.

"Did you give them my demands?" I ask him.

"Please, you think I'm a rookie?" he asks. "I'll let you know if they approve."

"I'll be on the ice," I say and disconnect. When I get to the rink, I walk in and say hello to a couple of kids who see me and then I walk into Caroline's office. She is sitting behind her desk typing away on the computer, and her eyes come up when I walk in her office. I smile when I think about her here with me.

"Hi," she says, smiling at me, and I walk over to her, turning her chair and kissing her on the lips. "It's not my lunch break," she says and wipes off the lip gloss that is now on my lips. "How'd it go?"

"It went the way it was supposed to go," I say, not telling her anything yet.

"Well, do you think they will still suspend you?" she asks, and I shrug. When I made the decision about quitting the team, I made one phone call and then decided not to tell her until the end. I didn't want her to think this was another thing I did for her. In reality, I wasn't doing it for her; I was doing it for us.

"No clue," I say, and I kiss her again.

"You look really sexy in a tie," she says. Twirling the tie between her fingers, she looks around. "Maybe tonight I can take it off you."

"Sweetheart," I say, looking around. "If you don't stop, I'm going to close the blinds on your window, lock the door, and then fuck you on this desk." I lean in now. "All while wearing the tie." She shudders in her chair. "That isn't helping." I'm actually thinking about how mad she would be if I did that when my phone beeps in my pocket.

"Saved by the bell," she says and pushes me away from her. "Now go teach hockey stuff so I can work."

"Fine," I say, kissing her one more time and then taking my phone out of my pocket and seeing it's a message from Carey.

Carey: Deal accepted. I'll send over the contract.

I look back now. "Change of plans tonight. The three of us will have dinner."

"The three of us always have dinner," she says, laughing.

"I mean out. Let's get pizza," I say, and she just shrugs.

"Whatever you want," she says, and I have to say in the past three weeks she's grown into her own. She's also started hanging around my sisters more, which makes it worse for me. You see, after everything that happened, they decided to spend the whole summer in Canada with me.

I don't get on the ice that day. Instead, I watch from the

stands and pick ten kids who I want to extend the program for. I had to choose, and it was the perfect day to do it.

When we finally decide dinner everyone agrees that we should just go home. Dylan starts talking about the weekend and how he wants to go to the cabin we went to last week and try fishing again.

"We can," I say. "I'm sure everyone is going again."

"Michael said he's going," Dylan tells me, and Caroline just looks at me.

"So," I start, and she looks at me. "I had a meeting with my team today."

"Are they still mad at you?" Dylan asks, and I look at him. He was very upset when some of the kids said I got kicked off the team. I had to explain to him that sometimes you get in trouble, and this was my time-out, which just made him even madder since he didn't understand any of it.

"No," I answer, and then I look at them both. "I'm mad at them."

Caroline just looks at me and waits. "Why?" Dylan asks me.

"Because when you are with a team, you expect them to have your back and be on your side," I tell him. "On that team, on the ice, they are your brothers." He just nods, and I decide I'm just going to have the rip off the Band-Aid moment. "I told them I was not getting on the ice in Edmonton anymore." Dylan opens his mouth, and Caroline gasps.

"What does that mean?" she asks quietly.

"It means that tomorrow, the whole world will know that I've been traded," I tell them, and Dylan starts to cry. "What's the matter, buddy?"

"You're going to move away from us," he says, "and you are going to get another family."

I decide that maybe doing this during dinner was not a good idea, and I get off my stool and take Dylan in my arms. "Let's sit on the couch."

I carry him to the couch, and Caroline walks behind me, her own tears hidden when she sits down and just holds Dylan's hand.

"I know that this is your home," I tell them. "I know that you love this city, and you have lots of friends here. But I was hoping ..." I start. "I was hoping you guys would come with me."

"You want to take us with you?" Dylan asks.

"Of course, I want to take you with me," I say, kissing his forehead. "Obviously, I want you guys with me always," I say, looking at Caroline who blinks away tears. "Would you be willing to move with me?"

"Yes," she whispers at the same time Dylan nods his head.

"Just like that?" I say, my heart finally beating. "Without even knowing where I'm going?"

"Doesn't matter," Caroline says, coming to me. My hand goes around her shoulders, and she puts her head on my shoulder. "Doesn't matter where it is, we'll follow you always."

I turn to look at her and kiss her lips softly. "I love you," I whisper.

"So where are we going?" Dylan asks.

"There was only one place I would accept," I tell them. "Home."

"What?" Caroline says, sitting up.

"Next stop," I tell them. "New York."

EPILOGUE ONE

CAROLINE

Six Months Later

"WHAT TIME ARE you going to be home?" I ask Justin, turning in the bed. He's on another road trip, and I'm not liking anything about him being gone right now. I mean, I thought it would be okay, a couple of games here and there, but the past two weeks have been brutal. He's been on the road, and the past two games have been crazy to watch, especially with him being in Edmonton and facing his old team.

"Does someone miss me?" he says, his voice low, and I roll my eyes.

"Yup, Dylan," I say, ignoring his laugh. "The bed is cold."

"I'll be home tomorrow night," he says. "I have to go."

"Love you," I say, and he disconnects, and I toss my phone on the empty side of the bed. I throw the white cover off me and walk to Dylan's bedroom. One thing that Justin did when he signed the contract with New York was get Zoe to get us a house. I was thinking maybe a nice two-story house, but when he brought me to see it, and we drove through the front gates, my mouth dropped to the ground.

Then he opened the front door, and the sweeping staircase made me fall in love. I didn't even know what to say. There was no way that I could help pay for this house. When he showed us the backyard, I cried. He held me in his arms while Dylan jumped into the pool fully dressed. I'm not even going to go into how much everything in the house cost. He sent me with Zara and Zoe and his credit card, and when I saw the price of the furniture, I felt sick and went back home with no furniture. But of course Zara and Zoe told him everything that I did like, and just like that, it was delivered without me even having a say.

I walk down the long-carpeted hallway to Dylan's room and peek my head in. He sleeps like a starfish in his king-size bed. His room is decked out in New York colors. I walk in and turn off the television and then go back downstairs to the kitchen. I make sure all the doors are locked and set the alarm. Walking back upstairs, I pass all the framed pictures on the wall. A picture of the three of us in the middle and then small pictures all around from everyone in the family. Turning off the lights I slide into our custom-made king-size bed, then put my phone on the bedside table next to a picture of us and then Dylan's school picture.

I close my eyes and think about how far Dylan's come. He's in a private school now, he's excelling at hockey to the level that his coaches are over the moon. Plus, he's started to grow like a weed, and he's going to be able to go up two levels, which people are saying is unheard of. He laughs all the time and eats more food than he's ever eaten. He's also just blended into the Stone family as if he was born a Stone. It takes me a couple of minutes to fall asleep.

"Sweetheart." I hear him whisper, and at first, I think I'm dreaming, but then he buries his face in my neck.

"You're home," I say, opening my eyes and seeing him. My hand comes out to touch his face. "I missed you."

He smiles. "I missed you more." He pulls me to him, and my leg hitches over his hip like it always does. His hand roams up my back, his fingertips giving me goose bumps, and he rips the shirt over my head and throws it over my head to the floor. "You were wearing my shirt."

"Yeah," I say of the tossed shirt. I always wear his shirts when he's away so I can smell him. My hands reach up to cup my tits, and he bends to take a nipple into his mouth.

"Sensitive," I hiss, and he flips me over on my back, and my legs open for him. I grip his cock in my hand, and I move my panties to the side. He slides in, and my back arches up. "Missed you." Wrapping my legs around his waist, I add, "So much."

He holds himself up on his arms, our lips lingering over each other. "Love you," he whispers, and my hand goes between us, and I play with my clit while he fucks me slowly, his tongue coming out to lick my lips. My tongue coming out to wrap with his. "Need you there."

"I'm there," I say. With him, I'm always there. "Right there." I lean up and kiss the necklace around his neck that I gave him, and he never takes it off. He pounds into me harder now, and I'm coming apart and tightening my legs around his waist. "Justin," I say while he kisses me and then buries his face into my neck. My fingers are going through his hair, and I play with the long ends. "Don't move," I say, enjoying him on me.

"I'm going to crush you," he says, and I moan when he gets off me and goes into the bathroom. He comes back with a rag like he always does. He walks back to the bathroom and tosses the rag and comes back and wraps his arms around me.

I turn to him, and I'm just so happy he's home. "Hmm," I say, cuddling into him and leaning up to kiss under his chin. "Hi."

He brings me closer. "Hi," he says softly. "Sweetheart."

"Why didn't you tell me you were coming home?" I ask.

"We were supposed to come home tomorrow," he starts and yawns. "But after the game, everyone just wanted to get home."

"Night," I say, my eyes closing now. "Love you."

"Forever," he says softly, and then the sound of his snores fills the room.

"And ever," I whisper to him and fall asleep in his arms.

EPILOGUE TWO

JUSTIN

Four months later

"GIVE ME A kiss." I walk to Caroline as she zips up the cooler for us to take on the boat. This is our first day on official vacation. My summer camp just wrapped up, and I surprised them with a getaway up north, joining the rest of the family.

"Be safe," she says and kisses me softly. "And can you text me."

"Yes," I say. "Have fun with my sisters."

"You know how much I love shopping," she says. "Do you think it's bad if I say I have a headache?"

"You know my sisters," I say. After moving to New York, they went above and beyond to make her feel at home. Including inviting her to every single girls' night they had until she slowly started feeling comfortable about it. If they wanted to go out and eat, she was always game, but shopping, not so much. Even though she had her own money now, and I gave her my credit card, she never ever bought anything. Enter Zara, who would just send her boxes of clothes every single month.

"Fine," she hisses. "I'll go, and I might even buy something this time."

I put my hands up. "Even if you don't, I'm sure someone will get you something."

"Your sister sent me a purse the other week," she says. "It was two thousand dollars."

"I mean, it's not that bad," I say, trying not to laugh.

"An evening purse, Justin," she shrieks. "I don't even go out."

"I take you out plenty," I say, and she rolls her eyes. "Dylan!" I yell back for him, and he comes down the stairs, and I swear he grew overnight.

"Coming," he says, grabbing his baseball hat and putting it on. "Are we fishing today?"

"That's the plan," I say. "Give Mom a kiss."

He walks over to her and kisses her on the cheek and then walks out of the house. "What time will you be back?"

"Not late," I say, and then I kiss her. "Love you."

"Love you more," she says. I walk out of the house and down the steps to the boat where Dylan is already getting in. I hand him the cooler and jump in with him. Starting it up, I pull out and make my way over to the spot where we always fish.

"Where is everyone?" he asks from beside me.

"Maybe running late," I say and look over at him. "Gives

us extra time to talk." My palms are suddenly sweaty. "You doing okay?" Jesus, I sound like an idiot.

"Yeah," he says, and I stop the boat in the middle of the lake and look over at him.

"You know that I love you, right?" I start at that part.

"Yeah," he says and then smiles. "I love you, too."

"And you know how much I love your mom, right?" I say, and he groans.

"I think you love her way too much. You really need to stop kissing all the time."

I laugh now. "Never going to happen, buddy." I look down and then up and reach into my shorts, taking out the ring box that I have had for the past six months.

"It's okay. Michael says that Max and Allison are always kissing also." He shrugs, and I think about how Michael and he are best friends on and off the ice, and I know next year is going to be a challenge for him since he's moving up in level and Michael still has another year.

"Well, I love her so much that I want to make her mine," I tell him. "Forever." I open the box and show him the ring, and he gasps.

"That's huge," he says, looking at it. "She's going to hate it."

I laugh, knowing she will freak out, but hoping she'll get over it and cherish it. "I want her to have my name and for the world to know that she belongs to me." He looks at me. "I want you both to belong to me." He looks at me. "I know you have a dad."

"Yeah," he says, and then whispers, "you." It's my time now to blink away the tears. He's always said he loves me, always hugs me, but never once did I push the idea of me being his dad on him. He had a dad, a shitty fucking excuse for a dad, but a dad nonetheless. "You are my dad."

"Dylan," I say now, not sure what else to say, and he doesn't give me the option.

"Andrew was never a father to me. He never brought me to practice, he never did homework with me, he never made sure I was okay, he never held my hand, he never put me to bed, or punished me because I played video games instead of reading. He only hugged me because he pretended that he liked me, and most of all, he never ever told me he loved me."

"Everyone shows their love differently," I try to defend him, and the words taste vile in my mouth even to me.

"Yeah, well, he has a shitty way of showing he loves anything except himself and his drugs." My head snaps up, and I look at him. "I thought that is what he did, and then I looked it up online."

"Dylan," I say to him.

"I know that you want Mom to have your name"—he looks down and then up and he has to blink away tears—"but can I have the name, too? I know that I have Mom's name now …" He doesn't finish his sentence. I just lean over to him and grab him, yanking him to me.

"I don't care what the fuck your last name is," I say to him, my arms around him and his arms around me. My hand goes to his head, and I take off his cap and kiss his head. Like I do every single day that we've been together. Like I'll be doing for the rest of his life. "You're mine."

"Thanks," he says, and then he says softly. "I won't tell

Mom you said the F word if you let me call you Dad," he says, and my eyes close, the tears now coming out. "And if it's okay, do you think Cooper will be okay if I called him Grandpa? And Parker, can I call her Grandma?"

"I'm going to say that he'll say yes, but you can ask him if you want," I say, and I hear a boat approaching with Matthew and Dad in it.

"What do we have here?" my father asks when he parks his boat next to ours. "What happened?" He whips off his glasses and looks at both of us.

"Nothing," I say while he ties his boat to ours. He then jumps into our boat with Matthew behind him.

"Why the tears?" he says to Dylan, and he turns to look at my father.

"Mom and me are going to be Stones," he says. Matthew looks up to the sky, and if I didn't know better, I would think he is crying.

"Is that so?" my father says, beaming.

"Yeah, and Justin is going to be my dad," he says, and I swear it just makes my heart feel fuller, bigger, complete.

"Well, son," my father says to me, "you've got a great family there."

"So since he's my dad, that kind of makes you my grandpa," Dylan says and then looks down. "Is it okay? If you don't want me to call you that, I won't."

My father gets down in front of him and holds his hands in his. "It would be my honor for you to call me your grandpa," he says, smiling. "We are so proud of you in so many ways. And family doesn't mean having the same blood," he says. "Matthew and Allison are mine, and I will fight anyone

415

who says they aren't. Family means protecting them, and most importantly, it means loving them with everything that you are." He nods his head at him. "My grandson," he says, grabbing him by the shoulder and bringing him to his chest.

"Wait a second," Matthew says from behind. "If you call him Grandpa and that one Dad." He points at me. "I want to be called uncle number one Matthew."

"You aren't calling him that," I say to Dylan, and the three of us laugh at Matthew. The rest of the crew gets here, and the day slides by with the kids swimming in the lake, then fishing, and when it's almost sunset, we make our way back home.

Getting Dylan off the boat is like pulling teeth. After all the sun and excitement and the swimming, he's already cranky and wants to go to bed. "What about dinner?" I ask, and he shakes his head as we walk up the steps to the house. I walk in, and the cold air hits me right away.

"Hey," Caroline says, getting off the couch and coming to us. Her long, tanned legs in the short white shorts that she is wearing with her blue tank top. She spots Dylan first, who just waves at her. "Oh, boy."

"He's tired," I say, dumping the cooler on the counter and emptying it, and then setting it outside to let it dry. When I come back into the house, Caroline is in the kitchen, putting away the things. I walk to her and wrap my arms around her waist and kiss her neck. "Did you have fun?"

"As much fun as one can have shopping for five hours," she says, and I laugh. "Go take a shower. You smell."

"Of what?" I ask, and she scrunches up her nose.

"Fish, water, and sunscreen." She shakes her head. "Not

a great trio."

"Fine," I say, walking to our bedroom and taking a shower. When I come back out, the house is quiet, and I look for Caroline everywhere. I even check in Dylan's room, and he's on his back in his boxers passed out. I pick up his wet towel by the bed and toss it in the laundry basket before I go outside and find her in the hammock, watching the stars. The soft tea lights hanging make it glow around her. "Hey," I say when I get to her side, and she looks at me.

"Hey." She moves over, and I get in with her. She cuddles with me, her leg hitching over mine and her arm going around my stomach. "It's a beautiful night."

"It is," I say, kissing the top of her head.

"I got a call today," she says five minutes later, "from Father Rolly." Her voice trails off. "Andrew died in an abandoned house. Someone called the ambulance, but he was dead for three days before someone was coherent enough to realize." She looks at me.

"I'm sorry," I say, and she shakes her head.

"Me, too," she says, "but he did it to himself." It's taken a lot for her to get over the fact that it was always his choice to do what he did.

We lie quietly together as the sun fades and the stars shine bright and then finally get up and walk inside, holding hands. My heart is heavy with the fact that Dylan's dad is gone, and this time for good. "I'll lock up. Go take a shower," I say, and she just walks ahead of me. I make sure everything is closed and check in on Dylan again, who is in the same position as he was before. I pull the door partially closed when I leave the room and walk to our room. The sound of the shower running tells me where she is as I grab the ring box and sit on the bed.

I look at the ring and wonder if there will ever be a good time to give it to her. I imagine her standing in front of me wearing a white dress and smiling. I'm so lost in my day-dream that I don't hear the shower turn off. I only look up when she opens the bathroom door and stands there in front of me wearing one of my shirts with her hair piled on top of her head.

"What?" she says, and she looks from the box in my hand and then up.

I guess there is no time like the present. "I had so many different ideas about how to do this," I say, and she stands there in front of me, not moving. "The whole romantic mo-ment, candles, roses, music, champagne." I shake my head. "You name it, the idea came to my head." Her lower lip trem-bles. "The rule is that you have to ask the father's permis-sion to marry their daughter." I swallow back the lump in my throat. "But I had someone more important to ask permis-sion of, and that was Dylan."

"Justin," she says with a tear streaming down her face.

"I told him I wanted to marry you. That I wanted to make you mine forever." I smile. "That I want everyone in the whole world to know that you're mine. I mean, officially mine." She steps forward to come to me, but I hold up my hand. "I told him I wanted you to have my name, and he asked me if he can have my name also, and just like that, it made this so much more than just us getting married or you becoming my wife. It means becoming not just your husband but be-coming his father. He wants to call me dad."

"I know," she says. "He's been dying to ask you for the past four months."

"I said yes," I say. "I said yes to being his father, and I really hope," I say now, getting down on one knee in front of her, "that you'll say yes and marry me. Become my wife."

"This is really awkward," she starts, "but I have a counter."

"Of course, you do," I say, shaking my head.

"I'll only become your wife if ..." I wait for it. "If you give me a baby."

She smiles. "I want to have another baby."

"Only one?" I ask.

"We can start with one," she says. "I can be maybe persuaded to go up."

"Yes," I say, and then I open the box with the ring, and she sobs. "Caroline, will you be my wife?" She nods her head, her hands on her mouth, and tears streaming down her face. I take the ring out of the box, and she reaches her left hand out, and it's shaking like a leaf. I slide it on her finger and see the five-carat square diamond sitting on it. "This is forever."

"Forever," she whispers, leaning down and holding my face in her hands. "And ever." She kisses me.

———

Nine years later

"Good luck tonight," I tell Dylan as he slips on his suit jacket. He grew to be a full six feet, five inches, and he works out even harder, so not only is he tall, but he's also a rock. He was also drafted first overall, making him the fourth Stone to be drafted first.

"It will be what it will be." He smirks at me as we walk out of the hotel room, and he makes his way to the rink. He gives me a hug before he walks to the back and gets ready while I make my way to the box where my family will be joining me. "Hey," I say to Matthew who just sits there on the phone. I sit next to him, watching the ice, getting ready for the big game.

"How's your boy?" Matthew asks from beside me.

"Calm," I say. "Nothing like his father."

"It'll be okay," Matthew says, and I just look ahead. Slowly, the box fills with all the kids and the wives, and I look over when I hear my name being called. "Dad." My eight-year-old son, Christopher, calls my name, and he walks in wearing Dylan's jersey. He looks exactly like me.

The night we got engaged is the night we decided she would get her IUD removed, and we would see what happened. It took one month before she was pregnant, and nine months later, my son came into the world. "Hey, little man." I open my arm, and he gives me a side hug. "Where is your mom?"

"She's coming," he says. "She was crying, so Grandma is talking to her."

My head snaps up, and I'm about to go check on her when my twin girls, who just turned five, come into the room wearing Dylan's jersey also. To say everyone was surprised when we were told we would be having twins would be an understatement. Having them come out looking exactly like my sisters is something else. Their hair is just a touch darker, and where Zara and Zoe have green eyes, my girls have baby blue eyes. "Abigail and Gabriella, where is your mother?" They both shrug and run to the food.

I'm about to charge out when she comes into the room with my parents beside her. "Sweetheart," I say her name quietly, and she comes to me, and I lean in and kiss her lips. "What's the matter?"

"Nothing." She pretends she wasn't crying.

"Christopher told me you were crying," I say, and she glares.

"Christopher should mind his own business," she jokes, and the crowd starts to cheer so you know the team is going on the ice. I kiss her forehead, and we stand, watching Dylan take the ice. "It's a big night."

"Or not," I say, trying not to get my hopes up. "He just needs to do his thing."

The game starts, and the three Stone men stand side by side. My father is in the middle of Matthew and me. "You ready for this?" I look over at my father, who just smiles and beams with happiness.

"It's time," he says, and I just smile. The game is uneventful until the last two minutes of the game when Dylan takes the puck and skates it out of the zone, my stomach fluttering for him.

He passes the puck behind him to the defenseman and makes his way into position right inside the zone. They pass the puck from defenseman to defenseman and then they slip it to Dylan, who is winding up his stick for a one timer, and just like that, it hits the back of the net. His hands go up in the air, holding his stick, while the box erupts with shouts.

The sound of the announcer fills the box. "History is made. It only took fifty years, but Cooper Stone has been knocked off by none other than Dylan Stone. He now has the record as most points scored by a rookie."

I watch him celebrate on the ice, and Matthew puts his arm around my father, who is clapping with tears running down his face. My arm goes around him also now. When the game ends, they have Dylan skating to the center of the ice, and the reporter is there waiting for him.

"I've won two Stanley Cups, yet this moment is so much better." I look at my dad, the smile on my face hurting my cheeks.

Dylan skates to the reporter with his helmet off as he tries to catch his breath. "Well, it seems like you did it."

"Apparently," he says, smiling, and he looks up at me. His hands are on his waist.

"It must be surreal," the reporter says.

"It is," he says, and the crowd starts to chant his name. "But I wouldn't be here without my family and their support," he says and looks at me again and points. "But most importantly, my dad."

Books By Natasha Madison

This Is

This is Crazy

This Is Wild

This Is Love

This Is Forever

Hollywood Royalty

Hollywood Playboy

Hollywood Princess

Hollywood Prince

Something So Series

Something So Right

Something So Perfect

Something So Irresistible

Something So Unscripted

Tempt Series

Tempt The Boss

Tempt The Playboy

Tempt The Ex

Tempt The Hookup

Heaven & Hell Series

Hell And Back

Pieces Of Heaven

Love Series

Perfect Love Story

Unexpected Love Story

Broken Love Story

Standalones

Faux Pas

Mixed Up Love

Until Brandon

Made in the USA
Columbia, SC
27 September 2023